Ouida

Chandos

A novel. Vol. 2

Ouida

Chandos
A novel. Vol. 2

ISBN/EAN: 9783337067199

Printed in Europe, USA, Canada, Australia, Japan

Cover: Foto ©Andreas Hilbeck / pixelio.de

More available books at **www.hansebooks.com**

CHANDOS

A Novel.

By OUIDA,

AUTHOR OF "STRATHMORE," "GRANVILLE DE VIGNE," &c.

God and man and hope abandon me,
But I to them and to myself remain
Constant.
SHELLEY.

Treason doth never prosper. What's the reason?
Why, when it prospers, none dare call it treason!
SIR JOHN HARRINGTON.

IN THREE VOLUMES.

VOL. II.

LONDON:

CHAPMAN AND HALL, 193, PICCADILLY.

1866.

LONDON:
PRINTED BY C. WHITING, BEAUFORT HOUSE, STRAND.

CONTENTS OF VOL. II.

BOOK THE THIRD.

CHAPTER I.

PAGE

"Spes et fortuna valete" 3

CHAPTER II.

"Tout est perdu fors l'Honneur" 29

CHAPTER III.

The Love of Woman 60

CHAPTER IV.

The last Night among the Purples 71

CHAPTER V.

The Death of the Titan 84

CHAPTER VI.

"And the Spoilers came down" 96

CHAPTER VII.

The Few who were faithful 114

CHAPTER VIII.

The Crowd in the Cour des Princes. . . . 140

BOOK THE FOURTH.

CHAPTER I.

"Facilis descensus Averni". 173

CHAPTER II.

"Where all Life dies, Death lives" . . . 190

CHAPTER III.

In the Net of the Retiarius 216

CHAPTER IV.

"Sin shall not have Dominion over You" . . 244

BOOK THE FIFTH.

CHAPTER I.

In Exile 261

CHAPTER II.

In Triumph 270

BOOK THE SIXTH.

CHAPTER I.

"Primavera! Gioventu dell' Anno!" . . . 281

CHAPTER II.

Castalia 287

CHAPTER III.

"Giuventu! Primavera della Vita!" . . . 309

CHAPTER IV.

"Seigneur! ayez Pitié" 323

BOOK THE THIRD.

il avait joui de son rêve insensé;
Du trône et de la gloire il savait le mensonge,
Il avait vu de près ce que c'est un tel songe,
Et quel est le néant d'un avenir passé.

Victor Hugo.

L'honneur parle ; il suffit.

Racine.

VOL. II.   B

CHANDOS.

CHAPTER I.

" SPES ET FORTUNA VALETE."

" COME early to-morrow," murmured the Queen of
Lilies, as her lover led her to her carriage, lifting
her fair eyes, lustrous as those of the daughter of
D'Orléans she personated.

Chandos stooped his head, so that his voice in its
soft answer only reached her ear.

" Would that to-morrow were here, or, rather, that
now we did not part!"

If he had ever doubted that he was loved, he could
not have doubted it now, as he watched the warmth
that flushed her face, the light over which her lashes
drooped, the half smile, half sigh, which with that
divine blush replied to him.

The costume-ball had been magnificent as though
it had been given in the Regency age it celebrated,

and the Louis Quinze quadrille had been the most
splendid of all the square dances. The Richelieu
dress excelled all others in the costly glitter of its
grace; the Clarencieux diamonds outshone all others
there. Royal women flattered him on " Lucrèce;"
the greatest statesman of the day pressed on him the
restoration of his Marquisate; the world adored him
as it had ever done, and feminine lips breathed him
his most delicate and most dulcet incense. The night
lived long in his memory. It was the last of his
reign—the last in which he loved the world, and the
world loved him.

It was late when the guests of the Italian Princess
left her imitation of the fêtes of Sceaux and of Versailles; the long line of carriage-lamps glittered far
down to the right and left in the uncertain light of
an early summer morning. Among the crowd of
horses, of lacqueys, of chasseurs, and of police, a few
wandering night-birds crept in under the wheels and
almost under the hoofs, and stared blankly at the
glimpse of an unknown world caught through the
crevices of the awning, and at the warmth of light
and colour that streamed out on them from the opened
portals. Among them a boy, of such beauty as
belongs to the canvas of Spanish painters and to the
eyes of Spanish gaditâni, stole noiselessly near, and
looking on, crouched, almost kneeling, in the shadow
of the portico. One carriage rolled away, another
with the well-known white and silver liveries of

Clarencieux took its place; the name ran along the line of servants; the lad Agostino leaned eagerly forward. Down the steps of the entrance, under the awning, Chandos came; the gas-light shed full on the rich colours and the gleaming jewels of his dress, as Richelieu himself might have come leaving the gatherings of the Palais Royal. So near leaned the boy, that the gold and silk of the sword-knot touched his lifted forehead; the attendants ordered him sharply off the pavement. Chandos, struck by the look upon his face, so eager, so longing, so full of youth and misery, stopped them, and paused a moment.

"My poor boy," he said, gently, "do you want anything with me? Surely I have seen your face before?"

Agostino gazed up at him, pale to the lips, and with an utter abject wretchedness in the darkness of his eyes; he trembled violently. He would have given twenty years of his dawning life to have found courage for speech; yet now that the opportunity so yearned and sought for came to him, the cowardice of his feminine nature held him paralysed.

"Speak! Do not be afraid," said Chandos, kindly. "If you want anything from me, say it without fear."

The boy's lips parted, but only inarticulate Spanish words halted upon them; the dread of his father's forbiddance, the horror of his English task-master's vengeance, held him powerless and speechless.

" That lad suffers; have him looked to," said Chandos, turning to the footmen nearest him, while he stooped and touched Agostino's hand with some gold. " Take these; and if you need more help, come to my house in the morning. I will give orders for your admittance. What is your name?"

" Agostino Mathias."

The voice was husky and scarcely intelligible; a great terror—the terror of his tyrant—lay upon him; yet the strange sudden loyalty and love he had conceived for the English stranger, with the face like Guido Reni's golden-haired St. Michael, whom he had seen among the vine-fields of the Vega, looked upward longingly and piteously from his eyes.

"I shall remember," said Chandos, as he stooped nearer and put the sovereign or two that he had with him against the boy's closed hand. "So much wretchedness in one so young must come," he thought, "from some such pangs of want and poverty as sent Chatterton and Hégiseppe Moreau to their graves."

But Agostino shuddered from the touch of the gold, and shrank back against the stone of the portico.

"Not your money—not *your* money!" he muttered incoherently in his Spanish tongue, while he cowered away as though the sovereigns were some leprous thing.

Chandos saw the gesture; he did not hear the

murmured answer. He turned and dropped the pieces in the hand of the servant closest to him.

" That poor boy can be scarcely, I fear, in his right mind. See to him, will you ? " he said, as he went down the few remaining steps and entered his carriage, which stopped the way of others. Agostino looked after him with passionate wistfulness, while the great tears gathered and brimmed over in his eyes : the footman touched him on the shoulder and addressed him. Like one roused out of fever and lethargy, the lad started and looked round, then wrenched himself out of the hold the man had laid on him, and fled like a frightened deer down into the darkness of the street. The servant let him go, and slipped the sovereigns in his waistcoat-pocket.

" He's that uncommon proud, he won't know new 'uns like the Earl of Clydesmore," mused the man, wonderingly, of him by whom they had been given ; " and yet he is always willin' to speak to such helpless street-trash as that."

Such a code as this, which could show an hauteur so aristocratic to the plutocracy, yet show a sympathy so democratic to the needs of youth and poverty, was a social anomaly that sorely perplexed the powdered functionary. In any one less fashionable, less famous, and less proverbially exclusive than Chandos, he would have set it down, without a second's hesitation, as evident insanity. The world would not much have differed with him.

"If a boy who calls himself Agostino Mathias come here to-morrow, receive him, and let me know," said Chandos to his maître d'hôtel, as he passed up the staircase of his own house.

The quick ear of John Trevenna, where he sat below, waiting in the library, with the door a little open, caught the name, and his white teeth set like a bulldog's.

"Ah, young one, curse you! you try that game?" he thought. "You will find out what it is to rebel against *me*, with a convict's chain ready for your mischievous baby-hands."

The man bowed as he heard Chandos' command.

"I will be very careful he is admitted, sir. I beg your pardon, but Mr. Trevenna bade me tell you he is waiting."

Chandos paused in astonishment.

"Mr. Trevenna? Why, it is past four o'clock. Is Clarencieux burnt down, that he comes here at such a time?"

"I believe he said, sir, his business was urgent; he entreated to see you."

"Inconsiderate fellow! I am half asleep," thought Chandos, as he passed up the stairs. "Well, say he can come to me for ten minutes—in my own room."

"A very good fellow, a very clever fellow, but a man with one failing; he never knows when he is *de trop*," he mused, as he went on into his own chamber, that was library, atelier, smoking-room, and art-gallery, all in one. It was always ready lighted, and, without waiting to take off his Richelieu dress, he stood against the mantelpiece, striking a match for a cigarette, and thinking, as his hand caressed the eagerly-lifted head of the dog, Beau Sire, less of what Trevenna could need him for, than of how lovely the Daphne looked in the mellow gleam of the light.

"Who would care for life without Art and Pleasure?" he thought.

The handles of the double doors turned sharply; the massive fall of the blue velvet *contre-vent* was thrust hastily aside; Trevenna entered. The retriever dropped, "down-charging," with a fierce, repressed growl; Chandos looked up, and laughed.

"Adieu to peace! You can't open a door, Trevenna, without jarring a room. What can possibly bring you here at this time in the morning? Is Clarencieux burnt, a racer dead, my Titians stolen? or, what is it?"

"I beg your pardon for disturbing you, my dear Chandos," returned the other, with more gravity than had ever been seen in him before, "but it is very imperative that I should talk to you."

"Talk away, then!" rejoined Chandos, with a sigh of ennui and resignation; "but, for Heaven's sake, shake off that most unusual and unbecoming solemnity. Whoever would have thought a single week of St. Stephen's would have been enough to make a man so prosy! Or perhaps **it's** only training for future 'office,' is it?"

Trevenna was silent; he came and stood on the hearth-rug, with so rare and grave a seriousness upon him, that he gave **no light or** humorous answer; he looked at his host where he leaned against the marble, his form, in the Louis Quinze dress, thrown out against the background of the blue velvet hangings of this favourite chamber; then he bent his **eyes downward on the carpet:** he feared they might betray the thirsty exultation, the eager sleuth-hound longing, that were hidden in his heart.

"Come, Trevenna!" said Chandos, in some surprise and a little impatience, "silence is **never** your forte. Say what you have to say."

"Well,—I'm **a** blunt man," answered his friend, as with some effort. "Plainly and briefly, I'm come on a disagreeable errand."

Chandos shrugged his shoulders:

"I'd a presentiment **of that.** People don't stay up for one **on** pleasant ones. Après?"

"Après?" said Trevenna, with something of his old malicious humour gleaming out in the corners of **his mouth.** "It *is* just the 'après' that I'm come to talk **about.** You've had a comet-like course, mon Prince; did you ever speculate how comets end?"

Chandos looked at him in supreme astonishment; he almost thought, **for** the moment, that Trevenna's habitual sobriety had given way, and that some hot wines heated his fancies.

"My dear fellow," he said, with a touch of stronger impatience, "you must really pardon me ; but if you only keep out of bed to propose me astronomical riddles, I must, with all courtesy, bid you good night !"

"Monseigneur, have a little patience. I come on grave matters, and you must hear them," said Trevenna, quietly. "You lock annoyances out with double doors in this chamber ; but I fear, do what you will, they will ferret through and follow you at last. I asked you, before you went to your fancy ball, if you knew at what rate you have lived and are living ; I ask you, now you have come back from it, the same thing."

"And I give you the same answer ; I do not know."

"Shall I tell you ?"

"If you please."

"I will, then ; but wait one moment. You are perfectly happy, Chandos ?"

Chandos looked at him again, in an astonishment not unmixed with amusement.

"I ? Perfectly ! I don't think I would live a day longer, if I were not."

Trevenna watched him as he spoke, leaning against the marble, with the deep glow of colour, the strewn

treasures of art and wealth, the white grace of the
statues, and the intense hues of the painted ceiling
around and above. In the Court costume, with the
diamonds flashing through the lace and gold em-
broideries, the strong resemblance he bore to the last
Marquis was as great as though the dead man lived
again. Trevenna watched him, recompensed at last
for a long decade of patient tact, for a lifetime of
bitter envy, of gnawing mortification, of impotent
hate, of festering jealousy—watched him as the jungle-
cheetah watches his prey before the final spring. He
went leisurely about his work : the treasured preparation of such long and thirsty toil was not to be devoured in an instant, but tasted slowly in its wicked
sweetness, drop by drop. He changed his own posi-
tion slightly nearer; his features wore a gravity such
as became the matters he approached, but a quicker
or a more suspicious observer than the man who trusted
him so freely might have noticed that in the glisten
of his clear bold eyes there was a look of eager
expectation, and about the firm humorous lines of
his lips there was a lurking triumph, a cynical, malicious relish.

"You would not live a day, if your fortunes altered?
I am sorry to hear that ; for the world, then, may lose
you soon. We must take those pretty ivory-handled
pistols out of sight; for, though you are so happy
now, I fear you will not be so happy in the future."

Chandos rose from the easy indolence of his resting attitude, and looked at him, with a new light rising in his eyes—a light of anger and of impatience very seldom there.

“ Jesters are privileged proverbially,” he said, coldly; “ but there are limits to their allowance when their jests have no wit and much insolence. If you have anything to say, say it plainly, and make an end.”

Trevenna’s words had angered and astonished him; but they had in no sense alarmed him. In his careless peace and his total ignorance of calamity, their meaning could not possibly suggest itself ever so dimly.

“ Très-cher !” replied Trevenna, with an irresistible lapse into his habitual manner—for, though the man was a foul traitor and an unblushing liar, it was against the cynical candour of his nature to be a hypocrite, though he could be one with great effect and success, if it were absolutely needed—“ that confounded hauteur of you thorough-breds is deuced provoking—it is, indeed ; and people won’t put up with it, perhaps, quite so patiently in future. As for saying plainly what I have to say, I suppose you will not believe me if I tell you that your expenditure is, and has been for many years, about quadruple what your income is?”

Chandos started, some faint perception of the de-

struction that must follow such a course arresting
even his careless indifference and ignorance on all
things financial. The next moment he smiled con-
temptuously at the thought.

"My expenditure? Impossible."

"Only too possible, unhappily. Even a Chandos
of Clarencieux cannot live like an emperor with
impunity. Royalties come expensive, mon Prince;
and who wears the purples must pay for them. Your
fortune was fine, but not large enough to bear such a
strain as you have put upon it. You have no notion,
you say, of all that you have spent. What comes of
a man's not knowing the rate at which he lives?
Why that, sooner or later, the last rope-strand gives
way, and he is—ruined."

The word fell strangely on the silence of that tranquil chamber, bringing, like the stroke of death, desolation where all was peace.

Yet still the word passed by him whom it should
have warned; his confidence was too secure, his carelessness too entire, his possession of all that was
highest and richest and brightest of too long custom
for the first presage of the storm to have power to
force its meaning on him.

A flush of amazed anger passed over his face; he
stood erect upon his hearth in a haughty and intole-
rant annoyance.

"Have you drunk too much, or are you mad?
This sort of fooling passes all licence. If you, in-

deed, know what you are saying, I must beg you to leave my presence."

Trevenna, in answer, stood in a firmer, sturdier attitude, with his feet apart, and his arms folded like the Napoleonic statuettes.

"I am neither mad nor drunk, and I am not fooling. I wish, for your sake, I could discover it were a nightmare after two dozen oysters; but I can't. I digest everything, and I don't dream! Briefly, Chandos, I must tell you what I have staved off perhaps too long; but I shrank from the task. I let time pass. I thought you might marry some rich or even royal bride, whose alliance would change the whole aspect; but your bidding me arrange the settlements for Lady Valencia compels me to withhold the truth no longer from you. There is nothing to settle on her!"

"Nothing to settle on her? What can you mean?"

Still, no doubt, no prescience of the truth came to him. He looked at Trevenna with a wonder in which some disgust and more pity were mingled; he thought that the strangeness of his sudden mania rose from some unusual indulgence in drink, that filled his brain with these singular, distorted phantasies.

"I mean what I say, monseigneur. There is not a sou's worth—not even those diamonds that glitter so bravely on your dainty dress—that is *free* to go to her dower. Can you not understand me when I tell you that you have lived at the rate of four times the amount of your annual income? What history does that simple fact suggest? You must be financier enough to know *that?* Hang it, Chandos! I am not a deep-feeling man—I don't go in for all that, as you know; but I wish from my soul that I could spare you, or that some other could better break to you the news you must hear to-night."

Chandos listened; a grey, deadly pallor came on his lips, his lips grew white, his heart almost ceased to beat; the first shadow of this dim horror stole on him. A glimpse of its meaning was forced at length upon him : he had heard of such fates for other men.

He drew his breath with a gasping effort. "If you speak truth, speak out," he said, in that strange and deadly calmness which falls upon the mind and senses before the visitation of some great calamity. A faint sense of this evil approaching him was all he felt; it was not possible that it could come to him yet more fixedly or fully.

"I speak the sad and sober truth," returned Trevenna, far more quietly than he had ever spoken, his eyes still resting on the Daphne opposite, as though to guard against a tell-tale flash from them of that lustful exultation that he knew was in their glance. "I can't speak to you as coyly and as delicately as your patrician friends and relatives would do. I'm a plain, frank man, Chandos, and I've the very devil's own mischief-making to tell you of now ; but, believe

me once for all, it costs me almost as much to tell as
it can do you to hear. There is no good in beating
about the bush—no good in being discursive over a
thing so horrible as this ; you must know the worst at
once, and it is better, perhaps, told without varnish or
veil ; a short shrieve and a quick death. That is
truer mercy, after all, than all the endless preparation
your fellow-aristocrats might give you. Listen !——"

He paused a moment, as though that which he had
to bring bore even him down in its bitter burden ;
but his eyes glanced swiftly and longingly at the man
he tortured : he loved this protracted torment. Like
a cat, he played with his victim's misery before he
killed him ; and if, without suspicion, he could have
prolonged it through hours of ignorance and dread,
he would have done so with all the endless patience
of hate.

" Listen," he said more softly ; " as I have said,
you have long lived—indeed, I think since your
majority—at the rate of four times your income.
You have kept two households in England nearly
such as princes keep ; you have had your Paris
hôtel, your Turkish palace ; you have lavished money
on art, like another Beckford ; you have spent God
knows what on women ; you have given entertainments that cost you (though you never asked the
cost) a couple of thousand a night ; you have played
the patron to every starving genius you met ; in a
word, you have lived like a king, my dear Ernest,

and not being a king, but only an English gentleman, your royalty has broken down, and will, I fear, end in a very unavoidable abdication. In a word, you are in debt to an extent I hardly dare compute to you. To sell everything you possess will hardly satisfy your claimants; bill-discounters and money-lenders have your signature in their hands, and will call for payment without mercy. Briefly, you have sold your birthright for ten years' enjoyment, and you now are, beyond all hope of ransom, irrevocably and most utterly—*ruined*."

The word cut down again upon the stillness with a shrill, sharp, pitiless echo, as a sword cuts down through the air before it falls on the bowed neck of the doomed.

Its utterance repaid its speaker for all he had fore-gone, for all he had forborne, for every slight endured in silence from the world he hated, for every benefit taken with an inward curse from the man he hunted down. He loved that word so well, he could have dinned it on the silence in incessant repetition, hurling down with it the brilliant and gracious life he had so long envied from the thrones of pleasure and of power into the nethermost darkness of a hopeless desolation.

" Ruined! *I?*"

Chandos echoed the word hoarsely, faintly, scarcely with any comprehension of it, as a man suddenly wakened from a deep sweet sleep to learn some un-utterable shame or misery that has befallen him repeats the phrase that tells it, mechanically and without sense. The agony of horror that gathered, white and bewildered, on the gallant beauty of his face was in as ghastly a contrast with the glittering splendour of his dress as though the face of a corpse gazed out from the laces and jewels of a gay masquerade.

"Yes; even you, my brilliant Lord of Clarencieux!" answered the friend who stood upon his hearth; and with the words went an irrepressible snarl and sneer of triumph and of mockery that passed him unnoted in that moment of breathless, burning, inconceivable anguish. "*Even* you! Details you will learn for yourself hereafter; for to-night, the broad brief fact's enough. I would have warned you long ago, if you would only have listened; but you know as well as I do, you would never hear of business, never think of money. Besides, in truth, I scarcely thought it was so very, so hopelessly bad as it seems now to be. I suppose your marriage with a bride who has no dower has set the fellows on : they are hounding for their moneys now like mad. I have had hard work to keep them even from arresting you ; I have, upon my honour! To-night, when you went out to your Princess's ball with all those thousands of pounds' worth of rose-diamonds about you, it was a wonder, on my life, that some one of your hungry creditors didn't stop those dainty jewels; you shall see to-morrow that I tell you but the plain, unvarnished truth. You are so deeply involved now, Chandos, that I doubt if there is a single little cabinet picture on these walls, or a single rood of land at your beloved Clarencieux, that in a month's time you will call your own ;——"

"Stop ;—O my God! have some mercy!"

The words broke out like the last cry wrung from one driven to the extremity of physical endurance —wrung from him in the abandonment of human misery against all strength of manhood and all power of will. He could bear no more; he was stunned and blinded like a man struck from behind him a murderous blow upon the brain which blasts his sight to darkness.

Ruin !—it had no meaning for him ; it came to him like some dim, shapeless, devil-begotten thing that had no form or substance, a hideous lemure of a night's delirious dream.

Trevenna stood by and watched him ; his hour had come at last, the hour which paid him back the canker-ous evil, the relentless toil, the unremitting chase of such long, wakeful, hungry years. This moment had been hoarded up by him as a miser hoards his gold, and now, in its full seizure, he was repaid for all his studied craft, for all his fondly nursed revenge, for all his unrelinquished hatred ; repaid to the uttermost coin by every gasped breath that he counted, by every shiver of the voiceless anguish that he watched.

He did not heed the prayer for silence, but took

up the broken thread of his discourse, and played with it as though loving it in every shape and on every side.

"Your property, you see, was fine, no doubt; but fine properties are not Monte-Christo caverns of exhaustless wealth. Dipped into, they will waste. You have eclipsed Princes, and starred through all Europe; you pay now for the pre-eminence. You have had women's love—no toy so costly! you have had the great world's worship—no clientela so expensive! you have been a dilettante, a *lion*, a leader of fashion, a man of endless pleasures—no pursuits take so much gold! You have lived in such a style that you would have run through millions, had you had them; and you had not one million, though you had a noble inheritance. Of course you possess such quantities of pictures and statues, and all that kind of thing, and your estate itself is such an untouched mine, that there can be no fear of your personal liberty ever being endangered; but I am grievously afraid, I am indeed, that you will be obliged to give up almost everything—give up even Clarencieux!"

The words, so deftly strung together to goad, and taunt, and add misery to misery, wound their pitiless speech, unchecked, with all the fiendish ingenuity of hatred that could not sate itself enough in the vastness of this wreck it wrought.

Chandos heard them, yet only dimly as men hear in whose ears the noise of great sea-waves is surging.

He raised himself erect, rigid in an unnatural calm. Years of age and wretchedness could not have changed his face as this brief moment had changed it; its radiance and its splendour had died out as though the breath of death had passed on it; its ashen white looked ghastlier beside the ball-room gaiety of his dress, and in the stillness that followed the loud, slow, laboured beatings of his heart were audible—each throb a pang.

"You swear that this is truth?"

His voice was broken and strained, like the voice of a man just arisen from a bed of lengthened sickness; and his hot lips had parted twice before words came to them.

"To the uttermost letter."

Chandos' head drooped as though he had been suddenly stabbed; all the vigour, and grace, and perfection of his frame seemed to wither and grow old; a shudder, such as the limbs shiver with involuntarily under some unendurable bodily torment of the flames or of the knife, shook him from head to foot.

" Clarencieux lost! O God !"

The words died in his throat—the stifled cry of a vain agony for his lost birthright. This alone, through all the blindness and the stupor of misery that had fallen on him, rose out clear before him in its burning torture—the passionate yearning of his heart towards his home.

As the flare **of** a torch suddenly shows the abyss that yawns beneath **the** traveller's feet, so **the** glare and the shame of the sentence he heard showed him the bottomless desolation over which he stood. He **was** wakened **from his** dreamful ease to be flung **face to** face with an absolute despair. For the moment strength gave way, manhood was shattered **down,** consciousness **itself could** keep no hold on **life; the** lights of the chamber reeled in giddy gyrations round **him, a sound like rushing** waters beat in on his brain, **a darkness** like the **darkness of** death fell upon him. **He** swayed forward, **like a** drunken man, against **the broad** marble **ledge above the** hearth; his hands in- stinctively clenched on the stone as the hands of those sinking **to their grave down the glassy slope of an** Alpine mountain clench **on the ice-ridge that** they **meet; his head** sunk on his arms, the suffocated labour **of each** breath panted out on **the silence** like a death-spasm :—at **one** stroke **he was** bereaved **of all !**

His torturer looked on; **never in** the cells **of** the Inquisition **could** Franciscan **or** Dominican have watched the gradual wrenching **of the rack,** the winding-out of the strained limbs till they broke, the wringing, and bruising, and slaying of the quivering nerves till they could bear no more, as Trevenna watched this moral torment, this assassination of **joy,** and honour, **peace,** and love, and fame, and every fair **thing of** a gracious world, laid desert and desolate at his word. He looked on, as in the legends of the early Church devils looked on at the impotent despair of those whose souls they had lured, and tempted, and meshed in their net, and made their own. He looked on, and was repaid.

"Chandos," he said, gravely, almost softly, pouring the last drop of burning oil into the fresh wound his stab had dealt—"Chandos, believe me,—from my soul I *pity* you!"

He had studied long the nature of the man now in his power, and he knew the keenest sting to give. Yet for once his greed erred in its mark; the last bolt shortened the hour of his rich, insatiate enjoyment.

It roused Chandos as the bay of the pack rouses the dying stag from its mortal throes to stagger up and drag its bleeding limbs to solitude, where it can die alone. It pierced his stupefaction; it told him more widely than all other words could tell, how mighty was his fall, how utter his desolation.

This man *pitied* him! He raised himself with sudden force; the pride of his race was not dead in him, and the same courage in the teeth of calamity, which had sent the last Marquis with a smile to the Tower scaffold, was in him now under the lash of his dependent's mockery of compassion. His face was strangely and terribly calm, but a premature age seemed to have withered all life from it; his lips were colourless, and on his forehead alone the dark congested blood flushed heavily, red and burning as in the heat of fever.

"If this *be* the truth," he said, hoarsely, while his throat was parched and almost voiceless, " you have had little mercy in the telling! Go—take the town your story; it will startle them. Spare more of it to me !"

The words were spoken with a tranquillity more horrible than the fiercest outbreaks of delirium or the most hopeless abandonment of woe. He stood as, in the days of Philip the Fair, one of his race had stood to be bound to the Templars' pyre; his hand was clenched on the marble ledge, and every now and then a quick shudder ran through all his limbs, shaking him as with the shudder of an icy cold; but his eyes were dry, and fronted his tormenter with a look under which the other shrank, and no sign or sigh of pain escaped him.

Trevenna moved slightly; he could not meet the gaze of those calm, tearless eyes, from whose depths there looked so wide a world of unuttered reproach, of unuttered agony.

" Chandos—Chandos ! There will be no need for *me* to tell the town; it will be whispered soon enough ! Would you give the task to your debtor, your guest, your friend ? No ! There are too many who will take it fast enough. Leave it to the men you have outrivalled, and the women you have forsaken ; those are the glib tongues for such a theme ! As for mercy in the telling, what mercy can the man show who has to bring his death-warrant to another? I would have warned you long ago, and you would not be warned. Is it my fault that you have wasted your princely substance, and are a beggar now? Oh, my friend!—there is no error in this thing save your own."

He toyed too long with the theme that was so sweet to him; he counted too surely on the endurance of the man he lashed, and stung, and stretched upon the rack of his subtle mockery of pity and of sympathy; there was a latent force he had not known, a latent passion he had not divined, in the pleasure-steeped softness of his victim's nature.

Chandos gave a forward gesture, like a maddened animal rising to its spring; he did not reel, or stagger, or let escape one sign of the anguish within him, but he stood there upon his desolated hearth erect, brought to bay as the deer by the sleuth-hounds, livid to the lips, with only the blood burning like fire across his brow, his golden hair dashed back disordered, his eyes proud and fearless even in their misery. It was no longer Alcibiades amidst the gay levity, the dreamy languor, the fragrant rose-crowns, and the laurel-wreathed amphoræ of the revels of his youth; it was Alcibiades, grander in his fall than in his reign, facing alone the dead cold of the winter's night and the unsheathed circle of his assassins' steel, until they cowed and fell asunder, and pierced him with dastard surety from afar off with the arrows of the Bactrian bows. He raised his right hand and pointed to the door.

"If you are man, not devil, let me be! Go! I command you—go!"

Bold though they were, his torturer's eyes could not meet his; victorious though he was, Trevenna dared not dispute that bidding; insatiate though his greed for this exhaustless triumph would still have been for hour upon hour, he was forced to obey that gesture of command. Mastiff-like both in courage and ferocity, he was still driven out as a murderous animal is driven out by the *will* it reads in a human gaze. He longed to linger there the whole night through, and ring every change upon that note of ruin, and watch every spasm of the overburdened life, and turn every screw and wheel in that rack on which he stretched his friend. But he dared not; he felt that he must leave his work to bear its fruit and harvest of misery unwatched; he knew it as the murderers of Alcibiades knew that none could come near, with life, to the menaced danger and the mighty woe that looked unquailing on them from the flaming eyes of the roused Sybarite, the discrowned idol, the awakened Epicurean, called out in the dead of night to stand face to face with his destruction. The hirelings of Pharnabazus slew the Greek; Trevenna, less merciful, left the living man to suffer.

The velvet swept down behind him, the door closed,

and he drew it softly after him ; then he paused in
the stillness of the breaking dawn that was rising on
all the sleeping world without, and listened with an
expectancy upon his face.

On the silence he heard a heavy crashing fall, like
the fall of a stricken tree; then all was still with the
stillness of the grave.

He smiled and passed onward through the second
door and down the corridor and staircase of the
house that had been opened to him night and day,
with a hospitality that no claims could weary, and no
exactions chill, and went out through the lighted hall,
with its bloom of exotic colour and its richness of
jasper and porphyry.   As he passed the statue of the
great Minister standing there, white and majestic,
amidst the foliage of American plants and the glow
of Eastern flowers, he looked upward to the sculp-
tured face with a glance of triumph, of achievement,
of satisfied revenge, that in the intensity of its evil
and its cruelty was almost grand by the sheer force
of strength and purpose.

" Monseigneur—monseigneur !" he murmured, in
that thirsty exultation, flinging his victory and his
mockery in the face of the lifeless marble, " how is
it with your beloved one *now?*"

CHAPTER II.

"TOUT EST PERDU FORS L'HONNEUR."

THE morning sun straying fitfully in through the thick leafy shades and trellised creepers of the winter-garden beyond, as the day rose high and bright over a busy waking world, found the ruined man lying where he had fallen, struck down by the blow that had beggared him of all, as a cedar is struck by the lightning. He lay there insensible to all except his agony, his hands clenched upon the leopard-skins that strewed his hearth, his brain heavy with the pent blood that seemed on fire.

The shock had fallen on his life as suddenly as, in tropic latitudes, the black tempestuous night falls down upon the shadowless day. Yesterday he had been rich in every earthly treasure; to-day he was beggared, shamed, dishonoured. Ruin!—it was upon

him like the confused horror of a nightmare whose
bonds he could not break; he could not realise its
despair, nor measure its desolation; he felt like one
drugged with opiate poisons that bring a thousand
loathsome shapes thronging between their dreamer
and the light of day and the world of men. He had
been a stranger to the mere pain of transient human
sorrow; he was stunned to unconsciousness by the
world-wide misery that felled him down at a stroke as
the iron mace fells an ox. Hours passed; he knew
nothing of their flight; the gas burned in the
chandeliers above him, still shedding its flood of
light that looked garish and yellow beside the brightness of morning that streamed in from the garden
beyond. There was profound silence round him,
broken by nothing save the monotonous murmur of
the fountains falling yonder; the faint noise of the
streets could not penetrate here, and the sounds of
the moving household were shut out in a deathly
stillness. He was left to the solitude which was all
the mercy that life now could give him. The dog
alone was with him, and crouched, patient and
watchful, moaning now and then with sympathetic
pain for the misery it could not comprehend, and
gathered close against him where he lay.

As the sun grew brighter in the palm and flower
isles beyond, the retriever tried to rouse him as on a
battle-field dogs will essay to waken their slaughtered

masters ; it thrust its muzzle against his hands, and laid its broad head against the disordered richness of his hair, moaning with piteous entreaty and fond dumb caress. At last the patient efforts moved him ; he looked up in the dog's eyes with a blind, bewildered gaze, and rose slowly and staggeringly to his feet like a man feeble from protracted illness. He had no clear memory of what had passed ; he could have re-called nothing, save that one word in which all was told—" ruin ! "

He looked mechanically round the familiar beauty of the chamber ; the hues of the pictures, the grace of the sculpture, the lavish luxury of every detail, the peace and fairness of the charmed tranquillity seemed so many mockeries of his woe. In the midst of wealth he stood a beggared man ; with the world at his feet yesterday, he stood now dispossessed of every earthly thing.

He had sold his birthright for ten years' delight ! And not of the world, not of his wealth, not of the fame of his name, and the worship of men, not even of the woman whom he loved, did he think in that first moment of awaking to this mighty desola-tion that had fallen on him ;—it was of the trust of his fathers that he had forfeited, of the home of his race that he had lost.

Esau-like, he had bartered his kingly heritance for the sensuous pleasures of an hour ; and the sole

memory that lived through the stupor of his brain
were those brief brutal words that devils seemed to
hiss for ever in his ear—" You have lost all!"

A convulsion shook his limbs ; a great voiceless sob
rose in his throat; his head drooped upon his arms,
veiling his face as the Romans veiled theirs before
outrage and calamity. "O my God! my God!" he
prayed in his agony, "give me death—not *this!*"

*   *   *   *   *

The only mercy life had left him—the privilege to
suffer in solitude— could be his but a brief space.
After the bitterness of the night followed the worse
bitterness of the risen day, when its witnesses must
come about him, when its wretched tale must be rung
on his ear in all its changes ; when the world must
flood in to wonder, to smile, to sigh, to censure, and,
yet worse, to pity ; when the condemned must go out
to the cross, to be stretched and nailed and lifted up
in crucifixion within sight of the gathered crowds.
When he remembered all these things, it seemed to
him more than life could bear to go through them ;
when he slowly roused to the real meaning of this
beggary that had suddenly seized him in the midst of
his joyous and magnificent existence, he recoiled from
its endurance with a sickening shudder, as the bravest
man will recoil from the approach of a drawn-out and
excruciating death.

Once the thought passed him—why meet it ? Why
await this living grave which yawned for him, when

the rest of the dead might be taken—the blank, blest silence of the tomb be his, instead of the world's pillory and the exile's wretchedness?

Close at his hand lay the pistols to which his torturer had referred with a jest that might be his tempting; they were loaded to the muzzle, as they had been carelessly laid down the morning previous, after an hour's pistol-shooting in his gardens below with a gay party. His grasp mechanically closed on one of them. Over and over again, in his serene security of happiness, he had smiled and said he would not live to brook a single hour of pain; the jest had become a terrible reality. One touch—one moment's blindness—then oblivion; the world and his own ruin would be as nought, powerless to sting or harm. Were it not better than to live on to face all that must come to him with the rising day? The old weary wonder of Hamlet, that pursues every mind through every age, rose in him now; the old, eternal, never-answered question came to him as it comes to so many—why live when every breath of life is pain?

For a moment his worst foe was nigh the fulfilment of his worst wish; for a moment, in the devastation of every hope and every possession, death and its escape allured him with a horrible force. All that made life worth the living was dead in him; the body only was left to perish; why leave breath in it when to breathe was only to prolong and to intensify an anguish without hope? For a moment he lifted the weapon up, and pressed the cold ring of its steel tube against his brow ; its chill touch was the only kiss left to him now, the only caress of pity he could know. His head sunk down against it, leaning on its mouth as it had used to lean on the softly-beating hearts of women who loved him. A moment,—and his dead limbs would have been stretched there on his hearth in such a close to the history of his life as would have sated even the lust of his unrelenting foe.

A ray of the sun, straying in across the yellow heat of the chandelier-lights, fell across the white features of a bust that stood at the far end of the chamber— the same features and the same sculpture as the statue to which Trevenna had murmured his vale- diction. The light illumined the marble, giving to the mouth almost breath, to the eyes almost life, with its sweet spring-day warmth. Chandos saw it as his eyes stared vacantly and without sense into the empty space.

His arm dropped ; his hand unloosed its hold ; he laid the weapon down unused.

He had treasured his father's memory, he had vene- rated his father's fame, with a great love that no time weakened. He remembered how his father once had bidden him make " the people honour him for his own sake ; " and he was about to die a dog's death by his own act, lacking the courage to rise and meet the fate that his own madness brought him !

With that memory the temptation passed. Philip

Chandos had died, like Chatham, in his nation's cause; the last Marquis had died upon the scaffold to save his honour from forfeit, and those who had trusted him from betrayal; he would not put beside *those* deaths the history of a suicide's fall.

Such as his doom was, he accepted it.

He rose and walked towards the window, with the uncertain, tremulous gait of a man dead-drunk. He drew the heavy curtains aside and looked out with aching, scorching eyes. The hum of the streets in the distance rolled in on the morning air; the faint busy noises of life came across the stillness of the gardens; a clock was striking twelve. Each sound, each murmur, every echo of the existence stirring round him, every shiver of the linden leaves near him, throbbed through his brain as though they were the clanging, jangling iron strokes of deafening bells; every sense and pulse of living things came to him with an excruciating pain, like the touch of a knife on a bared nerve. The day was at its height; solitude could be no longer possible. Even now the woman whom he loved watched for his coming; in a few hours his world awaited him; even that very night, all that was highest and fairest in the land were bidden to his house; even that very night, the fame and the fashion of his name were to give success to the crippled artist's best-beloved creation. The world looked for him; to be alone was too rich a luxury, too merciful a sentence. He must go out and endure this thing which had come to him in the broadness of daylight—in the sight of all men.

As memory rushed on him of all that must be borne, of all that had been lost, he bent his head as though under the weight of some insupportable bodily burden; a sickness of horror was upon him; he strove to realise all that was ended for him, and he could not. Only yesterday his hands had been filled with every fairest gift of life; he could not bring himself to know that they were now stricken as empty as the outstretched hands of any beggar sitting at his gate.

The paralysis of an absolute despair fell on him, mute, tearless, unmoved—the rigidity that falls on mind and brain and heart under the pressure of some immeasurable adversity.

He had to hear the worst; with the rising day came all the day's course must unfold. He could not have the partial peace of loneliness; he could not have such comparative mercy as those have, who, bereaved of what they love, know their doom at once, and can seek solitude to bear it. Step by step, letter by letter, he must pass through every detail of his desolation; and, soon or late, publicity must proclaim it to all who should choose to listen. He could have no rest, no pause, no reprieve; his misery had hunted him down, and must be met and faced.

The sun shining in through the gas-light, that burned dull and lustreless in the noonday, shone on the diamonds glittering on his dress; his eyes fell on them as, in the extremity of wretchedness, the mind will strangely play with some trifle of which it has no consciousness. He looked at them dreamily, and wondered why he wore them: a blank had fallen between him and every memory; it seemed a lifetime since the night just passed; it seemed as though the life, that was parted from him by a few hours only, had been destroyed for an eternity. Yet with the sight of them came one remembrance; he heard, as if it stole on his ear now, the low whisper of the lips he loved, as they had murmured, " Come to me to-morrow "— murmured it with the softness of a good-night blush, with the lingering light of sweet eyes of farewell !

The morrow was now to-day. How had it dawned for each !

* * * * *

He had to hear the worst. In this thing there could be no delay ; under this sentence there could be no waiting-point of preparation or of hope. He must meet the gaze of other men, and listen while their voices coldly told the story of his ruin.

He bade them come and tell him all—to the furthest letter of his doom. Despair is often bitterly calm ; it was so now with him. In solitude, nature had given way, and sunk prostrated ; before another's eyes, pride supplied the place of strength, and lent him its fictitious force. He met his fate as the last Marquis had met his ; and, in the sight of men, the

enervated Epicurean showed the steel-like endurance
of the Spartan. With the noon Trevenna returned,
as a hound returns to the slot of his quarry, when
once loosed from the coursing-slip that has held it
back perforce. He re-entered the chamber as soon
as permission came to him. He was the holder of all
papers, the comptroller of all finance, the director of
all affairs connected with the Clarencieux properties ;
with him, even more than with the lawyers, lay the
knowledge of all their minutiæ; through him, more
than through any, must come the unfolding of the
million things that went to make up the one vast sum
of destruction. He could not be driven out from the
scene of his work ; for by him alone could the thousand meshes of the net which, unseen and unsuspected,
he had woven, be traced and moved. He had secured more than his victory and his vengeance; he
had secured the imperative necessity that he should
behold the fruits of both.

Yet even he, evil as was the brute greed in him,
pitiless as was the envious hatred which scarcely
success could slake, started, as he entered again the
room he had changed from its dreamful peace into a
torture-chamber as terrible as any that the will of
Torquemada ever shut in with iron-clamped walls,
and filled with human misery—started at sight of the
wreck that he had wrought. Last night he had
looked upon Chandos in the full brilliance of his
youth, of his splendour, of his fashion, of his shadow-

less content; he saw him now, broken, exhausted, aged, altered as the flight of twenty peaceful years could never have changed him. He was still in the Court dress of the ball he had quitted when his fate fell on him : its richness was disordered, its lace crushed and soiled, its ribbon-knots and broideries tangled; but its jewelled elegance set in deadlier contrast the haggard whiteness of his face, the shattered look of his whole form; it marked in ghastlier contrast what he had been and what he was.

But "calamity is man's true touchstone," as Beaumont and Fletcher wrote. Met by misfortune, he who had shunned every shadow and every weariness with all the indolence and fastidiousness of the voluptuary, faced it with a proud serenity from which no confession of suffering was wrung.

The gas was still burning in all the crystal globes and silver branches as Trevenna entered. Chandos had no sense of the things that were about him, of the dress he wore, of the passage of the noonday hours; and his household, who felt that some great adversity had suddenly befallen him, dared not venture nigh unsummoned. He stood against the hearth as his guest advanced; his eyes were bloodshot, his hair disordered and damp with the dew of his forehead; his face was bloodless : beyond these, he "gave no sign."

Trevenna stretched out his hand in their old friendship and familiarity of greeting. Chandos did not give his own : he looked at Trevenna with a tranquil, lingering gaze; if there were reproach in it, the reproach remained otherwise unspoken.

"Tell me all," he said, briefly; and his voice, faint though it was, did not falter.

For one instant his traitor was silent, baffled and wonder-struck.

Fine as were his intuition and insight into character, he had made an error common with men of his mould; he had undervalued a nature it was impossible he could comprehend. Studying the weaknesses of his patron's temper, he had not perceived that they were rather on the surface than ingrained; he had disdained the facility that had lent Chandos so willing a tool into his hands, the gentleness, the frankness, the generosity, the unsuspecting pliability of temper; he had looked with contempt on the imaginative, idealic mind and the effeminate softness of the man he hated. He had never perceived that there were qualities beneath these that might leap to life in an instant, if once roused; he had never dreamed that Alcibiades the voluptuary could ever become Alcibiades the warrior. Had he found Chandos shot by his own hand, in the light of the young day, he would have felt no surprise—he would have thought the close in fitting keeping with the tenor of his career; to find him braced to look his desolation calmly in the face staggered and almost unnerved him.

But in an instant he recovered himself. The ruin was complete; and it should go hard, he thought, if to it he did not drive his victim to add—dishonour!

With the concise rapidity of a mind trained to précis-writing and to logical analysis and compression, he had every detail clear as the daylight, proved to the letter; and he showed, with mathematical exactitude, that everything was gone. His papers were of the plainest, his accounts the most perfectly audited, his representation of others' statements lucid to a marvel. If he had been opening a budget to a crowded House, he could not have more finely mingled conciseness with comprehensiveness, geometrical exactitude with unerring quotation, than now, when he came to prove the hopelessness of his best friend's beggary.

Hopeless it was. The inheritance which Chandos and his world had thought so secure and so exhaustless had melted away as a summer evening's golden pomp and colour fade, till not a line of light is left to show where once it glowed. It was the old, worn-out, ever-recurring story of endless imprudence, of absolute destruction. If other hands had woven half the meshes of the net spread round him, if other hands had spread their snares and temptings to make the fatal descent the surer, if any villany were in this thing, there was no trace that could even hint it. It might even have been said that the best had been done, with patient labour, to arrest the downward and irresistible course of a blind and unthinking extravagance, and done wisely and toilsomely, though in vain.

It was true, as he had stated, that Chandos had lived at a rate of expenditure quadrupling his income; vast sums had been drawn out without thought or inquiry, and in many cases there was no record of why or how they had been used. He had lived with prodigal munificence; his houses had been as open night and day to all who chose to enjoy their hospitality, as the palace of Philip of Burgundy; his gold had been ever ready to aid his friend, or to assist his foe. None had come to him for help, and gone from him empty-handed; he had relieved the necessities of other men, without a memory that they might recoil on him and become his own. His households had been very large, and utterly unchecked; the maîtres d'hôtel, the butlers, the heads of every office, had exercised their own choice in the magnitude of their expenditure. No inquiry had ever been made as to the cost of all the princely entertainments for which each one of his residences had alike been noted. He had given money, drawn money, scattered money, as he was asked; and the indulgence in every fancy, and the ignorance of all wealth's worth, which were the fruit of the habits he had been bred in from his earliest childhood, had made him as unconscious that he was sapping the very root and foundation of his whole fortunes as the madman of the ancient fable, who sawed asunder the branch on which he rested,

and which alone held him suspended above a bottomless abyss.

It was true, as Trevenna had said, that having but
ordinary possessions of an English gentleman (and
much of Clarencieux was rendered, by its very
dower of wild beauty, in beach, and rock, and forest
wilderness, profitless in a monetary sense), he had
spent his years as though he had been a sovereign with
an exhaustless treasury. He had given as royally, he
had paid as lavishly, he had bought in every delicate
gem or priceless picture, he had offered his aid to
every unfriended talent or merit, as though he had
had, not the rent-roll of Clarencieux, but the exche-
quer of two kingdoms as the ever-filling well from
which to draw.

This having been done through ten years of an un-
chequered life, there was no wonder in the crash
which followed it. No warning had arrested him
midway in its ruinous course; Trevenna had uttered
none, and the remonstrance of any other could only
have reached him through Trevenna's medium.

The whole mass of the fortune was expended; the
debt-pressure had accumulated to an enormous extent.
Who could say where what was scattered was gone?
Who could check now the piled-up bills of hirelings
and kitchen-chiefs? Who could tell now whether all
the great sums paid had been paid rightly? Who
could know now whether the items of that magnificent prodigality were justly scored down or not?

It would have been as hopeless a task to thread the buried intricacies of all these things as to take the Danaïds' labours, and seek to fill with the waters of a too-late prudence the bottomless vessels through which this lost wealth had been poured.

Trevenna, indeed, had every detail at his fingers' end. He ran through them as rapidly and as accurately as though he told the details of a new tax to the benches. He showed how, when he had first come to share any management of these matters, the locust-swarm had already eaten far into the fair birthright that Philip Chandos had bequeathed. He failed to show why he had not forced the bitter knowledge on his friend's careless ease in time to save much, though not all; yet even this discrepancy in his narrative he glossed over with an orator's skill, a tactician's sophistry, until he seemed throughout it to have been the one steadfast, wise, and unheeded Artabanus who had vainly stood by the side of the crowned Xerxes, and pleaded with him not to fling riches and honour and life into the grave of the devouring Ægean.

Chandos heard in unbroken silence.

Gigantic sums were numbered and added before him in gigantic confusion. Tables of figures and of estimates were placed before his eyes, and told him nothing, save that their sum-total was—bankruptcy! He had never known or asked the cost of the pleasures he enjoyed; he had never speculated on the worth of

all the luxuries to which he had been surrounded from
his infancy. His mind had never been trained to
balance the comparisons of receipt and expenditure.
He could have told, to a marvel of accuracy, whether
a picture, a statue, a cameo, was worth its price,
through the fineness of a connoisseur's judgment;
but, beyond these, he knew no more than any child-
Dauphin in the Bourbon age what was the value of
all the things which made up the amusement and the
adornment of his life. A man well skilled in finance
finds it a hopeless task to glean the truth of squandered
moneys. To him only one thing could stand out clear
and immutable—the fact that all was gone. It was
impossible for him to dispute the mass of evidence
heaped before him, as impossible also to dispute the
mass of debt that was brought before him. He had
believed that no creditor had ever had claim on him
for a day; but, now that the demands were made, he
could not prove they were undue. Of receipts, of
accounts, he had never given a thought : his agents
and his stewards had been allowed carte blanche to do
as they would; they could not be blamed for having
used the power, and there was no evidence that they
had abused it. The demands of the debts were vast;
there was not a witness that could be brought to
their injustice or their illegality. There was nothing
with which to face or to deny them ; they must devour
as they would. He heard in unbroken silence : once
alone he spoke; it was as the name of Tindall and

Co., the bill-discounting firm, amongst his creditors, came into sight, pressing **for heavy** sums. "How are *they* amongst the swarm?" he said, with that unnatural serenity which he **had** preserved throughout the interview unmoved still. "I never in **my life** borrowed gold, either of Jew **or** Christian."

For an instant the **face of** his tormenter flushed **slightly** with the **same** transient emotion of **shame which** had moved **him** in the portrait-gallery **of** Clarencieux.

"For yourself? Perhaps not to your own knowledge," he answered, promptly; "**but** for your friends you have many a time. How **many bills** you have accepted for men **in** momentary **embarrassment!** In nine cases **out of** ten these **bills have never** been met **by those in** whose favour they **were** drawn. They have always been popular with the trade. **Your** signature was thought the signature **of** so rich a man! This firm has bought in most of that floating paper, **and has taken its own time** to press for payment: that time has come at last. There lies your writing; the bills cannot be dishonoured **without dis**honouring you. **No** loan was ever **so costly to its** lender **as** that loan which **looks so** slight at first—the loan of your mere **name!**"

Chandos heard him calmly still. The extremity of misery had reached him, and the peace **of** absolute hopelessness was on him.

"**You say,** 'perhaps **not to** my own knowledge;'

unknown to me, then, have I borrowed moneys of these usurers?"

"Once or twice lately—yes. Forgive me, Chandos, if, in my zeal to screen or save you, I plunged you deeper into this chaos. You sent over for great sums to be lodged in Turkish and Athenian banks, whilst you were abroad this winter; you wrote to me to lodge them there. I knew that if I sent, on your bidding, to your own bankers, the amounts you required from time to time would overdraw by thousands the little left of your original capital; and that the bank would inform you of your improvidence without delay or preparation. I could not tell how to spare you; and I always persuaded myself that in some way or other—mainly I thought by some very high marriage—you would rebuild your shattered fortunes. I went to these Tindall people; I effected arrangements with them to supply you with the moneys. They held my acknowledgments for the amounts till you returned; they knew me, and they knew you. When you came back, you may remember, I brought you papers to sign at Clarencieux, and pressed you to give me a business interview. You would not wait and hear me—you never would: you signed; and I had not heart or courage, I confess, to tell you then at how terrible a pass things were with you. I did wrong; I admit it frankly. I was guilty of what I should call the most villanous procrastination in another man; but I knew it was too late to save you. I was willing to let you have as long a reprieve in your soft pleasures as I could; and, until your engagement with the Lady Valencia, I always thought that some distinguished and rich alliance would restore the balance of your affairs. And there is this much to be said for it, the error I committed in essaying to save you added but very very little to the mountain already raised of inextricable debts and difficulties. It only gave you six months more of peace : you, self-indulgent as you have been, would have deemed even those worth the purchasing."

The sophistries were deftly spoken. To a man more aware of business customs and of monetary negotiations, Trevenna would have been too astute to offer such an untenable and unlikely explanation ; with Chandos the discrepancies passed unnoted, because he knew nothing of the method of pecuniary transactions. All he had known had been to draw money and to have it. But though the financial errors passed him, his instinct led him to feel the falsity and the hollowness of the arguments to himself. Suspicion was utterly foreign to him ; his attachment to Trevenna was genuine and of long date ; doubt forced itself slowly in on a nature to which it was alien ; yet a vague loathing of this man, who had let him go on unwarned to his destruction, began to steal on him ; a disbelief in his friend wound its way into his thoughts with an abhorrent strength. It had been there when he had refused his hand in the day's accustomed greeting.

His eyes dwelt on Trevenna now with a strange wistfulness, rather reproach than rebuke — a look which mutely said, “ Is it thee, Brutus?”

“ I understand,” he said, simply; “ you have betrayed me!”

For the instant his traitor's eyes drooped, his cheek flushed, his conscience smote him.   Under the accusation of the man to whom he owed all, and whom he had pursued with a bloodhound's lust, the baseness of his own treachery rose up for a single moment before his own sight.   But it passed; he even frankly met the eyes whose silent reproach condemned him more utterly than any words.

“ Betrayed?   Do you take me for a second Iscariot?   Betrayed! how so?   Because I tried to save you pain with means that proved at best fallacious? Because I was guilty of an error of judgment that I frankly regret, and as frankly condemn?   No! blame me as you will, I may have deserved it; but accuse me of disloyalty you shall not.   If every one had been as faithful to you, Ernest, as I have been, you would not now hear the history of your own ruin.”

There was a grim, ironic truth in the inverted meaning of the last sentence that the temper of the speaker relished with cynical humour.   If others had been as faithful to Chandos in friendship as he had been in hatred, the positions of both would have indeed been changed.

Chandos answered nothing; his eyes still rested with the same look on the man whom he had defended through all evil report, and enriched with such untiring gifts. The truth of his own nature instinctively felt the falsity of the loyalty avowed him; yet that such black ingratitude could live in men as would be present here, were his doubt real, took longer than these few hours—more evidence even than these testimonies—to be believed by him. He had loved humanity, and thought well of it, and served it with unexhausted charity.

Trevenna moved slightly; hardened and tempered as was the steel of his bright, bold audacity, even he could not bear the voiceless rebuke that asked still, "Et tu, Brute?"

"Let us speak of the future," he said, rapidly; "we have seen that the past is hopeless and irremediable. You know the worst now; how do you purpose to meet it?"

"You have said already, all must go."

The same perfect tranquillity was in the reply; it was the ossification of despair.

"True—even Clarencieux."

The deadliest words that he had spoken in the past night!—he could not resist the choice of them again. He knew the sharpest torture he could inflict lay in them.

An irrepressible shudder shook his listener's limbs, but he bent his head in unchanged silence.

" And will the woman you love not go with the rest ?"

Chandos moved involuntarily, so that his face was in the shadow.

" She will be given her freedom."

Trevenna looked at him with the same impatient amaze with which he had started as he had entered the chamber. He could not realise that the voluptuary whose weakness he had so long studied, that the pleasure-seeker whose pococurantism had so long been the subject of his scorn, could be the man who answered him now, thus calm in his endurance.

" But, if she love you, she will not take it.   If all that you poets say of the sex be true, she will cling but the closer to you in your fallen fortunes.   What think you? I, I confess, doubt it.   She is so poor; she is so ambitious; she has so sought the restoration of your Marquisate !"

Chandos stretched out his hand; his breath caught as with the pang of one who can endure no more.

" It matters nothing to speak of this. I have heard your worst tidings ; now leave me for a space."

" No ; hear me yet a little longer.   I fancy I see a way to spare you some portion, at least, of your heritance, and to spare you at least this loveliness you covet.   Will you listen ?"

He made a gesture of assent. Hope was dead in him ; but he was passive through the very exhaustion of extreme suffering.

E 2

"See here!" pursued his tempter. "If you go to her and say, 'I am a beggared man,' will her tenderness remain with you? You know her best. I trust it may; but, frankly, my friend, I fear! She loves you—yes, all women do. She loves you as well as *she* can love; but she loves power more. Tell her of this thing which has overtaken you, and I believe she will be lost to you for ever."

Chandos shrank from the words.

"Leave me—let me be! It avails nothing,——"

"Yes, it does. *Why need she know it?*"

The question stole out, tempting and alluring as the sophistries that beguiled Faust.

"Why?" He re-echoed the word almost in stupor.

"Ay, why? Who need tell her? Listen here. I can temporise with your creditors for a little while. Each does not know how heavy the claims of the rest are, and none wholly suspect—hell-hounds though they be—how complete is your beggary. Your marriage is fixed for an early date from this; let the settlements be drawn up as they *would have been*, and the ceremony concluded. A marriage, even though to a penniless bride, will throw your creditors off their cast. They will believe you are secure, or would you wed with one so portionless? You can leave for abroad on your marriage-day; I fancy I could quiet them enough to let you go. Take the Clarencieux diamonds with you. Meanwhile I will send off, under divers names and in secret, many treasures of yours, that will pass out of England unknown to those who have these claims, and will be sufficient by their sale to enable you to live in moderate ease, though, it is true, without affluence. The rest you must let go; but you will have secured much—your liberty, your love, and a remnant of your possessions."

"What! you would tempt me to dishonour!"

The temptation broke down the enforced serenity that Chandos had hitherto borne; the veins swelled out black upon his forehead, a shuddering passion seized him, his voice was hoarse and harsh.

"Dishonour? — whew!" answered Trevenna, lightly. "Call it so, if you like. *I* call it common sense. How many men, pray, quit England for their debts, and see nothing but a sensible care-taking for themselves in it? Doubtless there are in those bills and estimates very heavy overcharges—we can't check them now; but I don't doubt there are; a major-domo will cheat, butlers will charge per-centage, tradesmen will add compound interest, bill-discounters will demand usurer's toll; if you take a little from them, you only take your own. As regards your fair Queen of Lilies, if she love you, what wrong can you do her? Wed her, and she will be your own; and, granted, she is very lovely. Go to her now and say, 'I am a beggared, self-outlawed, ruined man,' and you must know as well as I, Chandos, that, in a few months' time, you will see her given to one of your rivals' arms."

Chandos swept round to face him, the fire of passion flashing into the weary pain of his eyes, the contraction of a great torture in the quivering lines of his lips.

"Are you a fiend? You would tempt me to disgrace, after having lured me into ruin ?——"

"Patience, *caro mio*," said his allurer, softly. "You are hard on your best friend. And *don't* be so disdainful. Men stood it while you dazzled the world; but they won't be so passive when the comet has taken its plunge into darkness. They'll bear the curb when it pays, but they won't when it don't! Tempt you? what is there of 'dishonour' in what I suggest? On my life, I see nothing. Last night you knew no more of your ruin than the world knows now; certainly, you are justified in withholding the world from your confidence as long as you choose. Is a man 'dishonoured' because, when he holds a bad hand at whist, he does not show the cards and tell his ill luck, but keeps his own counsel and plays the game out in the best way he can? *Your* cards are bad now; but you are no more bound to expose them than he. Men are not your keepers, that you are called on to proclaim to them that while you thought yourself a millionnaire you were, in truth, a beggar. You are proud; why give yourself this degradation, why pillory yourself for public mockery? You have dazzled them, and outshone them; will you bear their laugh and their sneer when the tables are turned? You have had homage from the highest; will you brook it when the lowest, unpunished, may jeer at your fall? You have lived with royal brilliance; will you feel no sting when society chatters of how rotten at core was the royalty? You love with all the blindness of passion; will you feel no sting when the beauty you covet is possessed and enjoyed by another?"

Blunt, sometimes coarse, in ordinary speech, when he saw occasion Trevenna could summon both eloquence of language and persuasiveness of phrase, could wind with subtle tact into the hearts of his listeners, and strike surely and softly what bolt he would home.

Chandos heard him; his head had sunk upon his breast, and from his white parched lips his breath came in painful, gasping spasms. His agony was mortal; his temptation, for the moment, was very great.

Subtilely and insidiously the words stole on his ear, goading pride, torturing passion, waking all the longing of desire, lulling and confusing every dictate of honour, like the dreamy potence of a nicotine, till cowardice looked strength, fraud looked wisdom—till a sin seemed just, a lie seemed holy.

"Because you have forfeited your birthright," pursued his Iscariot, "you are not called on to beggar yourself utterly, and to summon the world in to pity

and to jibe you.　That which you did not know yourself last night, it can be a small sin not to proclaim to
men to-day!　If she love you, she will thank you that
you do not mar her sweetest hours with your own
calamity.　If she love you, the blow will fall softened
on her if she only learn it when she is your wife,
whom no evil can part from you.　Conceal your ruin
but a few weeks—a few days—and the woman you
covet is yours; proclaim it now, and you will forfeit
her, with all the rest that you have gambled away in
ten mad years.　Do as I say, and her beauty is your
own."

A sigh, wrenched as in a death-pang, alone answered
him.　Chandos stood, still with his head sunk, and
great dews gathered on his brow : honour drifted from
his grasp, and paled and withered under this devilish
tempting; while passion, coiling round his strength,
numbed him to all memory save of its own burning
pain, its own imperious dictates.

"Can you hesitate?" said Trevenna ; and his eyes
gleamed with an eager light, as he lured his prey on.
"Only withhold for a few days the knowledge you
yourself had not last night, and she is given to you ;
tell it, and some other will taste the sweetness of her
lips, and rifle as his own the loveliness you covet.
Choose !"

A low moan broke from the man he tortured ; he
wavered—he almost yielded ; he was sorely tempted.

All his nobler, better instincts were forgotten

under the spell of that insidious tempting : all he knew was the yearning of his love; all he heard was the subtle voice that bade him take evil as his good, and hung out to him, as the sole price of all he longed for, one single sin—*a lie*—a sin so venial, as men hold it, a sin so familiar in the world, that every trader's ordinary commerce and every social difficulty's small entanglement are filled with it and solved by it—a sin so slight, as a baneful licence has decreed it, yet a sin in his eyes accursed as the vilest of dishonour; a sin, as he deemed it, that would mark him out for ever an alien to his blood and a disgrace to his name.

For the instant only it tempted him—tempted him with all the mad longing of passion that dulled and dwarfed all other thoughts in its own intensity; then the voluptuary, who had never in his life risen to front a painful thought, or to deny desire, had strength to overcome this allurement which came to lead him into shame and evil, whilst he was broken and worn out with misery. He lifted his head, and for the moment his voice rang out—all faint with pain and want of food and sleep as it was—with the old, clear melody of other days :

" Out of my presence ! Cease to tempt me—cease to torture me ! By God, I will *not* yield !"

Trevenna bowed, and backed towards the door; he was too careful a tactician to press what was useless, to pursue what was unasked.

"So be it, monseigneur; I have done! I spoke but in the roughness of my common sense, in the ignorance of my coarser nature of the fine porcelain you haughty gentlemen are made **of.** I would have served you, had you let me; but since you have such a fancy for flinging yourself to the crying pack, why it must be so—and *they* are ready! You have the last **Marquis's** superb consolation—'*Tout est perdu, fors l'honneur.*' I hope it may content you!"

Chandos, from where he stood, crossed the room **with a** sudden impulse, as a **stag,** driven from bay, springs at the hounds surrounding him.

"**If it** were not **to** make **you viler** than the beasts, I should think it failed to content *you,* and that, after the beggary **you** have let me drift to without **a word** of warning, **you** want to drive me further yet down into shame and shamelessness!"

Trevenna looked at him with a steady, unflinching gaze; he was on his guard now.

"You speak on the spur of pain, **mon Prince,** and wrong me. I sought to serve you. If my blunter, ruder senses failed to feel the 'dishonour' your aristocratic blood recoils from, put it down to my failure in **delicacy, not to** my lack of loyalty. One word more, **and I** leave you at your **wish.** Have you forgotten that this is the day of the new opera, and that all your world will be about you before many hours? **Without** you, the opera must fail; shall I give out that **you are** ill, and that the matter is postponed?"

Chandos shuddered involuntarily, and the nerves of his mouth quivered. All that had befallen him, all that the future held, had never stood out before him in its desolation as now, when he remembered—the world.

"Alter nothing," he said, with an effort. "Let them come."

"Come! What! can you meet them?"

He smiled, a smile more utterly haggard and heartbroken than any sign of grief. There was a meaning in it, too, from which the daring and hardy nature of his foe recoiled.

"I have neither killed myself nor you in these past hours. There is little that will be hard to endure, since I have withheld from *that!*"

Trevenna looked upward at him for one glance; then, silenced and with an unfamiliar awe and fear upon him, let fall the heavy velvet, and left him once more to his solitude.

CHAPTER III.

THE LOVE OF WOMAN.

SUCH temptation as Chandos now resisted is like an ordeal by fire to men of strong will and of braced endurance; with him, formed to yield and to enjoy, to surrender himself to pleasure and caprice, to be facilely persuaded, and to resist nothing that allured him, it was the first conflict that had ever come to him. Yet where men moral in their lives and stainless in their repute might not have shrunk from the lie, but might have eagerly embraced the expedient, he whom many called an effeminate libertine had found strength to save his honour from the shipwreck which swamped all beside.

The woman he loved he would not win by a fraud.

The day was far spent when his tempter left him. Of the flight of time he had no consciousness; one thing alone he remembered now—she must know it, and at once. The agony of the last few hours had kept him strong and braced, as men are with the burning strength of opium or brandy. When life has done its worst, it lends a singular power, for a brief time, to endure it. Nothing greater than this can come upon us; and we gain such a courage as that force of desperation with which Spartans and Thespians buckled on their shields and waited calmly in the Pass, for that certain death which Megistius had foretold to them. Thus it was now with him; he acted mechanically, and with a calmness that was horrible even to himself, as he left the favourite and luxurious chamber which had been fated to see suffering as intense as ever filled a lazar-ward, and went out into the bright air of the young summer.

As his carriage, with all its blinds down, rolled through the streets, he leaned his forehead on his hands, and wondered if he lived, or if he lay dreaming in his grave. Every sound, every sight of the familiar thoroughfares, seemed unreal and unknown to him, as to one who rises from a bed of fever; he felt to have no share in all the life about him, no more part with it, than though he came, a disembodied ghost, to gaze upon the scenes of his past life on earth. He had never known before this what it was to suffer for an hour: in the intensity of his present suffering, existence itself seemed paralysed in him. The light of the sun blinded him; the move-

ment and noise around seemed loud on his ear as the
roar of torrents—every sense and nerve were quick-
ened to acutest perception; yet he never lost the sensation of unreality, of consciousness completely severed
from corporeality.

The Queen of Lilies stood beside one of the windows
of her own boudoir, restless, disquieted, half swayed by
anger and half by anxiety. So many hours of the
day had passed, and her lover had not approached
her. Where she stood, there was nothing near her
but the foliage and clusters of innumerable flowers;
the brightness of the declining day was shed full on
hers. She looked a woman to satisfy a sculptor's dream,
to haunt an artist's thoughts, to be hymned in a poet's
cancion; yet there was about her that nameless and
fugitive coldness which, in the fairest statue, chills
the senses and the heart.

Her hand was listlessly wandering among the clusters of blossoms; and every now and then, as the impatience and disquiet of her thoughts increased, she
broke them off and cast them down, beating her foot
in haughty irritation on them till their fragrance and
their colour perished.

The door unclosed; she turned, a smile lighting her
eyes and lending a lovely warmth to her cheek. She
swept forward with the grace of her step, with half-
playful, half-proud words of reproach for such un-

explained desertion; quickly they paused upon her lips; she looked in his face, alarmed and amazed.

"Ernest! what has happened? You are ill?"

For all answer, he pressed her to his heart and kissed her many times with a passion almost terrible in its force, the fever of his lips scorching her own like fire. He held her as men hold the dead form of their mistress, which they must lay down and leave for ever, never again to meet their sight, never again to cling to their embrace.

Then in silence he released her, with his last caress upon her lips, and moved from her, while his limbs, weak with long fasting, shook like a woman's, and his head sank down upon his breast. He would sooner have gone out to his death upon a scaffold than have told her what he came to tell.

She watched him in fear and terror. She saw that he suffered, as no physical pain could make him suffer; she saw that he was altered, as no illness could have changed him. She swept softly to his side again; she laid her fair arms round him; she lifted to him her beautiful face, which, in that moment, tempted him to dishonour, as his betrayer's words had never done.

"My love, my love," she murmured, anxiously, "what is it?—what has grieved you?"

He turned his eyes on hers, and in them she read a look that paralysed her, that haunted her throughout her lifetime—a look of such unutterable anguish that she cowered down and shrank back as she met it, struck by it as by a blow.

"Calamity has come to me," he said, briefly, whilst his voice sounded hollow as a reed, and wrung from him as confessions were wrung from men upon the rack. "I have been a living lie to you and to the world. Listen."

Then, as he spoke the last word, his calm forsook and his strength failed him; he fell before her, his hands clenched in her dress, his head bowed down upon her feet. In a few broken, passionate, disconnected words, wild in their misery, yet burned into her mind for ever as aquafortis burns its record into steel, he told her all.

There was a profound silence in the chamber—a silence in which he only heard the dull oppressed beating of his heart—a silence in which his head was still bowed down as he knelt. He dared not look upward to her face. He loved her, and it passed the bitterness of death to bring this misery on her young life; he loved her, and he had to utter words that might divorce them for eternity.

For many moments the silence lasted—a silence so agonised to him that in it he seemed to live through years, as men in the moments of a violent death. He longed, as one perishing in the desert longs for water, for one word of tenderness, one promise of fidelity; he longed for them with an intensity great as the fall he bade her look upon.

None came.

She drew herself slowly from him where he knelt, and stood in the dignity of her matchless grace, mutely gazing at him with those eyes which had all the chilliness as they had all the lustre of the stars. Her face was white and drawn like his own; but in the amazed fixity into which it had set there was no trace of pity for him, there was no grief that sprang from tenderness.

"This is a strange tale," she said at last, and her voice was bitterly, bitterly cold, though it was tremulous with the tremour of incredulous rage. "A strange tale; you must pardon me if I fail to believe it."

He looked for the first time upward at her. All hope he might unconsciously have cherished that her love might be stronger than its trial, and vows that had been vowed him in his prosperity not prove false in his adversity, forsook him now. He rose slowly to his feet, and stood beside her; and in his eyes came the same wistful reproachful pain that had been in them when he had looked at his betrayer, the pain that silently said, "Dost thou, too, then, forsake me?"

"Believe!" he said, wearily—"believe! Can you look me in my face and doubt?"

She stood aloof from him, lifted in her full height, her foot beating the bruised colourless petals of the flowers she had destroyed, her fair face haggard and rigid; her gaze fixed on him pitiless yet passionate in the coldness of its unrelenting scorn.

"Believe," she repeated, while her lips shook and

her bosom heaved. "Believe that you are the ruined bankrupt that you tell me — yes; but believe that you have been in the ignorance of your own beggary that you plead — no! ten thousand times no!"

He looked at her in a mute amazed stupor that stilled the force of the anguish in which he had knelt before her into an icy serenity, such as that with which he had faced John Trevenna.

He had never known but the tenderness and the softness of women. This vileness of imputed fraud flung at him by the one who but a moment before had lifted her sweet lips for his kiss paralysed him with its wantonness of merciless indignity.

"Ruin does not fall in a day," she pursued, while the haughty acrid words came from her lips in a quiver of rage that her graceful breeding alone reined in from the violence of passion. "Such ruin as yours is, you confess, the work of years. How perfectly you have duped the world and me!"

He who had loved her with a great and most disinterested love, yet who had refused to win her through a falsehood, could have killed her in his agony as he heard her now, could have crushed her in his embrace, and trampled out this life that looked so fair and was so merciless, that had smiled on him with so divine a forgery of love, and that flung at him in his darkest hour a dishonour that his worst foe would never have dared to hint.

Yet he stood before her with a calm dignity, a proud reproach.

"Look in my eyes and see if I could lie! Had I chosen, I could have wedded you by a fraud, and made you mine, in ignorance of my fall. As it is, I set you free—it is your right."

"My right?" There in the glow of the late day's sunlight she stood amidst the flowers, her patrician beauty instinct with the scornful passion that her own lost ambitions, her own thwarted pride, made so intolerable a misery; fronting him with a gaze as unyielding as stone, scourging him with words clear and frozen in their utterance as ice. "Indeed, my right! The pity is you did not earlier remember what my rights and the world's both were, ere you chicaned us and misled us with the paste brilliance of your tinsel glitter. You could have wedded me by a fraud? I wonder you could hesitate at one fraud more when you were so long practised in so many."

"O God!—and yesterday you loved me!"

The cry broke out involuntarily from him. Yesterday her soft caresses had been his; a few days or weeks later and she had been his wife, and now—from *her* lips poured the cruelest invectives his ruin could ever hear, from *her* thoughts came the foulest taunt that could be thrown at him to goad his wretchedness.

"Yesterday, yes! Yesterday the world and I alike believed in your honour and your rank. Yesterday we did not know you as you are, a gamester, a trickster, a living falsehood to us both."

Men under less torture than he bore then have killed with a madman's blow the fair, false thing that taunted and that jibed them. A convulsive effort of self-restraint shuddered through him, then he stood tranquil still, and almost yielding to her still, the forbearance her sex claimed for her. She had no pity for him; he would claim none.

"Your insult is undeserved," he said, briefly, while his teeth clenched tight to hold back the flood of passionate yearning, of agonised reproach, that rushed to his utterance. "Believe or not, as you will: I have spoken truth, and all the truth. I sought you when my fate was such as all men envied me; it has changed, and I set you free. All I ask is, for the sake of others, keep these tidings back until to-morrow; and, for yourself, forgive me that I ever——"

His voice broke down; his control forsook him; he loved her, and he thought only of all they would have been, of all they never now could be, to one another, and his heart went out to her in a great resistless longing that shattered pride and forgot injury, and only craved one touch of tenderness, one echo of the fond faith but yesterday so lovingly vowed to him. *He* was not changed; were these accidents of fortune, this visitation of calamity, to make him loathsome where he had been adored?

He stretched out his arms involuntarily in the suffering of his passion.

"For the mercy of God, my love, my *wife!*—for sake of all we should have been!—speak gentler to me in our wretchedness."

It was the only prayer he ever prayed for pity. In the moment of its entreaty, something softer, some grief more piteous and less absorbed in selfish violence, passed over her face. In the moment of that gesture of beseeching tenderness she could have thrown herself upon his breast and given up the world for him. Trevenna had rightly said, she loved as well as *she* could love, and in this instant life asunder seemed a doom too terrible to bear. But the impulse passed swiftly: the weight of the world was heavier and stronger on her than her love for him; he had destroyed her ambitions, and had shattered her victory; she knew no thought save for what she deemed her wrong, no grief save for what she deemed her degradation; for her loveliness enshrined a heart of bronze, and her solitary idol was—herself. She stood unmoved, her head turned towards the light with a gesture of scorn, her foot still treading out the bruised fragments of the wasted flowers.

"Claim gentler words when you can prove juster deeds," she said, with a bitterness that seemed to leave her fair lips with the lash of a leaden-weighted scourge. "You have lived one long falsehood in the sight of men; *they* may believe your pleaded ignorance of your bankrupt shame; they have long been your dupes, and *they* may be so still—*I* shall not. The Premier offered you your Marquis's coronet : go take it! You refused it to my wish; you will accept it to screen you from the claimants of your debts !"

His gaze fastened on her, riveted there by a horrible fascination. Were those eyes, that froze him with so unpitying a hate, the eyes that yesterday had smiled up in his own; were those lips, that lashed him with such brutal taunts, the lips that yesterday had met his own in their last lingering caress?

His breath came slowly, and drawn with effort, as though life were ebbing out of him; yet he stood before her prouder and sterner in the extremity of insult than he had ever been in the full splendour of his power.

"Silence!—you shame your sex. I ask your forgiveness of any wrong I may, through my own improvidence, have wrought you; but I thank God that I have known you as you are before my life was cursed with you."

Without another word he turned and left her, left her with the crushed blossoms lying beneath her foot, and the summer light upon her loveliness.

CHAPTER IV.

THE LAST NIGHT AMONG THE PURPLES.

THE new opera began.

The house was crowded with all that had rank and had fashion to make their applause become renown. For sake of its patron, the aristocracies of England and of France came to its representation, willing to be charmed, and prepared to admire; for sake of its patron, Court beauties flocked thither, resolute to be enchanted though there were not a note of melody in it; and connoisseurs came in the gentlest, most generous of tempers, inclined to be lenient, indeed secure to be pleased. All the world was ready to be complacent to Genius, since Fashion had chanced to have lent it her bright-jewelled ægis. There is a sublime arrangement in this world: the greater thing must always be floated up by the lesser. Does not the world phrase it that a queen "honours" a great statesman with her presence, and that a prince "honours" a great artist with his sitting? The world always loves these transposed phrases, and clings to these inverted orders of precedence.

So Fashion was prepared to patronise Genius; happily for Genius, it does not do it very often.

The *Ariadne in Naxos* was commenced, and the most brilliant audience of the season glanced in surprise to the empty box of its patron. The grand swell of the overture rolled out, and thrilled through the silent house with a new emotion. Such marvellous poems of sound, such pathetic echoes of sadness, such intense vibrations of passion, such spiritual cadences of thought!—in the creation that had issued from the lonely chamber of suffering, from the dreamy mind of a feeble cripple, there was that which caught the ears of the hearers with a new voice, and spoke to them with a new eloquence. They came to patronise; they stayed to feel!

As the overture closed in the throbbing of the waves of melody that swelled with a mighty thunder through the stillness, into the dazzling light and glitter of the thronged theatre Chandos entered.

The fairness of his face was unusually pale and unusually cold; his eyes had dark shadows under them, and had a singular hectic brilliance; otherwise there was no change.

"Late he is; been drinking," said a person in the stalls, who did not know him.

"Never drinks," said one who did. "Been gambling."

Trevenna, sitting by, set his teeth while he smiled.

"Gambling '*au roi dépouillé.*' Curse him ! he dies game," he thought, while he looked upward to the box as Chandos advanced to the front and stood there for a second, as though blinded with the light, then seated himself in his accustomed chair and leaned slightly forward in full view of the thronged building, where there was scarce a seat in the grand tier but held some titled friend or foreign beauty who knew him familiarly, or loved him well. No other noticed that slight pause as he stood with a paralysed, dizzy stupefaction coming into that blaze of radiance and crash of sound; no one except his foe, who knew all that was suffered in it, and all it meant. There had never been a night in which Chandos had been more on people's lips, and more in their praise and babble, than he was to-night. The interest of the stage and of the artists whose un-rivalled talent had been brought together to do justice to the new opera was divided with the interest that the well-known box where he sat had for all present. Foreigners looked at him eagerly as the man with whose fêtes all Paris had rung; strangers had him pointed out to them as the leader of the aristocracy, the former of fashion, the author of "Lucrèce," the owner of Clarencieux. Peeresses wondered at the absence of his betrothed, and spoke of his appearance as the

Duc de Richelieu at the Princess's fancy ball; of his Watteau water-party at his Richmond bijou villa; of the magnificence of the bridal gifts he had ordered for the Queen of Lilies. Poor men envied him bitterly—bitterly; and rich men wondered why, with all their wealth, they could not buy his grace, his fame, his popularity. Women who had been loved by him, or had loved him vainly, looked at him, and alone were struck by some vague sense of pain and disquiet, at the serenity of his face, at the glitter in the blue depths of the eyes that had ever till now smiled at life with so careless a brilliance.

He sat unmoved. He spoke, listened, acted precisely as he had done on any other of the many nights when he had led the verdict of that house on some new talent; there was not even a tremor in his hand, not even a quiver in his voice. The intense strength of intense agony was lent him for a time; the world-wide desert of desolation that spread round him gave him the desert's arid and passionless calm; he had all the fictitious force, all the mechanical action, of fever. The recklessness of his nature was roused till he could have laughed aloud to think how he sat there, the observed of all eyes, the envied of all men, accredited by the world about him with every gift the gods could give, and knew himself that not a beggar in the streets was poorer, not a homeless dog starving to its death more wretched, than he was.

He had not come to play out his terrible comedy from mockery or desperation; he had come because even in his darkest hour he would not forsake the man who was dependent on him, and whose whole future hung on the success which his own presence here alone could be certain to secure. But passing through it for this man's sake, the gigantic gulf that yawned between what he seemed and what he was, the knowledge of what his world thought of him and said of him in this his last night's reign over it, and of the mighty lie that, all unwitting to him, his whole life had been and was, struck on him with the horrible jest which despair oftentimes will seem to itself, and woke in him the desperate and reckless laughter with which men of his race had ridden in the old days of warfare down on to the ring of spear-heads, down on to a certain death, to laugh still while the life-blood burst forth from a hundred wounds, and the hoofs of trampling chargers broke their bone and tore their nerve.

The music swelled out on the air, rising in aërial cadence and throbbing in eloquent passion, now clear and fresh as a spring bird's song, now supreme in its melancholy as the moan of autumn winds through western forests of pine. Every joy denied him, every hope forbidden him, every smile he sought in vain, every sigh he breathed in suffering, Guido Lulli seemed to have recorded here. The music was sublime as a song of David, pure as a young child's eyes. It might not throughout be coldly perfect for the ear, but it was far more ; it was passionately human for the heart, it was eternally true for every time.

Chandos sat unmoved to the end. To him, though his hand had moulded many of its parts, though his sympathy had cherished it from its earliest birth, though his thoughts had many a time vibrated to its every chord, it was without sense or melody or meaning now ; it was like the sound of rushing waters in his ear, no more. Yet he sat unwavering to the end, and led with an unerring precision the bursts of applause that ever and again rang through the Opera House.

It closed ; the last magnificent chords re-echoed through a dead silence ; then, through the thunder of public admiration, the name of Guido Lulli was given for ever to the fame he sought.

Chandos rose and left his box with an apology to the Duc d'Orvâle and a Russian Prince, who, with others, had joined him there. He went to one, small, obscure, shut wholly away from sight of the audience ; here, alone, Lulli had been placed, shunning the view of the glittering throng, and dreading the notice or the speech of any with the nervous terror of a recluse. He unclosed the door softly. Stretched senseless on the ground he saw the Provençale's form, his hands above his head as he had fallen in the moment of ecstasy, when for the first time the voices of the world had given him that promise of immortality of which he had so long and vainly dreamed.

Chandos stooped and raised him gently; the movement and the sweep of air from the open doorway roused him from his trance; his eyes unclosed, he looked upward, scarcely conscious still.

"It has triumphed!   Ah! I can die so happy."

The words left the cripple's lips with the sigh so rare in human life—the sigh of perfect joy.

His gaze, dreamy and distant, like one who sees the visions of the future, wandered back, and knew the features that bent above him. The smile that was like sunlight beamed upon his face; he took his bene-factor's hands and kissed them, the great tears coursing down his cheeks.

"Monseigneur, this is your gift!   I cannot thank you. What are words? You have given me life, and more than life; you have given me immortality! *I* cannot reward you, but night and day I pray that God may pay my debt."

A smile came on Chandos' lips—a smile so sad that it might have been either curse or prayer. He stooped over Lulli, and spoke with an infinite gentleness.

"You will be very famous in the years to come. Once or twice remember that I aided something to it. I shall be repaid enough."

And with those words of farewell—a last farewell, though the other knew it not—he left him before the musician could reply.

" You eclipse yourself to-night!" said a French Princess to him, when, an hour later, his great world, having ordained the triumph of the opera, came, as they had long been bidden, to an entertainment in celebration of the success of the *Ariadne in Naxos.* " You revive the fêtes of our Grand Siècle."

He bowed, and smiled slightly.

" You do me much honour, madame. It was in the Grand Siècle that a Chandos gave a supper to Marie Antoinette when she was Dauphiness, with which all Paris rang from the Court to the Cerveau, and—when his guests were gone, fell on his own sword!"

" How horrible!" murmured the lady. " Pray do not revive the century to that extent."

" Oh no. We wear no rapiers, and we make no scenes."

Every highest title, every fairest beauty, in the two aristocracies of which he was the idol came to his house that night; every distinction in intellect, or blood, or fashion, or loveliness met round him as they had met a thousand times. The gardens were lighted with innumerable lamps gleaming among the trees; the winter-garden glanced a very paradise of oriental colour; the wax radiance fell on fairest brows, and the diamonds and sapphires glistened among silkiest hair; the low, pleasant murmur of voices, with " fashion not with feeling softly freighted," filled the chambers; the echoes of music came from the ball-rooms beyond;

all the old life that he had known so well, and led so
dazzlingly, was about him now for the last time.

As the "thousand great lords" who "drank and
praised the gods of gold and silver" at Belshazzar's
banquet, while laughter and song echoed through the
high halls of Babylon, saw not the foreshadowed
doom written on the brow of the lord of the feast,
and read not among the jewelled arabesques of the
palace wall the "Mene Tekel Upharsin" that rose out
to his own sight, so those who came to Chandos to-
night saw no sign upon his face, and had no thought
that this was a farewell—a farewell to joy, and
peace, and women's love, and the honour of men, and
all the gracious gifts and treasures of his life. They
did not know. They saw no change in him. Great
ladies found his voice as soft, his courtesies as graceful; men thought his wit keener, his insouciance
lighter, than they had ever been. He had said in his
heart that none should be able on the morrow to
recal having noted in him one shadow of pain. The
men of his race had always been proud as they were
reckless, capable of intense endurance as they were
resigned to limitless indulgence; the spirit of his race
rose in him now. Throughout this night—a night
when such agony was on him as men of stronger will
and harder training might have sunk under without
shame—he let the world about see no trace that all
was not with him as it had ever been. His face was

quite colourless, and now and then he lost all sight or sense of where he was; yet he never let a word, a glance, a sigh escape him which could have told his deadly secret.

One only, mingled among the crowds of princes, peers, and statesmen by right of long-established footing and familiarity, noted the dark gleam in his eyes as of one who defied fate with all the delirious daring of desperation, and knew all that was suffered, all that was suppressed,—and was content.

Once their eyes met, with a swaying cloud of perfumed laces, and delicate hues, and fair faces, and glittering orders, and sparkling jewels parting them for the breadth of a chamber. It was a strange fellowship between the betrayer and the betrayed, this solitary knowledge of the doom that hung over the house that was now filled with light and melody and the music of women's voices, and the names of those who controlled nations—this mutual consciousness alone that as they met now they met for the last time for ever, that when this night should end with it would end for ever the shadowless life that had been here so long.

To-night was the supreme martyrdom of the one— the supreme triumph of the other.

"Finished at last!" thought the man who had never let go his vow of vengeance since the summer-night long before in his childhood when he had sworn it at his mother's instance. "All the toil, all the lie, all the envy, all the bitterness and the humiliation, finished for me—all the glory, all the peace, all the fame, all the luxurious ease, and the royal pride, and the world-wide love finished for you. After to-night we shall change parts, my proud, beautiful, caressed darling of women—my careless Chandos of Clarencieux! Ah, what a thing is patience! it sits and weaves so long in the gloom futilely, but it traps at the last. There is only one thing wanting—if you *would* wince. But you die like the last Marquis, curse you! you die game through it all!"

Imperceptibly, one by one, the aristocratic crowd thinned, and left the long vista of rooms that had so often and so long seen the most exclusive and the most superb entertainments of the time; they passed away seeing nothing, dreaming nothing, of the fate that had fallen on the man who thus took his farewell of them, but speaking only as their carriages rolled away of the new genius that he had introduced among them, and of the lavish and fantastic royalty of splendour with which his fêtes were always given. The murmur of the voices died away, the strains of the music ceased, the low subdued laughter sank to silence, the glittering throng dispersed; they left him —his long-familiar friends, companions, and associates—never again to rally round their Roi Gaillard, never again to be summoned at his bidding.

He stood alone—alone as he must ever be henceforth.

The perfect stillness followed strangely on the movement and melody and radiance of life that had all died out; a clock struck a mournful silvery chime upon the silence, the fall of the water splashed in the fountains; other sound there was none. The light from a million points fell on the clustering colours of the tropic flowers, the drooping fronds of the pale-green palms, the fair limbs **of** the statues, the deep **glow of** the paintings—he looked at these things, and **knew that from** this hour **they would be his** no more.

To-night, for **the last time, they were his own;** when the sun should rise the fiat would go forth that would scatter them abroad to strangers' hands and enemies' spoil. Henceforth they and he would be divided—the things that he gathered and cherished would be divided, broadcast to whoever should choose **to** buy—and under the roof that had known him so long his voice would be unheard, his face unseen, his **name** forgotten, his place behold him no more.

Far behind him, parted from him by an eternal gulf, lay the life of his past, which had been one glad and gorgeous revel, one cloudless and unthinking joy, and which he must now lay down, as the Discrowned whom the Prætorians summoned laid aside golden pomp, and Tyrian purples, and brimming amphoræ, and dew-laden rose-crowns, and went **out,** unpitied **and alone, to die.**

That sweet and cloudless life of his rich past!—
to-night he was dethroned and driven out from it for
ever; to-night, a living man, he knew all the desolation of death, and in the full glory of his youth was
condemned to the anguish and the beggary of im-
poverished and stricken age.

To-night he was driven out to exile; and behind
him closed for ever were the barred gates of his lost
Eden.

CHAPTER V.

THE DEATH OF THE TITAN.

THE Duke of Castlemaine sat in his library in his mighty Abbey of Warburne, whither he had come by his physician's counsels. He was alone; for secretaries and chaplains and stewards were no companions for the superb old Titan of the Regency. His bright blue eyes, so fiery and so eloquent still, were looking outward at the tumbled mass of rock and moorland and giant forest-breadths, that made the grandeur of Warburne; his head so stately, though white with eighty winters, was slightly bent; his thoughts were with dead days—days when his voice rang through the House of Peers, or wound its silky way to the hearts of women; days when he could riot in the wildest orgies through the night and dictate despatches on which the fate of Europe hung, with a clear brain and a calm pulse, when the morning rose—days when he had loitered laughingly over ladies' supper-tables with half a dozen duels on his hands, and looked in the soft eyes of cloistered Spaniards ere leading his Cavalry to the charge—days when his frame had been iron and his voice magic, when nations were guided by his will, and soft lips had been warm on his own—days, in one word, of his Youth.

Though in his extreme age, the Duke was a greater man yet than those of this generation; more powerful, more fearless, more full of fine wit, of stately cour-tesy, of haughty honour. He was of another breed, another creed, another age than ours—the age when men drank their brandy where we sip our claret; when men punished a lie with their sword, where we pass it over in prudence; when disgrace was washed out with life, where we bring it in court and make money of it; when, if their morals were more openly lax, their honour was more inexorably stringent; when, if their revels were wilder, their dealing was fairer; and when the same strength which made their orgies fiercer and their blow harder made their eloquence loftier, their mettle higher, their wit keener, their courage brighter than our own. And in his extreme grace the Titan was a Titan yet, dwarfing and paling those of weaklier stature and of more timorous breed. He sat there looking out at the brown moors, warm with the golden gorse; and he moved in surprise as the door opened, with a smile of pleasure lighting his eyes:

"*You!* Has an earthquake swallowed the town, that we see you in the country, my dear Ernest?"

Even as the first word was spoken, even as his first glance fell on Chandos, he knew vaguely but terribly that some calamity, vaster than his thoughts could compass, had fallen here, on the man whom he cared for as he cared for no other of his race. Chandos was the only one of his blood who had his own code, his own creed; the only one in whose companionship he heard the echoes of a long-passed age; and he was proud of him and built mighty hopes on him—proud of his eminence, of his brilliance, of his successes, proud even of his personal grace and beauty.

Chandos drew near without a word. Those who loved him as the old Duke loved saw a change on him more ghastly than though they had seen his face set in the colourless calm of sudden death.

Castlemaine leaned towards him, and his long white fingers closed with a convulsive pressure on the Mignard snuff-box that he held.

"*What is it?*"

Chandos answered nothing; he sank down into a seat, and his head fell forward on his arms. The recklessness of desperation, the fever of utter hopelessness, had given him strength to pass through the ordeal of the night before; but here his strength broke down. He knew how the pride of the gallant old man had been centred in him; he suffered for the pain that he must deal, not less than for the misery he bore.

The Duke's mellow voice shook huskily:

"Tell me in a word. I have never loved suspense."

Chandos did not lift his head; his answer came slowly dragged out, hoarse and faint from exhaustion, excitation, and long want of food and sleep; for he had tasted nothing from the hour that he had learned his fate, and his eyes had never closed.

"I *can* tell you in one word—ruin!"

The Duke's hand trembled, making the diamonds flash and glitter on the enamel lid; it had never so trembled when it had shaken the dice, though a fortune hung on a throw, when it had lifted a pistol, though a life hung on the shot, when it had pointed to a serried square of Soult's picked troops, though an Army hung on the charge.

"Ruin! A wide word. And for whom?"

"For me."

"*You?*"

"Yes!" he answered, with a reckless laugh—such a laugh as the gamester gives when his last coin is staked and gone, and no resource is left except the suicide's grave. "As Trevenna phrases it, 'Crœsus has ceased to reign in Sardis!' It will amuse the world—for a week at least. A long time for the absent to be remembered."

A deep oath sprang from the close-shut lips of the

old Duke; his face grew white as the hoary silky hair that shaded it, and the diamonds shook and glittered in the tremor of his hand. But he loved the temper that made a jest even of a death-blow; he had seen much of it in his early day; he followed the lead with gallant endurance.

"Ruin for *you?* It is very sudden, is it not? Tell me more; tell me more."

His voice was very faint, but it was steady; he loved the man of whom he heard this thing with the generous love of an age that kept all the warmth and all the fire of his youth; yet they were both of the same school—they both suppressed all sign of pain as shame. He heard; his head—the head of an Agamemnon—bowed; his hand closed convulsively on the Louis Quatorze toy; his breathing was quick and loud. Once alone he interrupted the recital; it was at Trevenna's name.

"That vile fellow!—I bade you beware of him. He hates you, Ernest."

"It may be," said Chandos, wearily. "I have almost thought so since—since this. And yet he owes me much—more than you know."

"Who hate us so remorselessly as those who owe us *anything?*"

"Then are men devils!"

"Most of them. Who doubts it? Did he ever owe you any grudge?"

"None—only benefits."

"They are the less easily forgiven of the two. Had you any mistress whom this man loved?"

"Never, to my knowledge."

"But you may have had, unknown to you? '*Who was the woman?*' may be asked well-nigh of every feud and misery! Whatever for, he hates you, haunts you, envies you ruthlessly—hates **you**, if only because his hands are large and coarse, and yours are long and slender!"

"You make him knave and fool in one."

"The combination is not rare! But, pardon me, go on. I will hear more patiently."

He heard very patiently—heard to the end.

His head sank, his breathing grew fast and laboured, the veins swelled on his still fair broad brow, his giant limbs trembled. It was the heaviest blow life had it in its power to deal him; and though still of the race of Titans, the Duke had lost something of the force of his manhood; the strength which had risen from the Regent's orgies unscathed, and borne unjaded the heat and burden of Vittoria and Waterloo, was not now what it had been.

"Great God! if Philip Chandos had foreseen——"

His voice faltered; his listener stretched out his hand in an involuntary supplication.

"In mercy spare me *that!* Do you think *I* have not remembered him?"

There was a piteous anguish in the few words that pierced the Duke's heart to the core; his own tones,

as he answered, were sorely enfeebled for the voice
that had used to roll its thunder through the Lords,
and peal down the ranks of " Castlemaine's Horse " in
the dauntless days of his manhood.

" I meant no reproach! You would have heard
none from your father's lips. He loved you well;
and though you have been improvident, you have not
lost all. You have been true to your house—you
have saved **your honour.** Pardon me, Ernest, your
news has left me scarcely myself. But—but—must
Clarencieux go?"

Where Chandos sat, **in the gloom of** the mullioned
window, the shiver passed over him that had always
come there at the name of his idolised inheritance; he
could better have borne to part from wealth, and
repute, and the love of the world, and the love **of
woman,** than he could bear to part from Clarencieux.

" **They say** so," he answered, simply.

" My God! **and** *we* cannot help you. Warburne
is mortgaged to its pettiest farm. We—of the Plantagenet blood!—are beggars! I would give my life
to aid you, and I have nothing."

The confession broke from him so low that it
barely was above his breath. It was very terrible to
the great **noble** to know that in the dire extremity of
the man he loved he could aid him no more than
though he were the poorest peasant on his lands.

Chandos looked up; the unnatural coldness and
fixity that had set upon the fairness of his face from

the moment this calamity had fallen on him, softened and changed; his lips trembled; he rose with a sudden impulse, and stooped over the Duke's chair, laying his hand tenderly on the old man's.

"Forgive me that I bring this shame and wretchedness upon you. I came here that you might learn it from no other first; not the least bitter of my memories has been the grief that I must entail on you."

The Duke's fingers grasped his hand close, and wrung it hard; no reproach, no rebuke came from *him*; he could not have raised his voice more than he could have lifted his arm against Chandos in his suffering.

"Do not think of me; I shall live but little time to suffer anything. One question more—she who is to be your wife?"

Chandos moved from him into the shadow that was thrown darkly across the casement by the great cedar-boughs without.

"She is dead to *me*."

Another oath, loud and deep, rattled in his hearer's throat; the fire of his manhood's wrath gleamed in his azure eyes; the haughty patrician could have borne anything sooner than this—that one of his blood should be *forsaken*. Still no recrimination escaped him; he never said, "*I* warned you!" The grand old Pagan of a colossal age, hardened by long combat, and used to the proud supreme dominion of

a great chieftainship through such long years of war
and of state power, was more merciful to adversity
than the young and delicate Lily Queen.

Silence fell between them.

The Duke sat with his white crest bowed, and an
unusual dimness over the brightness of his Plantagenet eyes; and every now and then the diamonds in
the box he held shook with a quick tremor in the sunlight.

"What will you do?" he asked, suddenly, shading
his glance with the enamelled box.

"Do!" echoed Chandos, wearily; it seemed to him
that his life was ended. "What is there to do?
Nothing; except—to end like the last Marquis. An
axe on Tower Hill was more dignified, but a dose of
laudanum will be as rapid. It would make the best
ending for the story for the clubs, and the sales will
realise better if their interest be heightened by a
suicide!"

The Duke looked hastily up, with that *fin sourire*
with which throughout his career his Grace of Castlemaine had veiled every deep agitation.

"Well, you would have precedent. You would
but do what Evelyn Chandos did after his master's
death—you remember? Doubtless it would finish the
melodrame well for the world. Still, were I you, I
would not. I am an old soldier, and I confess I do
not like *surrender*—to fortune or anything else. Your
father died in the Commons like a gladiator; I should

not like you to die in a ditch like a dog. They would
not be meet companion-pictures. Besides—I do not
wish to see your grave; I have seen so many!"

Calmly, dispassionately, the old soldier spoke, toying
with his Bourbon box. None could have guessed the
intense anxiety hidden under that courtly manner, the
yearning emotion concealed under that serene smile.
Once only his voice shook: he had seen the graves of
so many!—of the friends of his youth, of his brothers
in council, of the comrades who had fought and fallen
beside him, of the women who had lain in his bosom,
and smiled in his eyes. He had seen so many!

Chandos knew his meaning—knew all that was veiled
under the gracious courtesy, the gentle smile; those
brief and tranquil words to him bore an unspeakable
eloquence—an eloquence which moved him as no
insult, no indignity, no adversity had power to move
him.

Where he stood, he bowed low, very low, till his
head was stooped and his lips touched the aged noble's
hand.

"You are right, and I thank you. Have no fear;
your words shall be remembered. Whatever my fate
is, I will accept it and endure it."

The Duke looked upward at him.

"I am glad," he said, almost faintly. "*Contre fortune bon cœur.* Pardon me if I intrude my counsels;
it is the privilege of Nestors to prose! You go now?
I shall see you again?"

" Surely." Chandos' voice sank very low as he stood before the grand old man. " Before I go—forgive me."

The Duke's eyes, so blue, so fiery still, dwelt on him with a great unuttered tenderness ; and the tones, that had used to ring like a clarion down the battle-fields, were gentle as a woman's.

" I have nothing to forgive. Had you loved and served yourself as you have loved and served others, it would not be thus with you now."

Then they parted, never to meet again.

The Duke sat listening to the last echo of his foot-steps, then, with a slight sigh, he leaned back in his arm-chair, his hand relaxed its clasp upon the jewelled box, a weariness came over him new to his nerve of steel, a mist stole before his eyes, shutting from his sight the flickering leaves, and the purple moorlands, and all the light and movement of the forest-world.

The summer light quivered through innumerable boughs, young fawns played in the warmth, white clouds drifted over sunny skies, and a nest-bird above in the cedar's branches sang low and softly, as though not to break the rest of the sleeper within. And the Duke still leaned back in his ebony chair, with the slight smile about his lips, and the diamonds flashing in the box that was lying at his feet.

The golden day stole onward, the shadows length-ened, the birds sought their roost, and the young

fawns their couches; the peace of evening brooded on
the earth, all things were at rest, and so was he; for
he still sat there, motionless and with the jewels
gleaming at his feet.

The sunset faded, and the twilight came, the
purple haze upon the moorlands deepening to night.
Still he sat there while the shadows stole the brilliance
from the diamonds and softly veiled his face as
though in reverence. And when some of his wide
household, who were so nigh, yet whom he could not
lift his hand to summon, dared to venture at length
unbidden to his presence, they found him thus; and
a great awe fell on them, and the hush of a breathless dread; for they knew that they were standing in
the presence of death.

The last of a race of Titans had died, as well became him, in silence and alone, without a sign, and
with a smile upon his lips.

CHAPTER VI.

"AND THE SPOILERS CAME DOWN."

IT was night at Clarencieux.

In the Greuze cabinet, where a few weeks before Chandos had stood lightly glancing through the French novel, with the warmth of its fire shed mellow and ruddy about him, he stood now. The twilight of the summer evening had but just fallen; the pale moon streamed in through the oriels; even the fair rich hues of the French painter's women looked ashen and weary in the misty half-light that was alone in the chamber. Chandos leaned against the high carved marble of the mantelpiece; his chest was bowed as with the weight of age; he breathed heavily, and with each breath pain; his face was white as the sculpture he rested on, and set into that deadly calm which had never left him when in others' sight. The tidings of the Duke’s death had reached him some days, and had filled up the measure of his anguish, adding to it the torture of a passionate regret, of an eternal remorse. He had loved the grand old man from whose fearless fiery eyes no glance but one of kindness and of gentleness had looked on him from his earliest childhood; and he knew that the shock of his own ruin had slain the mighty strength of the old noble, if ever grief killed age.

He stood alone ; his heart seemed numb and dead with misery, he gave no sign of emotion; no tears had ever come into his eyes since the hour in which his fate fell on him. The nights had passed pacing sleepless to and fro his chamber, or heavily drugged to rest with opium; the days had passed almost fasting, and in an apathy that awed those about him with a vague terror lest his end should be in the vacant gloom of madness. He was self-possessed, self-controlled ; he answered tranquilly, he heard patiently ; but there was that in this mechanical action, this unnatural serenity, that had a more horrible dread for those who saw him than all the ravings of delirium, all the passion of grief, could ever have had.

The door unclosed ; John Trevenna entered.

“They are all here,” he said, more softly than he had ever spoken.

Chandos bent his head and followed him out of the chamber. They who waited were his creditors.

In a day, with the rush of hell-hounds let out of leash, and as though at a given unanimous signal, his claimants had poured and pressed in on him, baying with one tongue for their one quarry—money. He had bidden them **all** meet here, and they had come without one missing—a strange gathering **for the halls of Clarencieux, where** Kings had used to find their **surest** shelter, and Courts had been entertained through Plantagenet and Elizabethan and Stuart days.

They were collected in **the** great banqueting-hall; a mob **of more** than a hundred **men—men** who had come down **on** the same errand, **in the** same temper, sullen yet eager, defiant yet **suspicious,** savage yet audacious—men who had **no** mercy on a dethroned royalty, **and** who had no sight save for the deficit they pushed to claim. Still even on them the **solemn** and venerable beauty of Clarencieux had a quieting spell. As they had entered their voices unconsciously had **sunk lower, their gait** involuntarily **had** grown **less swaggering;** and **as they** stood now, **counting** with **greedy eyes the** worth **and** magnificence **of the** banqueting-room, a silence had fallen **on** them.

"**Feels** a'most **like a church,**" whispered one, a **picture-dealer, as** he looked **down the vista of** the double porphyry columns.

As he spoke, Chandos entered.

He bowed to them with **a** grave and courteous grace; all had their hats on, even those better **bred,** from the sense of scorn in which they held a debtor, and for the sake of vaunting a nd of claiming their own superiority. Involuntarily, as they saw him, they uncovered in respectful silence, the Jew, Ignatius Mathias, who represented the bill-discounting firm, alone remaining the exception. Trevenna's eye had glanced at him as his hand went to his velvet cap, and his arm had dropped as though paralysed.

In the stillness Chandos advanced up the hall, his eyes resting unmoved on the strange and motley group that filled with their uncomely forms, and with almost every type of European nationality, the porphyry chamber where King and Prince and Peer had used to sit, his guests and his boon friends. His perfect calmness was unchanged; his bearing was grave and proud; his face looked white as the marble of a statue against which he paused, death-white beside the black velvet of the morning-dress he wore, but it was composed, haughty, thoughtful —strangely like the face of the last Marquis. There was not a murmur, not a whisper, raised; there was that in his look which held the coarsest, the greediest, the most pitiless, silent.

He stood beside the statue (it was that of his father) and turned towards them. He was at the upper end of the porphyry hall, and the multitude faced him in the glow of the lights that were illumined here.

"Gentlemen," he said, calmly, without a tremor in his voice, though it was faint as after long illness, "I have but a few words to say to you. You are here to enforce your claims; of any one of those claims I was in ignorance a few days since; but I dispute none of them, the improvidence of my life has left me no title to do so. You will doubt me perhaps when I say I never knew I owed a single debt; yet such is the truth."

There was a stir amongst the crowd, restless, pained, yet curious; they could not tell the meaning of this, yet they were stirred with a singular awe and wonder. One voice, the picture-dealer's, rough yet cordial, broke the silence :

"We believe you, damned if we don't! You hain't got a face what lies!"

Chandos bent his head in silent acknowledgment.

"For the rest," he continued, still with that unchanged tranquillity, "I have but little to add. The amount of your claims on me is, in the aggregate, sufficient to wreck fortunes ten times larger than mine has been; yet, as I understand, you can be paid in full by my entire surrender of all that I possess. This surrender I make; my lawyers will explain its value better than I can do. I resign everything unconditionally to you; it has become no longer mine, but yours. I believe there will be enough to satisfy you to the uttermost farthing."

The murmur rose deeper and louder in the hall;

the mass of men swayed together as though stirred by an universal impulse. They had come prepared to bully, to bluster, to demand, to enforce, and they were disarmed. Moreover, as he stood against the statue, they remembered the fame of Philip Chandos; the coarsest amongst them felt a pang of shame that his only son should be standing thus before them now.

They looked at one another; they could not comprehend this man who voluntarily came and laid down all his possessions at their feet, and yet in their own rough way they understood him; they would fain now have sympathised with him had they knew how. The picture-dealer—a rude broad boar who was worth near a million, and whose claims were the largest of any there, save the Jew's—pressed himself forward again, and spoke what all there felt, spoke with a genuine emotion in his harsh voice, with a mist before his sharp and eager eyes.

“Sir, you're a gentleman, and have behaved like one. We thank you, all on us. If we'd a' known, we'd a' waited—ay, bless you, we would; but that ain't here nor there. Your father was a great man, but damn me if I don't think you're a greater; and if there's any little matter—any picter or that like— that you set particular store on, say the word, and it shall be kept for you, or I'll know the reason why.”

“Spoke up right well, Caleb—hear, hear,” muttered another; and the applause was echoed and murmured down the whole body of the hall, till even the fashionable tradesmen, who had heard and had looked on supercilious and impassive, were moved by it, and joined it.

Chandos bowed his head again.

"I thank you for your good will and for the belief you give me. I will leave you now. My men of business will conclude all arrangements with you, and my servants will bring you refreshments here. For your offer, there is nothing I would claim. I have said, I give up all; but if there be any surplus left, I will ask you to do me the favour to sink it in an annuity for one who has been long dependent upon me, and whose health can never let him be as other men are; I mean, the musician, Guido Lulli."

A profound silence followed on his words, the silence of supreme astonishment. He might have taken advantage of their offer to ask anything, and he thought only of providing for a foreign cripple!

Caleb, the dealer, broke the stillness as before, dashing his hat down on the mosaic with a stormy oath.

"I wore that hat afore you;—I'd sooner uncover to you than to all the kings. Lulli shall be took care of; *I*'ll go bail for that."

Chandos turned with that royal grace which had made him the darling of Courts, and could never leave him while he had life, and silently stretched out his hand—the delicate patrician hand which his foe had hated—to the rough, uncleanly, hairy palm of the dealer. Then, with a bow to the standing multitude, he passed out of the porphyry chamber; and they made way for their debtor as men make way for monarchs.

The Israelite, Ignatius, smothered a sigh in his patriarchal beard.

"Agostino was right. It is worse than murder!" he thought.

Trevenna ground his teeth, baffled even in the sweetness of his utter victory.

"Curse him! Do what you will, you can't *lower* him!" he mused.

Caleb, the dealer, stood curiously looking at and touching with a sort of wonder his own tough broad right hand.

"He shook it, he did," he murmured; "and they call him as proud as the devil. He warn't above taking it. Damn me if it shall ever do so much dirty work agen."

A few hours later Trevenna re-entered the Greuze cabinet.

Chandos sat alone before the still-opened window; there was even now no light except the pale radiance of the moon, in which the fair women of the French painter lost life and colour, and smiled a deathly smile. His head was drooped forward; his eyes fixed on the moonlit forest and river scenes beyond.

In his hand was the tube of a great Eastern narghilé, and the smoke that curled from it was suffocating in its perfume; it was the smoke of opium. Thus, hour after hour of night or day, in solitude, he would sit and gaze out at the lands he had lost, and strive to steep his senses and his agony in the insensibility of the nicotine.

Trevenna looked at him and smiled.

"Ah, monseigneur," he thought, "you are proud as the devil, and calm as a statue, and unmoved as ice before the eyes of the world; but you suffer the worse for *that*. You bear it grandly now, and will not show that you are fallen; but you will go to wrack and ruin body and soul in no time, for all that. You have taken to opium, have you? There will not be much left of your beauty and your genius in twelve months' time. You had better have shot yourself that night you were so minded to; it would have saved you a world of trouble, and could not have destroyed you more utterly than *that* will do!"

He moved forward; Chandos neither heard nor saw him. Trevenna called him by his name; he did not raise his head nor give a sign of knowledge; he sat, bent forward, looking dreamily out at the night-world of dew-laden grasses, and mighty forests bathed in starlight, and dark skies with wreathing mists of white summer vapour, and beyond all the silver line of the calm sea.

Trevenna touched him on the shoulder; then he

raised his eyes; there was in them so senseless, so sightless a look of intolerable pain, yet almost utter unconsciousness, while, dilated by the opiate, the pupils were twice their natural size, that the man who had pursued him might well have thought his pursuit would end in the chambers of a madhouse.

"Chandos, can't you hear me?"

"Hear!" he echoed wearily. "Shall I *never* have heard all? What more can there be?"

"What more? Then have you no heed as to what becomes of Clarencieux?"

Trevenna saw the shudder which always passed over him at the name shake him from head to foot.

"No heed? *I!*"

In the stifled words there was a piteous anguish that might have moved his torturer to mercy, were not the man who hates, a blood-hound whom no death-struggles will sate till the last drop of life-blood has ebbed out.

"Well, it must go," he went on, without remorse; he had had many a pleasant banquet in that choice Greuze room, but none so full of flavour to him as the banquet he enjoyed now. "The men are in a good mood; you have pleased them mightily; and it's a great pity when you had the offer that you didn't clinch it and ask 'em straight off for the Clarencieux diamonds. I do believe you might have had them. Englishmen are such almighty fools when they once get soft and sentimental! Still, though they've taken such a fancy to you, they won't do without their money. Park-lane must go, and Clarencieux must go!"

Chandos rose to his feet; his large eyes, looking twice as large with the dark dreamy gaze the opiate gave them, dwelt with weary, **heart-sick** pain on his tormenter.

"Why come to tell me this? You heard me. I gave them all."

Trevenna shrugged his shoulders.

" Très-cher, you did. It was just as well to give it them with a good grace, seeing that they would assuredly have taken it. But the point that concerns Clarencieux is, how will it go? It *may* go by private contract, if they're all of one mind, which no set of Britons ever was yet; if not, it goes by public auction."

Chandos drew his breath with a sharp contraction. Despite the dull, heavy, half-drunk stupor of the opium, each one of these phrases quivered through him with a fearful force.

" And if it go by public auction, they will divide it," pursued Trevenna, while almost unconsciously in his triumph he lost his caution, and in his friend's ruin eased himself for the yoke so long borne before his friend's superiority by an indulgence in a contemptuous authoritative insolence that prudence would have forbidden him, precious as its enjoyment was.

" Divide it !"

The echoed words were hollow and inarticulate ; a fresh misery faced him. He knew that he and his home must part, that strangers must rule in his father's heritage, and that the place he loved most see his face no more ; but he had never thought that this heritage could be parcelled out and severed amongst the spoilers, and scattered north and south, east and west.

"Yes, divided."

The certain vulgarity which had always underlaid the tone of Trevenna's manner, though his scholarly culture had counterbalanced it, and his familiarity with good society almost effaced it, came out now almost unconsciously to himself, as he stood on the hearth, with the careless insolence of a coarse temper to adversity, and addressed, with a roughness he had never dared to use, the man who now had no power and no title in the home that had so long called him master.

"*You* won't be consulted, you know ; it's theirs now, and of course they'll go the best way to work to make money by it. We can't help that—wish we could ! It will bring most so, sold in lots. The castle will go with the home-park, of course ; some millionnaire will buy it, very likely, just as it stands, furniture, pictures, and all ; or else they say it may be bought by Government for a new military hospital. I don't know about that myself, but some say so. The rest will go in lots ; the forests will fetch no end for timber ; those oaks and elms are worth any money for ship-building and railway-carriages. The deer-park they'll turn into a sheep-walk, kill the herds, and drain the land ; and all that waste part by the sea, so pretty to look at, you know, and worth just nothing at all for agriculture, they'll sell for building purposes. All that rock, and gorse, and moor, and pine-wood will tell uncommonly well in an auctioneer's periods. The air's beautiful; the sea runs right up under the trees. It will take the public mightily as a bathing-place. I'll be bound, in ten years' time, villas will cover the whole sea-line, and hotels will be cropping up among the firs like mad. A company's sure to dart at it."

For his life he could not restrain the merciless jocularity ; it was so delicious to him to stand there in that Greuze cabinet where the pangs of envy had gnawed him so bitterly many a time, and parcel out by his words the magnificent demesne he had longed so savagely to see sold to the Egyptians and divided among the thieves, as the sons of Jacob longed to tear the many-coloured coat in rags and sell the favourite of Israel into bondage.

Chandos, standing where he had risen, heard in silence, his teeth clenched on his under-lip till the blood started among the golden luxuriance of his beard, and his breath came slow, loud, and stertorously.

" Best thing that can be done with it for you,"

went on Trevenna, standing at ease there, with his hands behind his back, and in his whole attitude the insolence of a coarse triumph more legibly spoken than he knew. "There *may* be a surplus if it sell well, and of course that will come to you. I don't think there can be much; but still something, ever so little, if it's only just as much as you used to give for an actress's bracelet, of course we shall be glad if we can save for you now. I suspect the building idea will be very profitable; there are always such a lot of builders ready to rush at a new place; and when the villas spring up like mushrooms, and the lodging-houses grow thick, I shouldn't be surprised if Clarencieux beats Ventnor. By Jove! what would the last Marquis have said if he'd foreseen bricks and mortar invading his mighty Druidic woods?"

Still Chandos said nothing; his eyes never left their gaze at Trevenna, but there was rising in them darker and darker that look which the Hanoverian nobles had seen in the eyes of the last Marquis, when he had sent them from his Tower-cell, with a single syllable, like lashed curs.

"But what I came to ask you, my dear Chandos," pursued his tormenter, "was, What will you do? What is your future to be?"

Still no word of answer escaped Chandos; and Trevenna's glance meeting his, his pitiless pursuer thought, "Small need to ask. Before another three months are out, he will be raving mad in some lunatic ward."

"You must do something," continued Trevenna, with a kick to the silver andirons. "You have not the worth of one of those fire-dogs now. If you had listened to me, you might have been living comfortably abroad, with the Lily-Queen to console you; but you wouldn't. You chose 'honour.' Now honour don't give us bread and cheese. It's quite a patrician luxury, and, I can assure you, you'll never get your salt out of it. There ain't anything the world pays so badly; you see, there ain't any demand for it! What's to be done? To be sure, you write; but now you're down in the world, très-cher, I'm sadly afraid your books will go down in the world too, and I shouldn't be at all surprised if the critics find you immoral. They always do, unless a writer gives 'em good dinners; they always shy that stone, unless their hands are filled with a claret-jug. Besides, as Scott says, 'literature's a good crutch, but a sorry staff,' unless you cant in it; and I don't suppose you'd ever cant, not if you were living on a loaf in a garret?"

Still there was no answer to him; only the gleam in his dilated eyes grew blacker as Chandos heard.

"Literature, of course, you can turn back to," resumed Trevenna, too appreciative of the satisfaction he enjoyed, and too absorbed in his ingenuity at stretching every pulley and turning every screw of the rack he had his prey stretched on, to note how dangerous a pastime he had chosen. "But I fear you won't be much able to write at present. Meanwhile, of course Warburne will be open **to you**; but I suppose you will hardly care to live there, a hanger-on upon your mother's family. Forgive me if I speak bluntly. I mean well! What remains? You can say with truth, if ever anybody could, 'I cannot work, to beg I am ashamed.' To be sure, the country —the Cabinet—would **give** you some post, perhaps, **out of respect to the great** Minister's name; but, on my life, **unless it's to** choose pictures for the nation, **or to** preside over a competitive examination of pretty **women for** the palm of beauty, **I don't know any public** office for which you've trained! **You're an** Epicurean, and there's no room for Epicureans **in** these busy, practical **days.** Your pride, **your** poco-curantism, **your art-fancies,** your fashionable caprices, were thought charming by the world, my dear Ernest, while you were rich and were its idol; but I am sadly afraid, now **that** you're a sold-up bankrupt, the world won't **care to** give you back your very good dinners, and **will** tell you, like Job's friends, that the best thing **you** can do to please them is to 'curse God and die.' "

He had gone one step too far—as the lion-tamer amuses himself with goading and insulting the fallen monarch that lies chained before him, till he forgets that the desert-blood is still there, and in incautious insolénce tampers and stings one moment too long, until the captive king, with a single leap, clears his barrier and breaks his bonds, and avenges his injuries with the old desert-might, so Trevenna had played for one moment too protracted with the man he tortured. With a spring light and long as a deer's, unerring and irresistible as a leopard's, Chandos threw himself on him, one hand grasping his shoulder, the other twisted tight in the linen at his throat, and silently, with a resistless force, strong as steel to clasp, thrust him downward across the painted cabinet towards the door, his height above the low square form of Trevenna like a Greek god's above a faun's.

"To-night at least this house is mine. If it were not that I have benefited you, if it were not that you are too vile to be avenged on, you should not leave me with life in you—you mocker, liar, traitor, you foul tempter who sold your friend!"

The words were uttered low in his throat, yet so distinct that every syllable in them vibrated on the other's ear; and, powerless, breathless, deprived of all his strength and all his self-possession by the amaze that seized him and by the force that hurled him out, Trevenna was thrust passive and without answer through the doorway of the Greuze cabinet, and flung down on to the floor of the corridor without.

The door closed, barring him out. He rose livid with rage, and passionately bitter that in one moment of thoughtless self-indulgence he should have undone the caution and the acumen of so many years, and betrayed the carefully veiled secret of his hate. Yet, as he shook himself, jarred but unbruised by the fall on the yielding velvet carpets, he smiled in a contemptuous triumph, a compensative satisfaction : he had what life could never take from him—his vengeance.

"The last exercise of your *droits de seigneur*, my beggared Lord of Clarencieux," he thought, content, though angered at himself. "You won't find any one put up with your pride now. You are bitter; yes, I dare say you are bitter; but all your misery won't prevent this haughty castle going to the hammer, and one day or other you shall see *me* in it! When I do come, I'll light my first fire with my Lord Marquis's Kneller picture, and I'll build my kennels with the pounded dust of Philip Chandos' statue ! "

CHAPTER VII.

THE FEW WHO WERE FAITHFUL.

THE morning came; a beautiful summer morning, with its light on the sea, and its west wind blowing over the limitless blossoms of acres on acres of lilies-of-the-valley and of wild dog-roses that filled the forest-glades with fragrance, and made their dewy couches for the deer, and their perfumed shelter for the earth-nesting birds. The earliest rays glancing in to the painted cabinet found Chandos sitting there as he had sat all the night through : he had never stirred: now and then his head had sunk forward on his breast, and the sleep of the opiate had fallen on him for an hour, heavy, dreamless, merciful, insomuch as it annihilated thought; at all other times he sat motionless, save once or twice when he drank off great floods of iced water or brimming draughts of

brandy, looking outward at all he loved so passionately
—at all he had lost for ever.

With that single roused action towards his traitor,
all revival of sense or movement seemed to have
ebbed out again in him. He sat dulling his senses
to insensibility with the nicotine, but never dulling
with it the pangs that ate at his heart, as the vulture
at Prometheus'.

Trevenna had not made a wide nor an unlikely
guess when he had thought to himself that the end of
the brilliant career he had so brutally and lustfully
envied would be a madhouse.

The joys of Chandos had been vivid and unshadowed
above all other men's; his suffering was proportionate.
The very nature which had rendered his pleasures so
perfect in the days that were gone, now only seemed
to render his torture ten thousand-fold more acute.
The opiate drugged his brain and his senses, but it
could not drug the mortal anguish that never for one
moment would be still.

He never noticed the rising of the day, he never
saw the sun grow brighter and higher in the west;
he knew nothing; his eyes only fastened with a look
that never left them on the sea and the woodland, and all the forest beauty that had been his
so long, that never now would be his own again.
Couched at his feet the dog Beau Sire lay, stirless
through the day and night, lifting his head now and
then with a low moan; the brute was faithful where

the hand he had filled with gifts and benefits num-
berless as the sands of the sea had turned against him.

All was very still. Trevenna, with the creditors
and lawyers, had left in the past night; the men whom
they placed in charge had been enjoined to show the
strictest respect for his privacy. The household—
amongst them old people who had known the great
Minister's youth, and had idolised his heir from the
cradle—were dumb and paralysed with amazement
and with grief; none of them dared venture near him.
Nothing roused him from his stupor—the stupor in
which the brain, the more finely it be organised, the
more vividly it imagines, and the more exquisitely it
creates, the more fatally still will lose its reason and
perish in delirium or in vacuity. Ignatius Mathias
was not in error when he had thought that his task-
master's work was worse than murder. The sharp
ringing shot, the certain mortal stab of the assassin,
would have been mercy to it. But Trevenna was too
wise and too ingenious for those; he slew more slowly,
and he kept within the law.

As the noon was high, and the sunlight without
shadow across the breadths of grass-land in the hush
in which the song-birds ceased, and even the busy
wild pigeons rested on the wing, the slow sullen
tramp of the steps of many men came on the stillness,
echoing dully on the road of the western avenue that
swept round by the western wing in which the
Greuze room was. The solid, measured beating of

the many feet did not awake him from his apathy of drugged unconsciousness; the noise of the irregular marching of varied steps as they crushed the ground beneath the woven boughs of the arched aisles of beech and chesnut did not reach his ear. The men came on to pass round the castle to the front; they were men of all ages and of different ranks, but well-nigh of all the same type—the type of the two classes of old England whom she never hears the name of now—the yeomen and the peasantry; the fair, florid, blue-eyed, broad-shouldered, bulldog type of what were once her franklins and her eorlmen; that now—here and there, fast fading out,—are still her tenant-farmers and her country cotters, still reap her yellow harvests, and still live in the green shadow of her woods.

They came on very slowly, their heads bent, their heavy steps dragging with a weary melancholy effort. They came as they had followed the bier of Philip Chandos, as they would have followed the funeral of his son.

They had learned that a worse thing than death had fallen on Clarencieux. They moved with a certain solemnity and dignity, rough and various as the men were in person and degree; for one emotion was upon them all, and a profound grief lent its sanctity, almost its majesty, to the weather-beaten faces on which the warmth of the early summer shone down through the leaves, and to the stalwart stature and the bent frames which were side by side as age and youth, as the tenant of thousands of acres and the peasant who lived in a shealing, advanced together in a long line up the double avenue.

At their head, walking alone, was a very old man of more than eighty-five years; his form gnarled and tough as one of the oaks of the deer-forest; his white hair on his shoulders like one of the patriarchs of Israel; his face tanned to a ruddy brown, that no near approach of death could pale. He leaned heavily on an elm staff, and the lines in his still comely face were deep-set, as though his own plough had riven them.

As they paced near, the loud swelling noise of their marching smote dully on the hushed noontide. At last it reached the ear of Chandos; he raised his head, heavy with the opium-fumes, and saw them. He knew them, every man of them; he had known them from the earliest moment when every creature on the broad lands of Clarencieux had striven with all the loving loyalty of feudal affection to do their best to please and to amuse the golden-haired young child of the great house of Claren-cieux.

The sight roused him in an instant, breaking away the mists, dissipating the lethargy gradually settling on his brain.

"O my God!" he moaned, aloud; "and they must suffer too."

Not alone could he bear his burden; not alone could his fate strike him; it would crush others in his fall, remove the landmark of the fatherless, drive out the old man from his lifelong hearth, send the worn-out peasant from the cottage hearthstone that had been his so long, and fell the green, glad welcome of the forests that the fathers' fathers of the most aged there had known and loved as familiar and venerable things.

He had thought of them before, thought often of all who must suffer through him; of the retainers made homeless in their old age; of the tenants given over to hard hands; of the men who had lived on those lands from their birth, like their fathers before them, condemned to see their roof-trees sold before their sight, and to be driven across the western seas to seek new homes, when they had had no other wish save to be laid in peace beside their people in the familiar graves beneath their village spire. He had thought of them; no pain could make him selfish; but he had never thought of them as he thought now when the three hundred south-countrymen, who held his fiefs, large or small, came up in the noontide through the western avenue. Involuntarily he rose; they saw him, and paused before the opened casement on the broad stretch of turf, all chequered with the shadows of the crossed branches. The oriels reached nearly to the ground; he was as much in their presence as though they had entered the building, and that which they came to say seemed best spoken under the summer freedom of the sky. With the same unanimous movement as his creditors, they uncovered to a man, standing with as much reverence before the ruined bankrupt as they had stood before the lord of Clarencieux. The sun shone clear upon his face, and at what they read there—the change so unutterable that a few days had sufficed to work—they were silenced with as unspeakable a horror. They knew then that this thing of which they had heard was true.

The old man who stood at their head advanced slightly. He was their spokesman, who had rented and farmed the greenest lands of Clarencieux, and had lived under the same broad thatch-roof as his ancestors had dwelt under since days beyond their memory, when the Chandos had been peers, and had marched with their brother-barons to win at the sword's point the chartered liberties of England. He was a brave and staunch old patriarch, holding himself proudly as any Saxon thane, yet loyal to the house he loved, as the Chandos had been loyal to their Plantagenet kinsmen and to their Stuart kings.

He—by name Harold Gelart—stood forward, his white hair floating in the soft west wind.

"My lord" (the owner of Clarencieux had been their lord to all the yeomen on the lands since that unforgotten, unforgiven day when the Hanover boor

had slaughtered in cold blood their last Marquis)—
" my lord, is this thing **true?**"

Harold Gelart could **not have put into clear** words
the shame and misery which he had heard had come
to Clarencieux.

Chandos bowed his head.

The dense throng gathered under the leafy shadow
of the elms, **moved with a** shuddering, swaying
motion. **Against** all witness they had disbelieved it
till **they should hear** its utterance from his own lips.
Its **blow to him was scarcely** less than was its blow to
them.

The old farmer bent over his elm staff as though
the shock that had been so deadly to him in the past
night smote him afresh.

" Will the lands be sold?"

His voice was hoarse, and panted slowly out, and he
covered his face as he asked it. To him it was such
unutterable shame, such insupportable disgrace, to
speak such words to the son of Philip Chandos, to
their beloved and honoured favourite, who had been
with them, and been dear to them, from the first
days of his bright childhood.

Chandos bowed his assent once more.

Speech would not come to him, and none was
needed as they looked upon his face.

They were strangely, terribly still—that mass of
toil-worn, air-freshened, stalwart men, whose strength
could have wrecked Clarencieux from terrace to

turret, had they hated its beauty with Trevenna's hate. What they heard might drive any or all of them out to new homes, might consign them to new and pitiless dealers, might level the homesteads they cherished, and might ruin them in many fatal and unlooked-for ways. But in this moment it was not of themselves they thought; it was for the great house that had fallen—for the dispossessed lord who stood before them.

Harold Gelart, the oldest amongst them, and elected their ambassador, a man of few words, tough in his mould as any oak that stood the shock of the sea-storms, yet tender at heart as any sapling fresh in its first green leaf, lifted his head, while great drops welled slowly out of his aged eyes and down the sunburnt furrows of his face.

"If it had pleased the Almighty God to have laid me in my grave before this day!"

It was the only moan that escaped the brave old yeoman. The honour of his "lords" had been his honour, their fame his fame; loyalty to them had been one, in his simple creed, with loyalty to his God; and though he knew not but that the old moated ivy-hidden Grange, where he and his had dwelt so long in peace, might be sold above his head and new landlords eject him to find a fresh resting-place in his last years, no syllable would ever have escaped him to add a blow to the misery that had fallen upon Clarencieux.

Chandos looked at him, and at the crowd that gathered so mutely under the elms; and the icy, stony rigidity, the almost senseless stupor, which had been upon his features, changed and softened as it had done at the dead Duke's words. He had known those furrowed bronzed faces ever since his youngest years; he had seen them gather round him in loyal attachment on every anniversary of his birth, at every return to his home, at every Christmas-tide that he had been amongst them. They were familiar to him as the venerable trees beneath which they stood; and he knew that they and he met for the last time.

" My friends," he said, gently (and his voice had not the composure with which he had addressed throughout his creditors, but shook slightly), " the worst that you can hear is true. You and I must part—for ever. I hope that my fate may not recoil on you; but it is too likely you may suffer through me. I have been blind and mad; forgive me that I thought too little of all I owed my heritage."

The words reached the farthest that stood on the outskirts of the throng, hollow and feeble though the once rich music of his tones was now. A single sound, like one deep vast sob, shook the crowd as they heard. They loved him well for his own sake, for his father's sake, for the sake of his great name and race, that had been part and share of their own honour for so long.

Harold Gelart lifted his white head, like the head

of a Saxon franklin, and spoke with the broad, marked dialect of the southern sea-board steeping his words in its accent.

"My lord, we aren't here to reproach of you; you have done what you will with your own. We are come to tender you our loyalty, to say a few words to you, an you will."

The old patriarch, whose life was spent amidst the woods and fields, whose rising and going to rest was with the larks of his corn-lands, found words with difficulty. His speech was ever laconic, and little above a peasant's; and the most silver-tongued orator would have found utterance hard under such grief as that he choked down now.

"Speak on," said Chandos, gently still. He knew that, bitterly as they tortured him, they came there out of love for him.

"My lord, it is just this—no more," said the old man; while the broad provincialism of his county-tone gave a rough imploring earnestness, beyond all oratory, to his words. "You tell us the lands must go; we have heard yesternight that a sore and wicked thing have befel you: it don't need to speak on it, it's too bitter in all our teeth; and them as has wrought it on you, may the vengeance of God overtake!"

Chandos stayed him with a gesture.

"No! to pray that were to call a curse on me. I but reap the harvest of my own utter madness."

Harold Gelart's eyes flashed with a fire that age could not wholly dim, and he struck his elm staff down into the turf with mighty force.

"Where be them that never warned you? Where be them that feasted at your cost? Where be them that knew all was rotting under you, and never spoke the word that might have saved you in good time? Where be *them?* Let their guilt find them out!"

There was a rude grandeur in the passionate imprecation, as the old man raised his head and looked upward at Clarencieux, where the colossal walls towered above him, as though marking the vengeance of the great dead who had reigned there. Then he turned his eyes on Chandos.

"I ask pardon, my lord; I feel dazed-like with the misery! What we come to say to you is only this. We hear a power of money is wanted; if the money was forthcoming any other way, the lands would be safe? We fancy so : we don't know much ; but we guess that. Now, we aren't rich men, none of us; but, put together, we're worth summat. We've saved a good bit, most of us ; and, clubbed together, it will make a bigger sum than maybe anybody'd think. Now, my lord, we don't mean no offence ; we've lived under you and yours all our lives, and we love you like as if you was our king. Now, will you let us pay the money? We'll clear the lands, any-how ; we'll clear summat, at least as far as it'll go. We'll give every penny we can scrape together ; and we'll bless you for using of it, as we used to bless your father's name when, let state and grandeur load him ever so, he never forgot *us*. Take it as we give it, right down with all **our** hearts; there ain't **a** man among us but what would go content, and feed with his dogs, and fodder with his cattle, to know that he'd been of **ever** such a littlest bit of help in saving **you and saving Clarencieux!"**

Harold Gelart paused—his voice shaken and stifled: **the** drops streaming unbidden, like a woman's, down **his** withered cheeks, in the passionate earnestness his errand **lent him.** Never, **in all** the years of his tough, sun-tanned, wind-beaten, healthy, vigorous life had such a weakness been wrung from him.

From the yeomen and peasant-throng a murmur came **such** as that which **the speech of** the dealer had **roused in the** porphyry chamber; **but louder,** bolder, rough, **and** honest, with the simple warmth of those who **gave it. It was** the ratification by **every** man present of the words and of the offer **of** their spokesman. **Every man** there bent his head, **as they bent it entering** their woodland church; so, **silently, they** registered their adhesion to his promise.

Chandos stood and heard. A strange alteration passed over his face; all **its** frozen calm changed; for the first time since the night that he had learned his doom, the blood rushed back in a hot flush over **his** features; he quivered through all his frame, as if they had struck him some heavy-weighted physical blow. He was silent.

At his silence, the throng stretching far away under the elm-glades before him surged nearer by one impulse; every unit of that swaying mass pressed forward to pledge his sincerity and the willingness of his gift, and from their throats, to a man, one shout broke:

"My lord! take it—take it, and buy back the lands! What is ours is yourn!"

"Ay, ay!" swore the staunch old Gelart, while with his brown horny hand he dashed back the salt from his lids. "And only just reckoning too. What was yourn have been ever free to us in your days and in your forefathers'; no soul was ever pressed, no soul ever hungered, no soul ever pined on these lands. What is ours is yourn."

Chandos was silent still. The change on his face grew softer, warmer, better with each moment; the vacant lethargy of the opiate cleared more and more away from his senses; but his head was sunk upon his chest, and for the first time since his ruin had been known to him tears gathered in his eyes and fell slowly one by one. The loyalty shown to him moved him as insult and as anguish had had no power to do; the rain of those bitter tears saved him from madness.

He stood back in the shadow, so that his face was concealed from them; the weakness he could not for

the instant control wrung his pride and wrung his
heart; with the warmer gratitude and emotion that
their generous fealty brought him, was blent the
shameful misery that he—the last Chandos of Clarencieux—should ever stand thus before the tenants of
his lands. Their love touched him with an intense
pain that he should ever have tried and proved it
thus.

They mistook his silence, and the movement with
which he involuntarily drew back into the gloom of
the Greuze chamber, for offence; and their spokesman, Gelart, pressed slightly nearer, laying hold, in
his earnestness, of the oak framework of the oriel.

"My lord, it sounds bold and coarse, maybe, as I
puts it, for we to come bringing our money to you,
but it ain't *meant* so; we come out o' love and loyalty
to you—just out o' that. Your house have been our
glory and our friend; we can't a-bear to see it fall
and not to heave a shoulder to its prop. Leastways,
my lord, if you'll just let us save the lands: we
shan't be a-doing it for you; we shall only be let
to save ourselves from new masters—nothing more.
The charity'll be to us."

The old yeoman was rude in speech and tough in
fibre, but a true inherent delicacy lived in him for all
that; he strove as far as his powers could to put the
service they came to render in the guise of a service
permitted them to aid themselves.

Chandos came forward, and took the old man's

brown hands in his, and pressed them silently; words were very hard to him to utter then.

"My friends," he said, unsteadily, while his voice vibrated on the quiet of the sunny summer day, "thank you I cannot; such service as you would render me is not to be recompensed by any gratitude. If I could take a debt from any man, I would take one from you. But were I to stoop so low as to rob you of your earnings to arrest my ruin, you would be right to deny that I could ever be the son of Philip Chandos."

A perplexed piteous pain cast its shadow over the honest ruddy faces upon which he looked; some perception of his meaning, some sense that could he take their offer he would be no longer what the men of his race had ever been, stole on them. They would have given their lives for him in that hour; and they had some faint knowledge that he was right—that his acceptance of what they tendered, in all the cordial singleness of their hearts, would stain the man they came to save more deeply than his calamity.

Old Gelart lifted his eyes.

"Master, master," he whispered, hoarsely, "it would be to save *his* name, *his* lands. I think he'd a let us do it?"

The yeoman had been of the same years with the great Minister, and had loved and honoured him with all a vassal's feudal strength.

Chandos shivered at his words.

"No," he said, gently, though in his voice there was an accent that pierced the hearts of the listening crowd. "I have dishonoured him enough; as I have sown, so I reap: it must be so. Yet, because I refuse you, do not think me dead to all your love—senseless to all your fidelity. We shall never meet again; but, to my dying day, I shall never forget you—never cease to honour and to thank you."

A mighty sob, like the wrung-out moan of a giant, shook the whole throng like one man. They had heard from his own voice the fiat of farewell; they had learnt from his own lips that the doom of Clarencieux was sealed, that they and the race they honoured would be severed for evermore.

They looked upon his face in as eternal a parting as the strong bold men who had dwelt upon his lands, and fought under his standard, had looked upon the face of the last Marquis when he had ridden forth to join the rallying—ridden forth never to return.

And they wept sorely like women.

The length of the summer-hours passed, the shadows of the clouds sweeping over the breezy uplands, the swathes of scythed grass, the golden gorse of the moors sloping to the sea, and the swelling woods of the deer-forests. A fairer day had never dawned and closed on Clarencieux. Far in the distance a white sail glided in the offing;

the stags couched slumbering under the umbrageous shelter of the greenwood aisles ; the brooks murmured their incessant song of joy, bubbling through the maiden-hair, and beneath the wild-rose boughs ; its beauty had never been more beautiful.

Like the youth whom the ancient Mexican world decked with roses, and led out in his loveliness in the light of the sun, ere the knife of the priestly slaughterer laid his dead limbs to be severed on the altar of sacrifice, the lands stretched smiling in the warmth, unshadowed by the doom that would dismember and destroy them.

To part from them for ever !—easier to lower the life best loved within the darkness of the grave, easier to lie down in the fulness of youth and die, easier to suffer all that the world can hold of suffering, than to leave the birthright every memory has hallowed, every thought cherished, every childhood's love endeared, every pride and honour of manhood centred in, and the one mad ruin of an Esau's barter lost.

The night was down—with the shine of the stars on the sea, and the call of the deer on the silence, with the grand woods bathed in dew, and the moorlands steeped in a hushing quiet ; and with the night he must pass out from Clarencieux a self-exiled and self-beggared man. All through the day he had wandered in monotonous, almost unconscious action amongst the places that he loved ; by the waves

where they stretched under endless crests of rock,
and below beetling walls of pine-topped granite; over
the heather, blossoming on leagues on leagues of
brown wet sand, where the grouse nested, and the
sea-swallow skimmed; through the dark, inter-
minable aisles of oaks without a memory that could
gauge their hoary age; through the rich, wild splendour of forest-growth, all melodious with birds and
with the noise of babbling waters; by the side of
lonely lakes belted in with leafy screens, under the
shelter of towering headlands, all clothed with fern
and pine, and with the fragrant wealth of linden-
flowers and the clinging luxuriance of summer-
creepers; through them he wandered, almost insen-
sibly, walking mile on mile without a sense of bodily
fatigue, wearing out physical strength without a
knowledge of its loss, beaten, strung, haggard, well-
nigh lifeless, yet conscious of nothing save that he
looked his last for ever on the place of his birth and
his heritage.

It was near midnight when he reached his home in
sheer exhaustion. Of the flight of time, of the
bodily suffering that racked his limbs, of the weakness upon him from want of food, he knew nothing;
he only knew that before the next day dawned he
must leave Clarencieux—his own no more, but given
over to the spoilers. All the familiar things must
pass from him, and be his no more. The trees that

had shed their shade over his childish play would fall under the axe; the roof under which kings had sought covert from the men of his blood would know him no longer; strangers would sit by the hearth to which hunted princes had fled knowing they were safer, trusting in the honour of a Chandos, than amidst the Guards of their lost throne-room. In the banqueting-hall, where his ancestors had gathered the chiefs of the nation, curious throngs would rush to stare and barter; the very marble that wore his father's semblance would be sold to whoever would buy; the very canvas from which his mother's eyes smiled on him would pass away to hang on dealers' walls. In the place that had been sacred to his race none would pause to recal his name; in the heritage where his sovereignty had been absolute, his lightest word treasured, his idlest wish fulfilled, he would have no power to bid a dog be cared for, no right to arrest a hand that should be raised to tear down with laugh and jibe the records and the symbols of the honour of his house.

Through the years, however many, that his life should stretch to, never again could he lay his head under the roof that had sheltered his childhood's sleep; never again could his eyes look upon the things beloved so long; never again could his steps come here, where every rood was hallowed, and where no race but his race had ever yet reigned.

In that hour nothing but his oath to the man who had bade him live on and meet his fate, whatever that fate should be, stood between him and a self-sought grave.

Death took the young, the fair, the well-beloved; O God! he thought, why would it pass him by? why would it leave him breath on his lips, strength in his limbs, consciousness in his brain, when all that was worth living for was dead, when every pulse of existence through his veins was but a fresh pang? Death! he had known its worst throes a thousand times with every familiar thing on which his eyes had looked their last; he had passed through its worst bitterness without a voice to comfort, without a hand to succour him, with every farewell gaze at all the living things, at all the forest haunts, at all the summer loveliness, with which he had parted as the dying Raphael parted, with longing, yearning love, from the glories of the canvas that the mists of dissolution blinded from his sight. Death! he had died a million deaths from the hour when he had known that he must part from Clarencieux.

It was long past midnight; all was very still. Through the opened casements came the lulling of the sea, and the faint, delicate murmur of leaves stirring in a windless air, moved only by the weight of their clinging dews or by a night-bird's wing. All in the vast building slept; all who loved him in the household (and they were many) had looked their last upon his face—the face that most of them had known since the laugh of its childhood had been on it. He could have no eyes upon him in this, the last hour. All was quite still; the moonlight streamed in, clear, and white, and cold, through the unclosed windows; the whole of the great limitless vista of chamber opening on chamber stretched on and on in the spectral silver light; the hush of the grave rested on the mighty halls where white-crossed Crusaders had defiled, and houseless monarchs been sheltered, and revellers feasted in the King's name through many a night of wassail, and his own life of careless, cloudless pleasure spent with so lavish a hand its golden moments. The quivering ashy gleam of the star-rays poured down the porphyry chamber, leaving deep breadths of gloom between the aisles of its columns, touching with a mournful light the drooping standards and the lost coronet of the last Marquis, shed full across Philip Chandos' statue, and leaving in its darkest shadow the motionless form of the exiled and beggared man by whose madness the honour had departed from their house.

Standing there before them—those memorials of the dead — he felt as though they drove him out, dishonoured, alien, accursed as any parricide. Through him had gone what had been dearer to them than life; through him had perished what they had trusted to him; through him their name must be tarnished by sneer, by scorn—worse yet, by pity; through him their might, their fame, their stainless heritage was dragged in the dust and parted amidst thieves. The crime of Orestes seemed scarce more of parricide than his crime.

Had not his oath held him, had not his word, pledged to one who now lay in his fresh grave, bound his arm powerless, in that hour he would have fallen, killed by his own hand, beneath his father's statue, where the moon touched with its brightest lustre the proud brow of the marble that stood there as though to bear witness against the wreck and shame of his ruined race, the desolation of his forsaken hearth.

The stillness of the after-midnight was unbroken; once the distant belling of a deer echoed over the park without: other sound there was none. He seemed alone with the dead he had dishonoured—with the great dead whose memories he had shamed, and whose treasures he had sold into bondage.

He looked at those lifeless symbols as though they were his judges and accusers; and a hoarse shudder-ing cry broke from him, and moaned down the silence of the porphyry hall.

"O God!—I saved our honour."

He felt as though he pleaded before their judg-ment-seat; as though he called on them to bear with him in his agony—to be merciful to him in his misery.

He had not bartered *all* their birthright; he had not given up his honour into slavery!

The hushed, grave-like calm that followed on the echo of his words was like the calm of a lone cathedral; it cast back upon his heart in terrible isolation the sense of how utterly he, who had loved men so well, and been the caressed of so many voices, stood in his poverty and his exile alone.

Slowly, very slowly, he looked once more at all that he must leave for ever; then turned to pass out from the porphyry chamber. But the tension of his strength gave way; weakened by little food, and worn out by exhaustion, his limbs shook, his frame reeled; he swayed aside like a tree under the blows of an axe, and fell prone across the threshold—the moonlight bathing him where he lay.

For hours he was stretched senseless there; the dog—the one friend faithful—couched down by him in a sleepless guard. The night passed lingeringly; the flicker of the gentle leaves, or the soft rush of an owl's wing, the only noise that stirred in it without. Now and then there was the sweeping beat of a flight of deer trooping across the sward that echoed from afar; once a nightingale sang her love-song with a music of passionate pain. There was no noise of life in the great forests without; there was none here in the moonlit banqueting-hall.

The wind freshened as the day drew near, blowing

through the vastness of the forsaken chambers down
the aisles of the porphyry columns; its cooler breath
breathed on him and revived him; he stirred with a
shuddering sigh.　His limbs were stiff and paralysed;
his blood seemed frozen—the warm air around felt
chill as a tomb. He rose with difficulty, and dragged
himself like a man crippled with age across the
threshold that his steps should never repass.　The
faint light of the young day was breaking, and shed
a colder, greyer hue on all its splendour, from
which the white majesty of the sculpture rose, like a
spectre keeping silent witness over the abandoned
solitude.

Thus, with his head bowed, and in his step the slow,
laborious, feeble effort of bodily prostration, he passed
onward—onward through all that never again could
his eyes look upon, save in such remembrance as
dreams lend to sleep, to mock the waking of despair—
onward through the mighty entrance-hall, in which
the silence as of death reigned, where the steel tramp
of the soldiers of the King had once re-echoed to its
vaulted roof.

He looked back, in longing as agonised, in thirst
as terrible, in yearning as speechless in its love as
that with which eyes look backward to the bier in
which all that made life worth its living to them lies
sightless, senseless, and for ever lost.　He looked back
once—in such a gaze as men upon the scaffold give

to the fairness of earth and the brilliance of sunlight, that they shall never gaze upon again. Then the doors closed on him with a hollow, sullen sound; he was driven out to exile, and his place would know him no more.

CHAPTER VIII.

THE CROWD IN THE COUR DES PRINCES.

WITH the day after his last entertainment the ruin, so sudden and so vast, had been rumoured on the town.

Convulsed with amaze, aghast with indignation, indignant in incredulity, the world at first refused to believe it; persuaded of its truth, it went as nearly mad with excitement as so languid and polite a world could.

Well as he had entertained the world, he had never, on the whole, so richly banqueted it as now, when it could surfeit itself upon a calamity so astounding. It was grateful to all, which no good news could ever claim to be; the story was so utterly undreamt of, so perfectly complete, without a flaw to make it less terrible, a loophole to make it less dark.

It was a boon beyond price in the hot languid days of a waning season; it only needed a suspicion of crime to be as refreshing as the sudden sweep of a *tramontana* through the sultry dulness of a Neapolitan noon. Just a thread of "something wicked" woven with it would have made it the "cause célèbre" of fashionable drawing-rooms. As it was, it was convulsingly amazing enough to be on the lips of every creature in the town; and inimitably coined rumours, turned out with an exquisite promptness and ingenuity from the mint of slander, soon supplied that sole deficiency of the scandalous element with an industry and adroitness beyond all praise. "In the misfortunes of our friends there is always some relish," says the Fronde Philosopher; and when this adversity piques the palate, amuses the ennui, and soothes the vanity, the wretchedness of a friend and brother may become very singularly acceptable.

It burst upon the town like the bursting of a shell. In its first rumour it was utterly discredited. "Absurd! Had they not been at his ball last night? Had not every one seen him at the new opera? Ruined?—preposterous! He could never be ruined. They knew better."

Then when the truth became indisputable, gossip-mongers quarrelled for it as a flock of street-sparrows quarrel for a crumb of bread; and the town felt virtuous and outraged. To have been led into offering such clouds of incense, year after year, to a man who

all the while was on the eve of bankruptcy!—society
felt morally indignant and unjustifiably treated. Nothing so marvellous, nothing so incredible, had startled
his order for many a long year; in the clubs and
the drawing-rooms, in the Rooms and the Lobby,
in the lounge of the Park and the' tête-à-tête of
the boudoirs, there was but one theme—his disappearance and his ruin. No loss could have been
so irreparable as the loss of their leader; no shock
could have been so intense as the fall of their idol; no
episode could have been so thrilling as their reception
by him the very night before his story was known.
Gourmets were in despair—there would be no such
dinners elsewhere; and club-wits were in paradise—
there could be no dearth of a topic. Ladies fainted
with grief, and revived to wonder if his Limoges-
ware would be sold; and wept their bright eyes dim,
to clear them again with eager speculation as to
the fate of the Clarencieux diamonds; divided interests reigned together in their hearts: it was agonis-
ing, it was terrible; no one would ever give them
such fêtes, but it was possible—all clouds have their
silver lining—that the Chandos jewels, perhaps, might
come into the market!

The Countess de la Vivarol set her delicate teeth
as she heard of it, and felt her cheek grow white,
rusée, dazzling young diplomatist as she was.

"I hate him; I have my vengeance. I ought to
rejoice," she thought, "and yet——" And yet in soli-

tude her tears fell. "Il est si beau!" she sighed to herself.

"He is ruined? Well, I have helped to do it," said Flora de l'Orme, with gay self-accusation.

"What a pity!" lamented Claire Rahel. "The art of opera-suppers will perish with him."

"There is an overruling Providence," sighed the worldly-holies; "his books are not fit to be read. Genius—yes, no doubt; but what is genius without principle?"

"Died game," said a Guardsman. "By George! one saw nothing last night."

"Always eccentric," hinted a club-lounger. "A little mad, *I* think; and, on my word, it's the most charitable thing to suppose."

"Deceived us shamefully; acted most dishonourably," wept Lady Chesterton to her allies. "My sister's peace is ruined for ever; indeed, I fear for her very life. But we may be thankful, perhaps, for even this terrible blow: it may have saved more. What happiness could she have looked for with a gambler, a libertine, a free-thinker, however brilliant his career?"

Two or three women—notably one beautiful Roman Princess, with the splendour of Rome in her eyes— suffered passionately in their solitude, passively though they had listened to the world on the subject, and thought, wearily pushing off their weighty hair from their brows, "*I* would have gone with him to his beggary."

For the rest, the world talked itself out of breath over its lost leader's **fall, and** picked the story of his calamity as a carrion picks the bones of the dead camel.   It flavoured their white soups, was the choicest olives to their wines, spared them silent moments, let the dull seem witty if he brought a piquant addition to it, and gave a lulling morphine to the pangs of jealous vanity.   The world was perfectly certain, of course, that the assertion of ignorance was merely a blind, and that they had been wittingly duped many years.   A man run through a fine fortune without knowing it?—ridiculous!   And the world began also, as Trevenna prophesied, **to find out that** "Lucrèce" was very immoral.

Thus the babble busied itself **over the wreck of** a life, denying **it even that** sanctity of solitude which even barbarians have conceded to calamity, and **ex-posing it far** and wide in those pillories where no adversity can veil, no misery can hallow, no dignity beneath misfortune can avail to shield those once given over to the mercy of insatiate tongues.

They were shocked, grieved, horrified, most com-passionately sympathetic of course; but they were quite of opinion that the idol they had followed had been utterly worthless, and began to discuss with unanimous vivacity the chances of who would be most likely to secure the prize of that inimitable genius—Dubosc.   It was perhaps regarded as almost the cruelest stroke of the whole fearful affair when the fact oozed out that the celebrated *chef* alleged his spirit to be broken, and announced his intention of retiring for the rest of his days to a villa at Anteuil, there to devote his mind primarily in uninterrupted study to the effects that might be produced by certain elements unrevealed on the red mullet—a problem which had long pursued him—and to indite a work which should annihilate Brillat-Savarin, and become the eternal Libro d'Oro of gastronomists.

The world altogether was harshly treated. There was no scandal or crime in the story of ruin, which omission rendered it curry without its cayenne; and the great coveted master—Dubosc—was lost to it. It could have lived without its late idol well enough; but it could not be reconciled to living without his cook. So it said one De Profundis over the virtually dead man and turned to his sales, much as it would have turned from his tomb to his catalogues. No one asked where he had gone; what did it matter? Take what route he would, he would be sure to go to Avernus.

Men there were, it is true, who took it strongly to heart in their own silent Quietist fashion, who smoked huge cigars over it in gloomy silence, who could not forget, try as they would, the voice that had always spoken them a gay welcome, the hand that had been always stretched out to aid them, the eyes that had never looked harshly on any living thing. There were men, many men of his own order, who loved him, who could not think of him without feeling like fools, as they phrased it ; and there were others not of his set, young men of talent and ambition, who had found an Augustus in this sparkling Catullus, who had been given fashion in their art by a word from him, and who had known no patron so sure, so generous, so omnipotent. These lamented him sorely, bewailed him bitterly in their souls; but their voices could not be heard amidst the veering wind of the condemning breath of many thousand lips; and the world in general fluttered the catalogue-leaves with raised eyebrows, and murmured its strictures on the morality of "Lucrèce." He was ruined, and they had been deceived; it was frightfully shocking, of course ; but meanwhile the virtuosi felt curious about the Quercia terra-cottas and the Fragonard medallions ; Turf-men could not but congratulate each other that the famous Clarencieux strains would become public property; dilettanti thought of the superb Titians and exquisite Petits Maîtres they had envied so long ; Pall-Mall loungers rumoured on his cabinets of cigars ; and epicures longed to read the catalogue of his Comet, his Regency, and his Imperial growth wines ; whilst ladies comforted themselves for their darling's loss by projects for securing his Della Robbia ware, his Evangeliarium in conical letters enriched with crystals *en cabochon*, his Cellini vases, or his Pompadour cabinets. He had amused them, no doubt, far more brilliantly than any other ever would do ; but, since he was gone, it was as well to console themselves with his collections. Chandos before had entertained but his order; now he furnished entertainment for all the world.

When the palace-gates were opened in the raw grey of the morning, and the Poissardes rushed in, eager, envious, insatiate, devouring, filling the Cour des Princes, what matter to them that the privacy of Versailles had never before been broken, save by laughter and music, and the soft fall of women's steps, and the glitter of a throng of nobles; what matter that Calamity held the Throne-room, that a mighty adversity had set its seal of sanctity upon the threshold? Like the Poissardes in the Cour des Princes, the crowds rushed to enjoy the ruin of the leader of fashion, and gave not one thought to the fate of the discrowned. His palaces were theirs to wreck and to burn as they would; they pillaged with both hands.

Moreover, as Philippe Egalité, if history bewray him not (which, sooth to say, it often does), took a latent pleasure in that rifling of his house, in that destruction of his order, and went up to see the crowd thronging through the dismantled palace-chambers with a smile on his lips, and his little cane swinging lightly between his fingers, to see the annihilation of the Eldest-born, to see the rooting up and trampling down of the White Lilies, even, like Monseigneur d'Orléans, some there were of his own relatives, of his own rank, who came up to watch the spoliation, and to view the wreckers among the household treasures of the fallen man, with a certain sense of gratification, with a certain self-congratulatory remembrance that he had most inconveniently outshone them.

The comet was quenched in the blackness of darkness. Well; on the whole, the stars felt they showed better.

And the *mondes* sympathised tenderly with the gross wrong done the Lily Queen, and said they were grieved that even the honour of his great father's name could not keep Chandos from such extravagance and such dissipations as had disgraced him ; and wondered whether those famous Titians of his really *were* genuine—they had their doubts; and murmured to each other in the fragrant air of their boudoirs, that there was a terrible story—very terrible—of one of his Eastern girls, hushed up and lying at the root of a great deal of this sudden disappearance. Then the papers, too, took up the theme and embellished it in leaders and notes of the week; and the *Hypercritic* recanted, and found the tone of " Lucrèce " most unhealthy.

" Dieu ! how droll an end to his royalty ! It is horrible, and yet it's amusing," said Flora de l'Orme, casting herself down, on the day of the first view, on one of the couches in his own room, while strangers stared up at the painted ceiling, tossed over his portfolios, appraised the bric-à-brac, wondered at the Daphne, and talked that the French Sovereign had bought all the Old Masters. What Demi-Monde said openly, a higher and more delicate Monde thought secretly—a point of coincidence common betwixt the two.

The world found it amusing, this discrowning and disrobing of its idol. His treasures were scattered far and wide; his favourite gems were numbered in lots; his pictures were borne from barren walls to hang under other roofs and in other lands; the Daphne was torn from her rose-hued shrine to pass to a Russian palace; the Danaïd was bought by an American fur-dealer to go to his mansion in the Fifth Avenue; the plate was bought by the great jewellers to be remelted; the Circassian girls were hired by a French Duc; the Park-lane house was let to strangers—new millionnaires of Melbourne-made fortunes—who had the painted ceiling gilded over, the winter-garden changed into a covered glass building for skittles, and the studio turned into a lumber-closet.

The world had followed him, worshipped him, caressed, quoted, courted, adored him; but when his catalogues closed, his interest for it had passed away. His closest friends were not altogether sorry to have his Titians in their galleries, his clarets in their cellars, the Clarencieux breed in their racing-establishments, and to feel that one who had eclipsed them had passed out of sight. His ruin was a nine days' wonder; then a Peeress ran away with a famous Tenor, and usurped the attention of society. Women taught themselves a pretty blush when that shocking work "Lucrèce" was spoken of; and men laid bets at evens that he had killed himself.

The world, indeed, felt that such an end for the tragedy **was** due to it, specially as it had been acutely disappointed in the fate of Clarencieux.

———————

The summer days found Trevenna at the place that was lost for ever to the great race which had reigned there since the thrones of **Rufus** and Beauclerc. Ostensibly he was there in a self-imposed devotion to his ruined friend's interests, keeping watch and ward over the spoilers. Indeed, the world altogether gave Trevenna credit for behaving very admirably in the matter—for showing an excellent spirit through-out. **He** seemed really grieved in his own manner; he confessed himself "cut **up**," lamented that Chandos never **would take his** warnings, and carried himself with so candid a contrition, so genuine a friendship, that society—who could learn more to gratify its curiosity through him than through any one—thought very well of him. Society naturally could not doubt his regret for a man with whom he had dined almost every day of his **life,** and began to discover that he **was** a very sensible and very entertaining person: he spoke with so much good feeling, and yet with so much just discrimination, of his friend's self-destruction. *He* would never have dissipated so royal a property.

It was thought, too, very delicate in him that, after the first shock of the town, he withdrew himself as much as possible to Clarencieux, to avoid hearing the misfortune discussed, and to guard, as far as he could, the conduct of the sales from dishonesty. Of course he had no power, as he said; still, if there were any residue, he should too gladly save it for his lost friend, though no one knew whither that friend had gone; and, at all events, it was as well to keep some note of the creditors' proceedings. In truth, in all his life Trevenna had never enjoyed himself so thoroughly.

To lounge through the porphyry chamber, with a bailiff eating his luncheon under the coronet of the last Marquis, to saunter through the portrait-gallery and hear dealers appraise the Lelys and Lawrences, the Vandykes and the Jamesones, to ride through the forests and know they would soon be felled as bare as a plateau, to feel his horse's hoofs sink into the rose and lilac heather-blooms, and think how building-lots would soon crush all that flower-fragrance out of sight, to look across from the deer-park over the sea and muse how the mighty herds would be driven out and dispersed, while scaffoldings of bathing-hotels would rise to front the waters, where now no step stirred the ospreys, and no sound scared the silver gulls, this was Trevenna's paradise—the paradise he had set himself to gain ever since the oath he had sworn in his childish vengeance, standing in the streets of Westminster. Hannibal-like, he had sworn in his boyhood to sack the citadel of his foes; more fortunate than Hannibal, he had seen his Rome fall.

All the cruelest traces of ruin were those which brought him most closely home the unction of his success: the Greuze room, with the writing-table strewn just as the pen had last been thrown down; the studio, with the unfinished picture on the easel, the unused colours dried upon the palette, the brushes scattered as they had been laid aside by a careless hand, the beautiful heads of women and the delicate grace of landscapes that never now would be completed by the fancy which had created them; the statues with their snow-white limbs smutched by the dirty fingers of appraisers; the treasures which had been the gift of monarchs noted down at their net value; the volumes that were the collections of centuries numbered and ticketed in lots; the rose-terraces, with all their luxuriance of blossom, their perfect sculpture, their summer sunlight, filled with the gathering of traders, Jews, and brokers—these were the things that brought to him the full realisation of his uttermost desires.

"We should put the escutcheon up, and paint

'Ichabod' under it; the glory has gone from your house, my superb aristocrats!" thought he, as he lounged down the façade of the building; and, but that it would have looked a strange lament for his ruined friend, he could have enjoyed doing that bit of buffoonery himself. Like many men of strong will and indomitable endurance—like Cromwell, and Napoleon, and Frederick—he had a dash of the broad jester in him, a love of comic, farcical bathos; it enters largely into many of the most powerful characters. For sheer schoolboy, devil-may-care love and zest in the devastation, he could have taken a brush himself and painted " Sic transit " on the white pedestal of the Minister's statue; for he was very human in his Mephistophelism, and jovial almost in the old rich Hellenic sense in his animal spirits. Besides, he had worn a curb so long; it was a delicious sensation to be utterly free and utterly victorious.

A good many of those into whose hands Clarencieux had fallen had made their camp there for a day or so, whilst the valuation was being made. It was given over to many masters; it had none in especial. Trevenna took his quarters there unmolested. He was, of course, closely allied with the lawyers, familiar for years with the agents; and he had a pleasant way with him that made him welcome, even to those whom ostensibly he came to inspect and control. He occupied the rooms Chandos had himself always used—that suite of the Greuze chambers looking out on the deer-park; and as he stretched his limbs on the bed, under the costly canopy of silk, and lace, and golden broideries, he could say to himself what few ever can say : " I have accomplished the dreams of my youth." He did not say so, so poetically ; but he thought, with a laugh of self-congratulation :

" My brilliant Chandos! which of us is the victor now ? "

And deeper than that jesting triumph, more bitter, more intense in exultation, more exhaustless in sovereign supremacy, was the sense in him of having struck down for ever the aristocrat he had hated, and of having alone, unaided, sheerly by force of his own masterly intelligence and his own matchless wit, pioneered himself a road on which he would distance the patrician he had so long and so futilely envied, and mount higher and higher, till he filled the void, and ascended the throne from which he had flung down his rival.

Thought of remorse, touch of self-condemnation, there were none in him; he had hugged what he deemed his own wrong till he had learned to look on treachery as a legitimate shield, and on chicanery as a legitimate weapon. Moreover, he was of a bright, world-wise, unerring, unscrupulous strength of nature, that never succumbed to weakness, and was never tainted by after-doubt.

That this nature was also one that no benefit could soften, no gratitude warm, was the most damning thing in the close-wrought steel of its formation.

The third day of his stay in the Greuze suite, he sat at dinner with the land-steward and one of the late lawyers of the ruined house.   He was popular with business-men of every class, though they sometimes shirked his pungent knowledge of them ; and, now that he was a Member, they in especial began to find out how racy his wit was, and how cordial his bonhomie.

The confusion that reigned in the building pleased him ; he would have liked to have seen the whole stripped and gutted by fire, if he could; he would have watched the leaping flames devour Clarencieux, as the Romans watched them devour the fair palace-walls of the city of the Barca brood. The old servants who came to him, homeless, with tears running down their cheeks, thinking little of their own fortunes, but begging him to tell them if he knew aught of their beloved lord, the weary, dejected faces of the keepers and the tenants when he met them in the shadowy woods, the emotion with which strong men shook like women as they spoke of the master they had lost—all these touched him not a whit.   They angered him, because there was one throne from which he could not oust Chandos—the hearts of his people ; but they touched him not a second.   And in like manner the desolation and confusion of the household pleased him ; and he would rather have seen a broker cracking a bottle of rum at the ebony tables of the banqueting-room, than he would have sat there to be entertained with all the sovereigns of Christendom.   Therefore his dinner in the Greuze cabinet to-night, though a hasty and ill-assorted one, had more flavour in it than all the delicate and unsurpassed tête-à-tête banquets which he had used to eat there with the owner of Clarencieux. He had never enjoyed himself more than as he leant back in the Louis Quinze armchair that Chandos had used to occupy, puffed his smoke into the fair eyes of the French painter's women, and ate his cutlet off the gold plate with the arms of Clarencieux raised in bas-relief upon it, which would soon pass to a millionnaire's ormolu buffet, or be melted down in the silversmith's smelting-room.

As he sat there, the crash of wheels driven at a gallop ground the avenue-road beneath the windows; a carriage swept round and paused. Silence followed. "Is it Esau come back to look at his lost land?" thought Trevenna. Audacious, bold as a lion, and masculine in all his courage and his powers as he was, he could never think but with a qualm of that night in which the hand of the man he had pursued and goaded had been upon his throat, forcing him backward out of his presence. It was bitter to his manhood that sudden surprise should have so thrown him off his guard, that he had endured the indignity of being thrust away like a cur; and even his fearless temper felt that it might be possible to jibe, and sting, and taunt a man made mad with misery one step too far. And yet the unsatisfied hatred in him, the love and zest in his conquest, made him think, despite that :

" I wish he might come back—just come back to see us here."

As the thought crossed him, the door of the Greuze cabinet was flung open, the Duc d'Orvâle strode in, his frank face flushed, his chesnut hair just dashed with a white thread here and there, tossed back disordered, his hazel eyes aflame.

" Where is Chandos ? "

His mellow voice rang out almost in the fierceness of a challenge. He entered without any of the ceremony customarily shown his rank, and without any of the formalities of greeting : " *le fou d'Orvâle*, as his world called him, disdained both ceremonies and formalities.

Trevenna rose and received him with that informal indifference with which (it was his best and highest point) he received a prince, as unembarrassedly as he would have done a sweep. Indeed, there was something grand and true, in his intense democratic scorn for titular differences, if he had not stifled his democracy when it was expedient, as he courted his hated aristocrats when it was lucrative.

" Where is Chandos ? " repeated D'Orvâle, imperiously.

" Don't know, M. le Duc," said Trevenna ; " perhaps in Hades."

" You don't know ? "

The eyes of Monseigneur Philippe began to sparkle dangerously.   Sweet-tempered **to** a fault, and wildly reckless of himself, he loved hotly, and hated hotly **too.**

“ Nobody knows, M. le Duc,” returned Trevenna, with a latent irrepressible delight at standing there on the hearth at Clarencieux, and saying this of its dispossessed and exiled lord, “ I suppose you will have heard——”

Philippe d’Orvâle stopped him with a passionate Parisian oath, and struck his **right** hand on the console by which he stood, till the room rang with the echo.

“ Heard ?   **Yes, I** have heard.   The news reached me in Russia.   I have travelled night and day since, without stopping, **though, till I** reached England, I believed the tale the blackest falsehood ever spawned. You do not *know* where he is gone ? ”

“ Nobody does, I have said, M. le Duc,” rejoined Trevenna, a little impatiently.   He held the French **Prince** in profound derision, as a man who, having the chance **to rule half** the Continent had he chosen, spent all his substance on café-singers and posture-dancers.   “ He is gone, I am sorry to say; and the world expects him to send it a sensational suicide.”

The brown eyes of Duc Philippe, so kindly and so full of gaiety and mirth at other times, grew full of ominous wrath, his colossal strength, that stood unimpaired all the wild excesses of his life, towered in the light against the violet hangings of the cabinet; he faced Trevenna with a superb disdain, mingled with the impatient grief that his face, mobile as a woman's and transparent as a child's, betrayed without disguise.

"What! what! Did every one forsake him in a single day?"

Trevenna shrugged his shoulders.

"Men are rats, monseigneur; scurry towards a full granary, and scamper away from a rotting house. As for the forsaking, I don't know about that. He gave a ball one night, and let the town hear next day he was all but bankrupt; he made a present of everything to his creditors, and disappeared another night, God knows where. Now a man who does that don't please society."

If Philippe d'Orvâle had doubted the fate that had befallen his friend, he could have doubted no longer when those words were spoken, under the roof of Clarencieux, by the man Chandos had protected, befriended, and benefited.

He shook with rage as he heard; the reckless and dissolute Prince-Bohemian might have many vices, but he had not the most dastardly vice on earth—he had no desertion for the fallen.

"You were his debtor, sir; of course you are but a time-server!" he said, with the haughty contempt of the Vieille Cour on his fine lips, the noblesse spirit waking in him, utterly as it was accused of slumbering whilst he drank with buffo-singers, laughed with polichinelle-showmen, danced the mad Rigolboche and Cancan at the Château Rouge, and learned their *argot de la Halle* oyster-feasting with blooming Poissardes, in all his headlong Paris orgies. "It is true, then, all this accursed history that I hear in every mouth?"

"Only too true," said Trevenna, more gravely. He would have rather had any eyes on him than those of this devil-may-care and dauntless noble, this eccentric and hare-brained original, this *bon enfant* of the Coulisses and the Chaumière, whom Europe had pronounced insane for inviting Barbary apes to breakfast; for he knew how Philippe d'Orvâle loved his friend. "Only too true, M. le Duc. Chandos has lost everything, and gone no one knows whither; out of England, no doubt. It was very suddenly that the crash came at last, though, of course, the extravagance of years had long led up to it."

Philippe d'Orvâle swung from him, and turned to the other men with the grand disdain with which he would have turned on to the Marseillaise swarming on the Terrasse des Feuillans, had he lived in the days of the Lilies.

"You were all the creatures of his bounty. Can you serve him no better way than by sitting drinking his wines in his chambers? Could he not be gone one hour before you carrion-crows came to pick your feast? Answer me in a word. What has been done to save him?"

"To save him!" echoed Trevenna, whose imperturbable nonchalance and good humour alone left him able to answer the sudden attack of the fiery southern noble, which had paralysed his companions. "Everything, M. le Duc, that tact and good sense could suggest. But you cannot dam up an avalanche once on its downward road; no mortal skill could arrest his ruin. It was far too vast, too complete."

Philippe d'Orvâle seemed as though he heard nothing; he stood there in his herculean stature, with his fiery glance flashing on the men before him, his lips drawn into a close tight line under the chesnut shower of his beard. So only had they set once before, when he had seen a young girl struck and kicked by her owners on a winter's night outside the *guingette*, where he had been as a Pierrot to a barrière-ball of ouvriers and grisettes; and the man, who had beaten her till she moaned where she lay like a shot fawn, had been felled down in the snow by a single crashing stroke from the arm in whose veins ran the blood of French nobles who had charged with Godefroi de Bouillon, and died with Bayard, and fought at Ivry under the White Plume.

"What is left him?" he asked, curtly. His breath came short and sharply drawn.

"Nothing, monseigneur."

Trevenna felt his hate rising against this haughty roysterer, this sobered reveller, who came to challenge the hopelessness and the completeness of the devastation he had wrought. He could not resist the malicious pleasure of standing there, face to face with the aristocrat-ally, the titled boon-companion of the ruined man, and dinning in his ear the total beggary that had fallen on his favourite and his friend.

"Nothing! Not a shilling!" he repeated, with the same relish with which a hound turns his tongue over his lips after a savoury, thirsty plunge of his fangs into the blood he is allowed to taste.

"'Nothing!' Is *this* place gone?"

"It is going by auction, M. le Duc."

The curt, caustic complacency of the answer was not to be restrained for all that prudence could suggest.

"Good God! what he has suffered!"

The words broke unconsciously from D'Orvâle's lips; he knew *how* he had suffered. In the moment he almost suffered as much. Duc Philippe was reckless, wayward, wasteful of the goods of the earth and the gifts of his brain, was eccentric to the verge of insanity, and fooled away his mature years in the follies of a Rochester, in the orgies of a Sheridan; but he had a generosity as wide, and a heart as warm, as the stretch of his southern lands, as the light of his southern suns. For a moment the grief on him had the mastery; then, shaking his hair as a lion shakes its tawny mane, he dashed his hand down again on the marble breadth of the console.

"Sold?   By the heaven above us, never!"

Trevenna bowed with a tinge of ironic insolence of which he was scarcely aware himself.

"It would be happy if monseigneur could make his words good; but, unfortunately, creditors are stubborn things.   Clarencieux is no longer our poor friend's, but belongs to his claimants.   It will be parcelled out by the auctioneer's hammer."

"*Never!*"

Trevenna bowed again.

"With every respect, **M. le Duc,** for your very strong negative, I fear it is quite impossible that it can take effect.   Clarencieux is doomed!"

D'Orvâle flashed his glance **over him** with that mute scorn which his grandfather **had given to** Sanson **when he sauntered up** the steps of the guillotine **as calmly as he had** gone through a minuette with Marie Antoinette or Lamballe.

"**You triumph in your** patron's adversity, sir! That is but inevitable; every jackal is content when the lion falls!   By the God above us, I tell **you** Clarencieux shall *not* be bartered!"

Trevenna shrugged his shoulders.

"**With every** deference, M. le Duc, your language, though you *are* **a** prince, is not polite.   With regard to Clarencieux——"

"It shall be mine."

M 2

The words were said as Philippe d'Orvâle could say such when he chose, with a dignity that none could have surpassed, with a sovereignty that sat finely on him in its negligent ease, with a force of will which now and then flashed out of his mad caprices and his fantastic vagaries, and showed what this man might have been, had he so willed to lead the world instead of to be the hero of a night's wild masking, the king of a score of wine-cup rioters.

"Yours? Impossible!"

Trevenna was startled almost into self-betrayal of the thirst that was upon him for the dispersion and destruction of the lands of Clarencieux—of the terror that seized him lest by some mischance any portion of the bitterness of his fate should be spared to Chandos, any fragment of the home he had been exiled from be saved from ignominy and outrage.

"Impossible?" echoed Philippe d'Orvâle. "No one ever says the word to me!"

There was all the superb defiance of the old nobles of Versailles, all the disdainful omnipotence of the Ancien Régime in the reply. When he would, he could exert his command as imperiously, as intolerantly, as any Marshal of Louis Quinze.

"Indeed! I fear his creditors will say it."

Trevenna could pause neither for the courtesies of custom nor the ceremonies to rank; he could have killed, if a glance would have slain, this loathed

French noble, who, with his seigneur's sympathies and his aristocrat's loyalty to his order and his friend, came to arrest the consummation of that unsurpassed edifice of vengeance which he had erected, at such labour and with such genius, to crush the might of Clarencieux, and lie heavy above a suicide's grave.

A fierce oath, passionate as a tornado, broke from under the sweeping beard of Duc Philippe where he stood.   But that his patrician honour forbade him to strike a man whom his patrician pride could not have met and satisfied as his equal, he could have dashed Trevenna down on the hearth he insulted, with a single blow of his stalwart right hand.

"Say it?" he repeated. "By God, then, they shall *not*. What! parcel his lands out among thieves? let a broker be master here in his stead? sell his home to some trader's new gold? Never, while there is life left in me! never, if my own castles are mortgaged over my head to get the money they ask! Where is your country's gratitude, that they let his father's memory go pawn? Where are all those he benefited, that there is not a voice lifted against such shame?"

Trevenna shrugged his shoulders. That this man was a prince and a millionnaire whom he bearded he cared not two straws; he only remembered Philippe d'Orvâle as a madman with whose outrageous follies all Europe had rung; he only remembered him as one who clung to the idol the world had dethroned, and who threatened to tear down the topmost laurel-wreath with which his **own** hand had crowned his labour of vengeance.

"Monseigneur d'Orvâle!" he said, with that malicious banter which Trevenna could **no** more **hold** back in his wrath than the leopard in his will hold back **his claws, "if the** country spent its money **on every great** man's extravagant scions, it would have some uncommonly uncomfortable legacies. **It** don't even **pay its own debt;** deuce take me **if I** can see why it should **pay Chandos'** because his **father** once was First Lord **of its Treasury, and he has seen** fit to squander as pretty a property as ever was **made ducks** and drakes of, for pictures, and dinners, **and women. As** for those he benefited—granted they're a **good** many; **but if** a lot of **artists, and** singers, and dancers, and shabby boys who think themselves Shakspeares, **and** bearded Bohemians who swig beer while they boast **themselves Raphaels, were** all to club together to help him **with a** shilling subscription, **I** don't suppose they'd manage to buy back **much** more than a shelf of his yellow French **novels. I'm** as sorry for him as you **can be (you can't** doubt my sincerity, I shall never get such good dinners); but I candidly confess I don't see, and can't **see,** why, just because he has been a **fool and** a spendthrift, a whole nation of sane people are bound **to rush** to his rescue with their purses wide open. **As** he sowed, so he reaps; nobody **can complain of that.**"

Duc Philippe shook in all his mighty limbs; and as he looked at the speaker planted **there** lightly, firmly, with his feet apart **and the** insolence of triumph irrepressibly spoken in **his face** and his attitude, **he** could have leapt forward like a staghound and shaken all **the** life out of him **with a single** gripe. It was with a mighty effort that he kept the longing in.

"If *you* reap **as** you sow, M. Trevenna, you will have a fine harvest of woven hemp!" he said, curtly, in the depths of his brown beard, as he swung with an undisguised loathing from him, and turned towards the other men, who, mute with astonishment, and out of deference for the rank of the mad noble who had broken in on them thus, stood passive. "You are his men of business, are you not?—wreckers enriched by the flotsom and jetsom you save out of his shipwreck? Listen to me, then. Whoever they be, or however his creditors hold this place, it shall be mine. Whatever price **they ask,** whatever liabilities be on it, I will give them and I will discharge. Let them name the **most** extravagant their extortion can grasp at, it shall not be checked; I will meet it. I will buy Clarencieux as it is, from its turrets to its moorlands; do you hear? Not a tree shall be touched, not a picture be moved, not a stone be displaced. It shall be mine. And, hark you here; I offer them their own terms— all their greed can crave or fancy; but tell them this, on **the** word of Philippe d'Orvâle, that if they do not part with it peaceably, if they do not send their hell-dogs out of its places and take the bidding I give them, I will so blast their names through Europe that their trade and their credit shall be gone for ever, and they shall perish in worse beggary than this that they have caused. Tell them that—Europe can let them know in what fashion I keep my oaths —and with to-morrow make Clarencieux mine."

The passionate words quivered out on the silence of the painted chamber, furious as a hound's bay, firm and ringing as an army's sound to assault. Then, without another syllable, Philippe d'Orvâle swung round and strode out of the cabinet, his lion eyes alight with a terrible menace, his lion's mane of hair tossed back. He had said enough. When once he roused from his wild masquerades and his headlong Bohemianism to use his lionine might, and to vindicate his princely blood, there was not a man in all the breadth of the nations that ever dared say nay to the " mad Duke."

He saved Clarencieux—saved it from being sundered in a thousand pieces and given over to the spoilers, though he could not save the honour of its house, the ruin of its race. The world was bitterly aggrieved—it was deprived of so absorbing a theme, of so precious a prize; and Trevenna could have killed him.

The pyramid of his vengeance had risen so perfectly, step by step, without a flaw, it was unbearable

to him that the one stone for its apex should be wanting, the one last line of the record of the triumphs
engraved on it should be missing. He had swept
all the herds away, leaving not one; it was unendurable to him that the last coveted ewe lamb
should alone have escaped him. He had destroyed
Chandos utterly, hopelessly, body and soul, as he
believed—slain honour and genius and life in him,
without a pause in his success. It was intolerable
to him that the last drop should not crown the
cup, that the green diadem of the Clarencieux woods
should wreath its castle untouched, that the royalties
of the exiled race should be left in sanctified solitude,
in lieu of being flung out to the crowds and parcelled
amongst the Marseillaise in the desolated courts of the
princes.

He had longed to see, had it been possible, the
plough pass over the lands, and the harrow rake
out every trace of the banished race; he had longed
to see, if he could, the flame of the culturer licking
up all the beautiful, wild, useless wealth of heather
and fern and forest lilies; he had longed to hear the
hammers clang among the woodland stillness, to watch
the oaks crash down under the axe, to behold the
beauty crushed out under the iron roll and the timber
scaffolding of the new speculators—to know that the
very place, and name, and relics of the exiled lord were
effaced and forgotten. Through Philippe d'Orvâle,
this last crowning luxury was denied.

Clarencieux, though he had driven from it the last
of its race, escaped him—escaped the indignity, the
oblivion, the desecration he had planned to heap on it;
he had made its hearths desolate, but his arm was
held back from the final blow with which he had
planned to make them also dishonoured, and to raze
their stones as though no fires had ever burned there—
till sheep should have grazed where kings had feasted,
and wheat have waved where its dead rulers had their
graves.

Through Philippe d'Orvâle, it was denied him.

Thus, some were faithful to the fallen idol: the
sun-browned men who toiled from dawn to evening
among the seas of seeding grass and the yellow oceans
of the swelling corn; the crippled dreamer whom his
fellows thought an idiot that a child might lead; the
reckless voluptuary, the Prince-Bohemian, whom the
world called a madman, and vested with every vice
that libertines can frame; the dog whom human
reason disdains as a brute without speech;—those were
faithful—those only. But they were many, as the
world stands.

The two who were deadliest against him, and
chiefest without pity or mercy in his fall, were the
man he had succoured with his friendship and his
gold, and the woman he had loved and honoured.

BOOK THE FOURTH.

CHAPTER I.

"FACILIS DESCENSUS AVERNI."

IT was far past midnight in **Paris**; a chilly, bitter winter's night, in the turn of the young year; a night without stars, in which the snow drifted slowly down, and the homeless couched down shivering into a traitorous sleep—a merciful sleep, from which they would wake no more ; an endless sleep, to be yearned for passionately when there can be no bread for the parching lips, if breath linger in them, no peace for the aching eyes, if they wake again to a world of want.

It was 'long past midnight in one of the gambling-dens which mock the law in the hidden darkness of their secret haunts—the dens which no code will ever suppress, which no legislature will ever prevent. Where any vice is demanded, there will be the supply ;

let every shape **of forbiddance** be exercised as it may, in vain. Wherever **men** be hungered **for** their own **ruin,** there will be also **those who bring** their ruin to **them.**

This was one of the worst hells in Paris—the worst in Europe. Men who dared venture nowhere else came here; men on whom the grasp of the law would be laid, were they seen, came here; men who, having exhausted every form of riot and debauchery, had nothing left except the gamester's excitation, came here; it embraced them all, and finished the wreck that other ruin had begun. Other places allured with colour, with glitter, with enticing temptations : this had none of these; it allured with its own deadly charm alone, it made its trade terribly naked and avowed; it let men come and stake their lives, and raked the stake in, and went on without a pause : it was a pandemoniac paradise only for those already cursed. It was hidden away in one of the foulest and most secret nests in Paris; its haunt was known to none save its frequenters, and none so frequented it save those whom some criminal brand or some desperate doom already had marked or claimed. Close at hand to it, in an outer chamber, were the hot drinks, the acrid wines, the absinthe, and the opiates that were drunk down by ashen lips and burning throats as though they were water; these alone broke the ceaseless tenor of the gambling; these alone shared with it the days and nights of those who plunged into the abyss it opened for them. Often all on through the dawn, and the noon, and the day, the flaring gas-jets of its burners would be kept alight: the crowd that filled its room would know nothing of time—not know even that the sun had risen. The gay tumult of the summer life of Paris would be waking and shining on all around it in the clear light of the fresh hours; and still here, where the sullen doors barred out all comers, the gamesters would play on—play on till they dropped down dead-drunk, or reeled insensible with want of food and drugs or nicotines. The Morgue had never owed so many visitants to any place as it had owed to this; the Bagne had never received so many desperadoes as it had received from here; the walls of Bicêtre had never been so filled with raving brainless lives as it had been filled with by the haunters of this den hidden in the midst of curling crooked streets and crowding roofs, like a viper's nest under the swathes of grass.

Those who owned it were never known; the longest frequenter of its room never knew who the bank was; it was a secret profound, impenetrable— guarded as closely as its own existence was guarded from the million eyes of the clairvoyant law. No one knew that in two or three superb hotels, with fine carriages, fine dinners, fine linen, with fashionable wives and blameless reputations, with a high name on the Bourse and a reception at the Tuileries, dwelt in peace and plenty—the proprietors.

Does the world ever guess how a millionth part of the money that fills it is made? The world at large, never!

It was far past midnight in the hell; the gas-glare fell on the painted faces of unsexed women and on the haggard brows of men who had played on here all through the day, and played on through the night. The croupiers were relieved at intervals: the gamblers never moved; they hung there till the sheer physical powers of life gave way, and famine forced them from the tables; stirless and breathless, only at long intervals rending themselves from it to take the drugs and the stimulants that soddened their senses, they were riveted there by one universal, irresistible fascination. Features of every varied kind were seen in the gaudy flare of the gas; but they all wore the same look—the thirsty, sleepless, intense look of ravenous excitement. It was not the polished serenity of fashionable kursaäls, the impassive languor of aristocratic gaming-tables, the self-destruction taken with a light word of the salles of Baden, of Homburg, of Monacco; it was gambling in all its unreined fever, in all its naked excitation, in all its headlong delirium, in all "its arid quest for wealth midst ruin."

There is a vast error in which the world believes, that gamesters are moved by the lust of gain only, by the desire of greed, by the longings of avarice. It is not so; the money won, they toss it back without an

instant's pause, to risk its loss at venture.   Avarice is
no part of the delirium which allures them with so
exhaustless a fascination ; the spell that binds them
is the *hazard*.   Give a gamester thousands, he cares
for the gold only to purchase with it that delicious,
feverish, intoxicating charm of chance.   There is
delight in its agony, a sweetness in its insanity, a
drunken, glorious intensity of *sensation* in its limitless
swing between a prince's treasures and a beggar's
death, which lends life a sense never known before—
rarely indeed, once tasted, ever abandoned.

There was scarcely even a sound in the fatal place.
Once now and then an oath, a blasphemy, or a shuddering gasping breath broke the charmed stillness, in
which the click of the roulette-ball, the rattle of the
dice, or the rapid monotone of the croupiers, reigned
otherwise alone.   The room was crowded.   Men who
had grown old and grey and palsied waiting on the
caprices of the colour; men who had wasted on the
framing of cabals intellects that might have rivalled
Newton's or Descartes'; men who had consumed
their youth in this madness, and, young yet, looked
for nothing save a death in a hospital and a pauper's
unowned grave ; men who had flung away high birth,
high gifts, high chances, and came here to wear out
the few last hours of dishonoured lives; men with
eyes in which the wasted genius of a mighty mind
looked wistfully out through the bloodshot mists of a
drunkard's sight; men who had the trackers of turf-

law or of social law in their trail, and, hiding for very life, knew no nest surer than this foul one,—all these were here in the tawdry glitter of the flaring gas-jets. And there were women, too—some young, some fearfully young—loveless and rouged, and hacking bitter coughs, or laughing ghastly laughs, playing, playing, playing insatiate, with the thirsty, eager, devilish glare aching in their painted eyes.

Among them stood Chandos.

The look which had set on his face the night that he had left Clarencieux had never left it; its glorious beauty survived the ravages of misery, the gaunt sleeplessness of a gamester's days, the wreck of all greater, better, higher things in him. Nothing could stamp it out utterly; but it had something more fearful than any one of the other faces crowded round them, though they would have furnished a painter with a thousand dreams for the Purgatorio, though they would have given an artist a throng of hope-forgotten, devil-tortured wretches fettered in the bottomless circle of Dante's Antenora. It survived to show all that he had been—to mark more utterly all he had become.

For he had fallen very low.

To meet his ruin, he had risen with the haughty pride, the reckless courage, of his race—risen to front it with a calmness and a force that none had looked for in him. He had met calamity greatly; he had been tempted to sell his honour for passion's sake, and he had repulsed the temptation : he had been allured to evade justice, and secure comparative peace, by acting a lie to the world; he had refused, and had given up all to remain with a stainless honesty and a conscience uncondemned. He had done these things with a sudden power of will, a sudden steel-knit strength of resolve, that had sprung in the instant of their need, giants full armed, from the voluptuous unheeding indolence and indulgence of his life. But characters cannot change in a day; endurance may be forged hard in the flame of adversity, but it will give way many a time first, and melt and writhe and bend and break at last. When all had been done, all ended, all sacrificed, all lost, the force which had sustained him had broken down, the utter reaction followed.

The habits of his life had left him with no shield, the temper of his creeds had left him with no shelter, against the storm that had burst over him. His only knowledge had been how to enjoy; none had ever taught him how to suffer. A limitless indulgence had been the master of his existence ; he had no comprehension of calamity. With latent greatness, he had dominant weakness ; as the limbs that lie ever on couches of down are enervated and sinewless, so his nature, that had basked ever in the warmth and the light of enjoyment, had no stamina to bear the crushing desolation that struck all from his hands at one blow. In the moment of emergence, of temptation, he had risen equal to it, risen above it, and been great; in the darkness that followed, in the darkness in which he was driven out into exile, stripped, mocked, abandoned, left in beggared solitude, to drift to his grave as he would, he sank under the burden that he bore. A strong man might have gone down powerless under the accumulated anguish, the blasted devastation, of such a fate. He who had known nothing but the caress of fortune from his birth, he who had all the loathing of pain and of deformity of the Achæan nature, he who had never felt a desire unfulfilled, a command unaccomplished, he who had been pliant to frailty, yielding to effeminacy, could have no sustaining force to enable him to face and to contend with the destruction that smote him to the earth. All who had kissed his feet forsook him as though he were plague-stricken; there was little marvel that he forsook himself.

He seemed to walk like a blind man through a starless night; he had neither sight nor knowledge: all that was left to him was the consciousness of misery, the power to suffer; the power to endure was dead. He drifted senselessly on, far on evil roads, far towards the murder in him of all that he had once been. He lived in infinite wretchedness, and the very memory of all better things died out in him. There is no arrest in a downward road. In the way of honour and honesty, and every holier thought and loftier effort, life piles obstacles breast high; but in descent there is no barrier, down the ice-slope there is no pause, till the broken limbs are dashed to pieces in the black crevasse below.

When his last step had passed the threshold of his home, he had left all likeness of what he once had been. There the proud blood of his race had taken the simulance of strength, and had upheld in him some likeness of their honour, of their power, of their grandeur, even beneath the strokes of his adversity; but once passed for ever from Clarencieux, the only influence that had sustained him was gone—he fell without an effort. His foe might have been consoled for the one failure which had saved the woods and the stones of his hatred from destruction, had he seen how courage, and reason, and genius, and manhood, were perishing with the body and the soul of the man he had betrayed.

In the sheer instinct for covert in which the hunted animal unconsciously finds his lair, he had made his way to the safe solitude and secresy of a great city. He shunned every sign, every sight, that could recal the world he had left to him, or him to it. The place of his refuge was known to none; it was hidden among the innumerable roofs of a close quarter; it was quitted only at night or in the earliest grey of the morning, and quitted then only for the gambling-dens. There was not a creature with him or near him that he had known or loved, save the fidelity of his dog. The animal never left him; he would lie at his feet in the gaming-hells, or would wait all day and all night outside the doors; he would crouch down by him on the cold and cheerless bed of some wretched lodging, as he had done under the silken hangings of a palace; he would watch with ever-wakeful eyes by his side where he was stretched in the stupor of an opiate or the heaviness of brandy-lulled sleep. The love even of the dog was precious to Chandos in his desolation; as far as he noted or felt anything, he was grateful for it. But he noted little. A burning fever consumed him at times; at all others he was sunk in lethargy more dangerous for his reason than even the oblivion of opium-dreams. The loss of lands, of wealth, of power, he would have met with the courage of race and of manhood; it was the desertion of every creature he had aided, of every life he had loved, it was the Judas-betrayal of all he had trusted, that had killed all strength and all life in him.

He lived in intense wretchedness; the little gold he had on his person was not so much as he had spent on a woman's bracelet, on an hour's entertainment. The absolute fangs of want might be upon him in a single day. He who had feasted Emperors more brilliantly than they reigned in their own Courts, and who had only spoken a wish to have it fulfilled as by enchantment, might any day want actually bread. Everything around him, everything touched, or seen, or heard, were such as would have been loathsome and unendurable to his voluptuous and fastidious habits a few short weeks before; yet these he was barely conscious of; he was lost in the stupefaction of a misery too great to have any other sense awake in it. Now and then he would glance with a shudder round the places to which he wandered; now and then he would turn sickening from the food offered him; more often all things passed him unnoted, and in his eyes there came gradually the lustreless dreamy vacancy which presages the rupture of the reason, the dulling of the brain. For hours he would lie prostrated. When he rose, it would only be to drag his limbs wearily out into the night and go to the gaming-hells, where intoxication as sure, and even yet more deadly, was to be found, where alone he gained such gold as sufficed to keep life in him, and to give him a stake to cast again.

Strangely enough, the temptress favoured him. Hazard often allures her prey with that merciless mercy, and fills his hands only to hold him closer in her coils. He won enough to keep life in him—such as life was now.

This was the issue to which his career had come; this was the fate to which he, who in his bright visionary childhood had vowed to rival in his nation's story the chivalrous honour of an Arthur's fame, had come; his pride trampled out; his genius drowned in drugs; his waking hours consumed in the gambler's delirium; almost all manhood slain in him. The Hebrew's thought was right; his enemy's work on him was worse than murder. It was a terrible abasement, a terrible surrender; it was frailty, cowardice, suicide; but the storm had beaten down on his once proud head till it hung in a slave's shame. Existence had grown so hideous to him that he sunk beneath its ceaseless torture, longing alone for death.

Those who have from early years been tried in the fires of affliction may grow the sterner, firmer, more highly tempered for it, like the wrought steel; but those to whom it has been wholly unknown in the soft sensuousness of a joyous life, stagger and fall swooning at the first intolerable breath of its blasting furnace. When a mortal is bound to the agony of Prometheus, the man may well succumb where the god could scarce endure.

Chandos stood now amidst the crowd about the play-tables, in companionship with much of all that was worst and most desperate in Paris. He did not know them; he scarcely knew how vile the character of many round him was. In the brilliance and the aristocratic exclusion of the life he had until now lived, he had been as ignorant of the world without his charmed circle, he had been as ignorant of all depravity that was unrefined, of all vices that were hidden away with poverty and criminality, as any one of the fair patrician women of the Courts. His licence had been the licence of a graceful Catullus; his sins had been the soft sins of an elegant Sardanapalus; he knew nothing of the ignominy of great cities; he knew nothing of the coarse infamy of such as those who harboured and gambled here. He had strayed to its haunt by chance; he returned again and again for sake of its secresy, its opium-drugged wines, its reckless play. He had no knowledge of the companions with whom he was thrown; he was too utterly lost in his own misery to note or to loathe them, whilst they looked on, half awed, half curious, at one whom all Paris knew by name and sight, whose history all knew also, as he came amongst them day after day, night after night, with that deathless beauty, that inextinguishable grace left in him, as they were left in the slaughtered body of Alcibiades, to show how royal a blood had run in his veins, how mighty, how majestic, how hopeless a wreck was there.

Once one of them touched his arm, a young girl, not twenty, but with long years of age and crime and shameless shame under the scarlet rouge that glowed upon her cheek, on the sallow, aching, burning brow from which her gold-hued, flower-decked hair was pushed.

"Why are you here? You are as beautiful as a god! You are not like us—yet."

He looked at her with a dull vacancy, and answered nothing, as he filled a glass with brandy. She thrust the opiate he had mixed with it back to his hand.

"Drink enough to kill yourself *at once*. Don't

live to be what you will be. Such as you go to a madhouse."

Her words dreamily pierced through the semi-insensibility of his brain; he set the opiate down undrunk—for that once. He thought of the dead man who had bade him meet his fate, whatever his fate became; but the next moment he was again at the gaming-table, the next moment only its mad tempting was remembered.

He never heeded what he won, what he lost, though he knew that the very food of the next day hung in the hazard; he would have blessed the famine that should have killed him. But he had the gamester's instinct in him; the gamester's peril alone gave him an oblivious intoxication; he never left it, except when he wandered out to some sleeping-place and flung himself down to sleep, well-nigh as lifelessly as the dead sleep, hours, perhaps days through.

So months had gone with him. The splendid strength and stamina of his frame resisted the ravages that were consuming them; but what was worse than the body perished—the mind decayed, swiftly, surely.

Months went by; he thought time would never end. The golden summer, the ruddy autumn, the bitterness of early winter had passed; he noted no change of seasons, night and day were alike to him; he only dully wondered how long life would curse him by leaving its throb in his heart, the breath in his lips.

He had played thirty-six hours now at a stretch, among the painted women and the haggard men who filled this pandemonium. He had played on till he had lost all—the only time that he had ever done so; the last franc was staked and swept away. He stood blankly gazing down at the tables; he felt that the means of gaining the one intoxication that was precious to him was gone, he had no remembrance that it turned him on the streets a beggar. The eager throngs, seeing the card pass without his stake being laid on it, pushed fiercely, ravenously, to get his nearer place. He let them take it, moving as a somnambulist, and made his way out down the staircase and through the low masked side-door that alone lent admittance to the gambling-rooms: the face of the house was merely a fruiterer's and a tobacconist's shops. He went out mechanically; he knew he must get more gold or go without this, which had become the single craving necessity of life. Where? He who had owned the aristocracies of whole nations as his friends, and had given to all who asked, as though the world were his, had not a shilling now to get him bread.

He walked on aimlessly, unheeding the snow which poured down on his bare head, the cutting north wind that blew like an ice-blast. It was between three and four in the morning; there was scarce a soul abroad. In the quarter where he was few carriages ever rolled, and the thieves and revellers who filled it were mostly

housed in some den or another in the inclement
weather. The dog followed him closely; otherwise
he was almost alone in the tortuous, endless streets,
whose windings he took without knowing whither
they led him. The bitter rush of the wind lifted the
masses of his hair, the sleet drove in his eyes, the cold
chilled him to the bone; he was adrift in the streets
of Paris, without a sou to get him food or bed—he
who a few months before had reigned there in a
splendour passing the splendour of princes!

He longed for death—longed as never man yet
longed for life. The unspeakable physical misery
alone passed his strength; to the nerves that had
shrunk from pain, to the senses that had been steeped
in every pleasure, to the tastes that had loathed un-
sightliness as a torture, to the habits that had been
enervated in all the richness of enjoyment, the wretchedness that was now his portion was horrible beyond
the utterance. He who had never known what an
hour's suffering, what a moment's denial were, now
endured cold, and exposure, and need of food, and
all the racking pangs of want and fever, like any
houseless beggar starving in the night.

He wandered on and on—still always in the same
quarter, still always keeping, by sheer instinct, far
from all that he had once known—far from all that
had so lately seen him in the magnificence of his
reign. He wandered on, under the lowering walls
of pent-up dwellings, through the driving of the

slowly-falling snow, against the cutting breath of the ice-chill air. A strange faintness stole on him, a strange numbness seized his limbs—he began to lose all sense of the keen blasts that blew against him ; the intensity of cold began to yield place to a dreamy exhaustion and prostration, half weary, half soothing : he felt sleep stealing on him—deep as death. He had no wish to resist, no power to overcome it ; the languor stole over all his frame, his limbs failed him ; he sank down and stretched himself out as on some welcome bed, with a heavy sigh, lying there on the snow-covered ground, with the snow falling on his closed eyes, and the wind winding among his hair. The dog couched down and pressed its silky warmth against his breast ; profound rest stole on him ;—he knew no more.

CHAPTER II.

"WHERE ALL LIFE DIES, DEATH LIVES."

THERE was intense solitude in the dark cheerless night; the snow drifted noiselessly down; now and then the wild winds broke and howled with a hollow moan: all else was very still—still as the starless, ink-black skies that bent above. One shadow alone moved through the gloom, that a yellow lamplight here and there only served to make more impenetrable—a shadow frail, bent, delicate as a woman's, feeble as that of age—the shadow of a cripple.

He dragged himself along with slow and painful effort; when he passed under one of the lamps, its glare shone on a face fair and spiritual, with great dark dreaming eyes, that looked out at the snow-

flakes wearily—the face of Guido Lulli.   The fragile,
helpless, pain-worn Provençale, who shuddered from
cold as a young fawn will shudder in it, and who had
barely till now quitted the chamber where he wove
his melodious fancies, and forgot a world with which
he could have no share, was out in the bitterness of
the winter's night, on a quest that his fidelity had
never slackened in through many months of vain
toil and fruitless search.   The search was ended
now.

His foot touched the outflung arm of the form
that lay prostrate—half on the stone of the steps on
which it had sunk, half on the road to which the
limbs had been stretched in the strange peace and
languor which had come with the slumber of cold and
fasting.

The snow had fallen faster and heavily in the last
few moments; it covered the hands, and was shed
white and thick upon the uncovered hair and up-
turned brow.   A lamp burned just above, its flicker,
glowing dully through the raw grey mist, shone on
the death-like calm of the features in the breathless
rest of sleep from which few ever waken.   Lulli
stooped and looked; then, with a great cry, sank
down on his knees beside the senseless form.   He
knew it in a glance, all changed though it was: his
search was over.

The dog lifted his head and gave a moaning

of recognition, half of joy, half of entreaty; but he
would not stir from where he crouched on his master's
breast, lending, with his warm breath and his curly
hair and his massive strength, such aid and protection as he could against the blasts of the storm and
the chills of the night. If any life lingered, he had
saved it.

"My master! Found at last; and found—O
God!—too late!" cried Lulli, as he strove, all weak
and feeble as he was, to raise the prostrate form
in his arms, to draw the limbs from the road, to rest
the head against his bosom, to dash the snow from
the wet hair, and to chafe the stagnant chillness of
the frozen hands.

"Monseigneur, monseigneur! is it thus with thee?"
murmured the Provençale, in the loving sweetness of
his southern tongue, while the great tears coursed
down his cheeks and fell fast as the snow-flakes on
the brow and eyes of Chandos—the brow that was
contracted even in senselessness as with an unbearable pain, the eyes that were closed so heavily, so
wearily, the long thick lashes lying on the cheek
white as the snow-covered stone on which it had been
resting.

The musician loved him with a tenderness intense
and enduring; and there was something that might
have moved a heart far less warm than the lonely
cripple's, in the sight of the magnificent limbs stretched
lifeless as a corpse, of the drooped head that hung

like the head of the dead, of the hair, that women had loved to toy with, dank and dogged with moisture, and of the features, only of late so brilliant with genius and with life, haggard, colourless, and drawn as by death, in the tawny flickering glare of the swinging lamp above.

Lulli laid his hand upon the heart—it beat dully, faintly; the dog's nestling body had preserved existence where otherwise in the bitter cold and dangerous sleep the pulse of the blood must have ceased.   Lulli looked round wildly, and raised his voice in a shout for aid; helpless and weak as he was in all actions for himself, loyalty and gratitude gave him the strength of giants to save the man who in his own extremity had saved him.

There was no answer to his call.   He was alone in the bleakness and the darkness of the wintry dawn, with one whom he firmly believed to be dying— dying of cold, of exposure, and of want; the man whom but a year before he had known in every luxury and every pleasure that the world could give! the man who had come to him in the summer-heats of Spain as the saviour of his life and art, who had seemed to him the very incarnation of beauty, of joy, of splendid manhood, of proud, rejoicing, perfect strength!

In his desperation he found the force that nature had denied his limbs and nerves; he raised the insensible form up from the snow in which it sank half buried; he stripped himself of the furs he wore and covered Chandos' chest with them; he chafed his hands and pressed them against his own lips to give them warmth; he shouted for help till his voice rang down the deserted street, waking all its hollow echoes, and died away—unanswered.

The roll of a carriage coming slowly, and muffled on the whitened roads, smote on his ear at last; he raised a louder cry, with all the power he could gather. He heard a woman's voice from the interior bid the coachman stop and wait. In the dull gleam of the lamp he could see the glitter of jewels flash as she leaned out; her words came strangely clear to him through the frosty darkness, as she asked in French:

"What is it?"

"One dying—and from cold!" he answered her; his voice thick and tremulous with the sobs that shook him like a child.

"Dying! wait while I see," said the voice he had heard, as the form he could dimly perceive through the gloom swayed from the carriage-steps and came towards him; a woman who had been, who indeed was still, very lovely; a woman whose youth was waning, but who still was young; a woman in rich costly draperies that the yellow light glittered on, and with the blue gleam of sapphires above her brow. She was the *lionne*, Beatrix Lennox.

A moment and she stood beside Lulli, disregarding the snow-flakes that drove against her, and the icy

wind that blew through her scarlet cashmeres. She
was a woman of swift impulse, of warm pity.

" Is he dying, you say ?" she asked, with an infinite gentleness in her voice, while she stooped to
look at the prostrate form. She started with a loud
cry.

" Chandos !—merciful Heaven !"

Her lips turned very pale—not her cheek, for that
was warm with a bright delicate bloom of rouge—and
into her eyes the tears sprang salt and full. Her
voice trembled.

" O Heaven, what a wreck ! I have seen so many,
yet never one like this !"

She was silent a moment, gazing down at the
senseless features, and softly touching, with a caressing
hand, the dead gold of the hair, all wet and whitened
by the driving of the snow. Then she turned with a
nervous energy; she was impetuous and rapid, and
firm in act.

" He is not dead," she said, impatiently; " but he
will die if he stays there. Lift him into my carriage
—quick! We must get him warmth and stimulants;
my house is so far off, and there is no fit place
here——"

" My lodging is not distant. Let him come there,"
pleaded Lulli, piteously, while he drew the inanimate
hands closer into his own, as though afraid he should
be robbed again of the one so long lost, so terribly
found.

"Yes, yes; anywhere that is near!" she answered, rapidly, while she flung the scarlet down-lined draperies she wore about the half-dead limbs, and stood, regardless of the blasts that howled, and of the heavy icy mists that descended on the earth like sheets of solid water, as her servants, at her bidding, raised him and laid him gently down upon the cushions of her carriage. She felt nothing of the searching wind, nothing of the drenching storm, nothing of the flakes that were driven against her delicate skin and her masked-ball dress. Her eyes were dim with tears; her lips shook; her heart ached.

"How many fallen I have seen!" her thoughts ran; "yet never such a fall as his."

When life and sense returned to Chandos he was stretched before a wood fire, that shed its ruddy, uncertain light over a darkened room, the dog was licking his hands and murmuring its love over him where he lay, and beside him, watching him, were the musician and the richly hued and delicate form of the famous Bohemian, Beatrix Lennox.

He looked up with a weary sigh; he knew neither of them; his mind was dull, and wandering far in the past.

"Clarencieux?" he muttered, dreamily. It was the one loss ever at his heart, the one name ever in his thoughts.

It struck those who heard it with a pang; they

knew how endless must be this longing, how endless this loss.

Lulli stooped over him, his voice very broken.

"Monseigneur! do you not know me?"

Chandos looked at him dreamily, blindly; his head fell back with a sigh of weariness.

"No, no; if you had been merciful, you would have let me die."

The words told his listeners more mournfully, more utterly, than any others could have done, how bitter to him had become the burden of the life once so rich and gracious.

Beatrix Lennox, albeit a woman who had known the world in phases that harden and chill, and fill with an ironic mockery for most emotions those who do so know it, looked on at him, where he lay, with eyes of pathetic pain, dim and aching with unshed tears. She had seen him but so late in all of the glory of his kingly manhood, of his unshadowed youth! She thought in that strange blending of assimilation and of incongruity, which not seldom accompanies hours of profound suffering, of the old words of the Romaunt de Duguesclin:

N'a filairesse en France qui sache fil filer
Qui me gagnait ainçois ma finance à filer.

"There is not the woman living," she thought, " who could look on him now and not give her all to gain him ransom from his misery, if she could."

Lulli, his voice broken with the weeping that shook him like a young child, stooped over him in the same entreaty, passionately praying for his recognition.

"Monseigneur! my master, my friend, my saviour! look at me; you know me?"

The long-familiar tones reached the brain, dulled by cold and want of food. Chandos raised himself and looked at him, vacantly yet wonderingly, but with a half-smile that passed over his face a moment to fade the next. "Is it you?" he said, faintly. "Where am I? What has happened?"

Lulli could not answer him: the musician had been strong to save him while danger nerved and emergency compelled him; but now the reaction told on him, his old weakness returned, he wept, trembling sorely like a woman. The affections and the feebleness of his nature were both very feminine; and it was an anguish beyond his strength to see stretched before him in that senseless wretchedness the man to whom he owed all, and whom he had last beheld the idol of a brilliant world, the darling of a throng of friends, the caressed sovereign of a limitless homage.

Chandos lifted his eyelids, laden still with the sleep that had been so nearly the sleep of death, and saw Beatrix Lennox. He remembered them both then, and, in the old instincts of his marked courtesy to women, strove to rise. With an effort he staggered to his feet, and leant heavily against the high slate shelf above the warm wood-piled blazing hearth.   He could not speak; the sight of these two faces so well known in his past—that past which seemed severed from him as by the gulf of a lifetime—brought back with a flood of memories on his slowly waking thoughts what he had been, what he was. They, looking on him and seeing the ruin a few months had wrought, did not know how vast, how terrible the change was in him more utterly than he himself.

His eyes closed involuntarily with a shudder. He had buried his life in the dens of the populous city to escape all sight of those once familiar to and with him. That any of those should meet him now was torture almost unbearable to the pride which survived in him above all that had sought to shame and stay it.

“ How do I come here ? ” he said, feebly, while his gaze wandered towards them with the pathetic glance of a man paralysed, whose eyes alone can speak.

“ The cold had struck you, and you had fallen,” answered Beatrix Lennox, in her voice that fell on him like soothing music. “ My carriage was near; we brought you to M. Lulli’s room. You are weak still; the night was so bitter. Wait and rest before you speak.”

She restrained the tears that choked her utterance; for with the tact that nature gave her, she divined how terrible must be to him the knowledge that they had found him in his destitution and his suffering—

they, who had been the companions of his glittering prosperity, the one the recipient of his widest charity, the other the guest of his gayest hours. She sought to hide her own knowledge of it as she could.

Lulli, the impressionable, transparent, childlike southern, could exercise no such self-restraint; he knelt at Chandos' feet, his head bowed in his hands, his heart half broken.

"Oh, monseigneur," he murmured, passionately, piteously, "how have I searched for you! how have I grieved for you! I sought you night and day; sought you living or dead. Could you not have trusted *me*? Could you not have let *me* go out with you to your exile?"

Chandos looked down on him, and a sigh, quivering as a sob, broke from him unconsciously.

"Forgive me, Lulli," he said, gently; "I was selfish; I forgot you; I forgot *you* would be faithful."

"You never forgot!" cried the musician, lifting his head eagerly, while he flung back the silky masses of his dark hair off his eyes. "You never forgot me; you only forgot yourself! You remembered my needs, you remembered my helplessness, you remembered to save me and serve me to the last; all you forgot was how I loved you!"

Chandos stretched out his hand to him with his old gesture; he could not answer, the Provençale's fidelity moved him too deeply, stirred him too bitterly in its contrast with the abandonment of well-nigh every other.

Beatrix Lennox drew nearer and laid her hand softly on his arm.

“You were very near death an hour ago. Rest now, and take what I bring you.”

With the skill and the speed of her sex—though some there were who said the *lionne* had left far behind in other years the softness of her sex—she brought him with her own hands some delicate food and some warm and fragrant coffee, standing there in her masquerade-dress all glittering with Venetian gems and Venetian grace, with the ruddy wood-fire light upon her, as she had stood in the driving downpour of the snow-storm. The hand that held him the food so tenderly had but just laid aside the black coquette Venetian mask of her opera-ball; but of a surety the ministration was not less gentle, the heart that prompted it not less full of divine charity, than if it had just cast aside the grey serge of a religious recluse.

It was the first food for months from which he had not turned in loathing; he took it with a gratitude that, though his eyes alone spoke, sank into her memory for ever. She saw what Lulli did not see, that it was the first he had taken for many hours, and that long fasting had done its work on him not less surely than the winter night.

“Can he want bread?” she thought, with a quiver

of horror. Heartless though the world called her, this Reine Gaillarde of a lawless court, she would have gone and sold her jewels and her cashmeres to bring him gold, had she not known by instinct that, though he might die of hunger, he would never take an alms.

"I owe you a great debt, Mrs. Lennox," he said, simply, as his eyes rested on her, all the light dead in them, a heavy languor weighing down their lids, and a haggard darkness circling them, but with their weariness a look of infinite thankfulness to her and to the one man who alone had never forsaken and reviled his memory.

"You owe me none." The words were very low, as she stood swaying to and fro the gold strings of her Venetian mask. "Chandos,—I owed you some time ago a far greater one."

"Owed me?"

His senses and his memory were still dim; warmth and, with warmth, life were fast flowing back into his veins, but he felt as one in a dream; the faces he looked on were so familiar, the place was so strange, he could not disentangle fact from phantasy.

"Yes!"

She came closer towards him, standing there in the reflexion of the blazing wood, with the scarlet and black folds of her masquerade-dress sweeping downward in the glow, and her haughty, handsome face turned to him with an inexpressible sweetness and tenderness tremulous upon it.   The thought woke in him vaguely, even in that moment, had this woman loved him? She, swift to read unspoken thoughts, guessed it.

"Do not think that," she said, with a smile of infinite sadness.   "I never loved you; it is very long since *my* heart beat. But I would serve you anyhow —anywhere—if **I could. Do you** remember being with **me at an opera-supper at** the Maison Dorée, **years and years ago? No!** how should you? It was only memorable to me. Some German Prince gave the supper—who, I forget now—but there were women present, with whom even I abhorred association.   The jests were very free, the licence very unchecked, and I—I had forfeited the right to *resent*. You alone noticed it—you alone pitied me ; **you** went and spoke in a whisper to the Prince. He laughed aloud. 'The Lennox, who is she to——' You silenced him. 'She was at least the daughter of a gallant gentleman ; that should not be forgotten.' Then you came to me with your gentle courtesy, and offered to take me to my carriage. Ah ! I was wrong to say I never loved you. I loved you *then !* I never forgot it—I never shall."

Chandos looked at her with **a** great gratitude, and yet a pain well-nigh as great; tenderness shown him subdued and touched him as it subdues and touches **a** woman.

"God knows it was trifle enough. If others remembered as you do——"

He paused; no words ever escaped him that could sound like a lament for the ingratitude that had forsaken him on every side.

"Ah!" she said, passionately, "it was no trifle to *me*. If ever I can repay it—if it be twenty years hence—I will, let the payment cost what it may."

The promise was very hurried and broken in its utterance for the most fluent and most eloquent woman of her time; she took her hands in his, and bent over them.

"If you could let me serve you!" she murmured, as softly as his mother could have breathed him her farewell; then, with a long, loving gaze, she left him, the black and scarlet hues of her draperies lost in the gloom of the fire-shadows. She could have stayed with him, stayed with him willingly, to aid, to tend on, to assist him with every ministry that a love, with which no touch of passion blent, could give; but she knew him to be very proud; she saw that pride was not dead, but lived in passionate pain beneath calamity; she felt that the fewer eyes there were upon him now, the better could he bear the knowledge that they had found him, a homeless wanderer, dying in the streets of Paris. So, true to her unselfish instinct, and guided by a tenderness higher than compassion, she left him— she whom the world called an adventuress, without pity and without conscience.

As she passed from the chamber, he sank down wearily and faintly, his head bowed on his breast, his limbs stretched out in racking misery from cold and stiffness in the heat of the leaping flames. He, who in his superb completeness of strength and of health had never known what the illness of a day was, suffered now every ill of mind and body—suffered almost more in this moment, when the reviving warmth and the stimulant of the choicer food gave him the power of vivid consciousness, than he had done in the stupor of his opium-drugged senses. Yet no word, scarcely any sign, escaped him of what he suffered; there was too proud an instinct in him still. Lulli watched him silently; the dog nestled close in the light of the hearth. For many moments there was not a sound in the chamber; sheer physical aching pain wore Chandos down, seeming to load him with the weight of iron chains, to burn him with the scorch of fire. He wished—he wished to God—that they had left him in that dreamless slumber upon the snow to die, with no more knowledge of the life he quitted than the frozen stag that stretches out its stiffened limbs upon some desolate moor-side.

Gradually, slowly, bodily exhaustion conquered; the pangs that racked his frame were soothed to comparative peace by the after-action of the opiates he had so long taken; the warmth of the hearth lulled him to rest; his eyes closed, his breathing grew gentler and more even; he stretched himself out with a weary sigh, as he had done in the darkness of the streets, and he slept at last as he had never slept since the night he learned the story of his ruin—slept for hour on hour, with scarce a breath that stirred the stillness of his repose, or could be heard upon the silence. That sleep saved him from the fate which the girl in the gaming-den had foreseen for him if he lived.

When he awoke, the sun was high in the western skies; it was far after noon. Lulli sat beside him, watching with a patience no length of vigil could exhaust; the dog lay asleep; the ruddy glow of the great fire on the hearth was dying down, though its intense heat still filled the chamber. His eyes, as they unclosed, met Lulli's resting on him with that unwearied spaniel look which had scarce ever relaxed its watch over that repose which so resembled death.

"Is it you, Guido?" he asked, faintly. "Ah— yes, I remember. And you have been waiting by me there so many hours!"

The Provençale strove to smile, though the tears stood thick in his eyes.

"Monseigneur, I would never weary of *that*."

"I know! There are few like you."

"Monseigneur, if all those whom you once served were like me, there would be many throngs."

Chandos answered nothing; he raised himself on his left arm, and lay on the hearth gazing at the flicker of the crimson flame, at the fall of the grey noiseless ash.

The deadliest pang to Richard Plantagenet, in all the bitterness of his discrowned fortunes, was when his hound, who loved him, **who** caressed him, who had been fed from his hand, **and** had slept by his pillow, went from him to fawn on Bolingbroke.   "*Il vous suivra, il m'éloignera*," said the forsaken King—a whole history of infidelity in the brief pathetic words.   The deadliest pang **of his lost royalties** to Chandos lay in the abandonment of all save this poor cripple, whom he **had loved** and **saved**, and who had caressed him in the days of his purple and his power.

"You can tell me," he said, suddenly—his voice was very hushed, and came with effort through his lips—"what is the fate of—of——"

His lips could not phrase, but his listener divined the word.

"Clarencieux?" asked Lulli.

He bent his head.

The musician looked at him eagerly.

"Did **you not** know?   Monseigneur d'Orvâle has bought the whole."

Chandos looked up, a flush of breathless gratitude, **of** incredulous relief, banishing for the moment all the broken, aged, colourless pain from his face.

"Is it true?   Philippe d'Orvâle?" he panted, with a thirsty anguish that told how more at his heart than any other thing had lain the weight of his home's loss.

"Would I cheat you?   True as that we live.   He forced them to surrender it to him; bought it untouched, undespoiled."

"Thank God!"

He covered his face with his hands, and for the only time in all his adversity, save the moment when old Harold Gelart had spoken under the elms of the western terrace, great storm-drops forced themselves through his closed lids and his clenched fingers, and fell one by one, like the rain before a tempest.

Far more to him than any mercy to himself was the mercy which had saved Clarencieux from sacrilege, and barter, and destruction.

"Monseigneur d'Orvâle has it," pursued the swift sweet voice of the Provençale. "Not a tree will be touched, not a thing be displaced. He sent for me, and bade me live there; but I could not—it would have broken my heart. He has sought for you everywhere; he has longed to find you; he would have you return to it as though it were your own still."

Chandos shivered where he sat.

"*I!* I am dead to it for ever."

He could not have borne to look upon the purple distance of its woods, he could not have borne to stand beside the far-off course of the mere river that flowed towards it—he who had forfeited his birthright.

Lulli was silent; his eyes watched ever, with a dog-like love, the form of Chandos, where he lay at length in the dying glow of the flames, his face hidden, his frame shaken now and then with an irrepressible shudder. An unutterable thanksgiving was in his heart for the fate which had spared his home and his lands from the shame and the ruin of dissolution; yet the knowledge that another dwelt there, that another had bought his heritage for ever, brought in him, as it had never come before, the full realisation of his own eternal exile.

He raised his head after many moments, and strove to steady his voice.

"Thank him from me; he will know *how* I thank him. I used to feel how true, how generous, his heart was; how noble a friend he would ever be. Tell him he is merciful beyond men's mercy——"

"*You* will tell him?" asked Lulli, softly; "you will see him? He loves you so well."

Chandos gave an irrepressible gesture of pain.

"Not yet; not yet," he said, hurriedly. "I doubt if ever——"

The words were unfinished; in his own soul he felt as though never could he force himself to look on the friends and companions of that lost life which seemed to lie so far behind him in a limitless distance, dead and past for ever. Nor in himself did he think that he would long live—long bear this burden of hopeless wretchedness—long endure this existence which was unceasingly upon the verge of madness or of death.

What had he now? The food that he ate here might be the last ever to pass his lips. He had not a farthing wherewith to buy bread even for his dog.

Lulli looked at him wistfully, and stooped forward nearer, a kindling light on his face.

"Monseigneur, hear me!" he said, very low, with a fervent, touching entreaty in his whispered southern tongue. "When I was dying, you saved me; when I was in beggary, you gave me food and shelter; when I was poor and friendless and alone, you were the world to me. You found me in misery, and pitied me; and for the art that is my life and my soul you gained me hearing and you gave me fame. Through you I am no more poor; they talk of me; my *Ariadne* has been heard through all the width of Europe, and they have paid her beauty with their gold, though *that* was never my thought with her. Listen! Pay my debt to you I never can; I love to owe it and to cherish it. But in some little sense I may serve you; in some degree you can make me happy by letting me ask you to remember it. Stay with me; let me toil for you, labour for you, wait on you, gather the gold they offer me for you. It will be such joy to me! Without the sound of your voice, I am like a blind man lost in this wide world; if you will only wait with me, you can give me back strength, power, ambition, everything, and I shall love the coins that I hate now, if you will let me glean them all for you, let me do for you in some little kind all that you did for me when I was a homeless cripple, dying, with all the music that was in me killed and silenced by my hunger and my poverty."

His voice rose in his impassioned entreaty, till it thrilled through the still chamber like one of his own melodies; he would have slaved, have starved, have killed himself, to have saved or served the man who had had pity on his youth.

Chandos heard, and the words moved him deeply as the words of the old yeoman had done. He never lifted his head, but he stretched out his right hand silently, and grasped the frail, nervous, transparent hand of the musician in a close clasp.

" What you wish cannot be," he said, huskily. " I should be lost to shame indeed! But from my heart I bless you for your fidelity—for your love."

" Cannot be? Why not? In *my* need you aided me?" pleaded Lulli, his wistful eyes pleading more fervently than his words. He knew too little of the world to know why, in his own sight, Chandos would have felt himself shamed beyond all humiliation had he listened to his prayer.

The blood flushed his listener's forehead with a pang of the old pride of his proud race; he could not tell this guileless, generous, devoted creature that he would sooner die like a dog, die of famine in the streets, than live on upon the alms of his debtor.

" It cannot be," he said, gently. "Do not ask it, Lulli. If you have fame and comfort, I am more than rewarded by you."

The Provençale's face darkened mournfully; the whole of many months had been passed in a vain quest for his lost master, in an unwearied, though, as it had seemed, hopeless search, through which his sole sustaining thought had been to find his solitary friend, and to repay in some faint measure all the gifts he owed.

Chandos rose slowly from where he leaned upon the hearth; his limbs were still stiff and weak, though the profound repose of long unbroken sleep had restored him something of strength, and the life-giving warmth in which he had rested had lessened the pain in his brow and eyes, and the oppressive weight on his lungs.

"You are not going? you will not leave me?" cried Lulli, with an accent almost piteous. He had ever before his thoughts the senseless form on which by so hazardous a chance his search had led him in the snow-storm of the past night; he could not bear to let him go from his sight to risk the same fate in loneliness and misery again.

Chandos looked at him with something bewildered in his glance; the question brought back on him the full sense of his own aimless and hopeless life. Where should he go? what should he do? In the desert of the world he stood alone; he had not enough to get him bread.

"Stay with me! oh, for pity's sake, stay with me," pleaded Lulli, passionately. So willingly would he have given up everything on earth to be allowed to starve for the only living creature who had ever pitied him.

Chandos gave a faint sign of dissent; he knew not what he should do, he knew not whether in the next day and night he might not perish of the same exposure and want he had been now rescued from ; but his highest instincts were not dead in him ; he would not linger here, though for one moment physical weakness and all the long habit of physical indulgence came upon him with a fearful longing to lie down and rest without effort in the soothing heat of the hearth, to stay in the lulling peace and shelter of the quiet chamber.

Serious illness was on him, as well as the inertia of fever and of languor. For the moment he felt it beyond his strength to pass out into the bleak biting wind, to face the homeless night, to accept the fate that drove him out into the wilderness of the great city, with none to give him rest, with nothing to buy him food. He longed to turn back, and lie down and die in the dreamy comfort of that calming fire-glow.

But he moved away, only pausing one moment to droop his head to Lulli's ear with a single question more.

" Tell me before I go, what of *her* ? "

The musician knew that he meant the woman he had loved; he was silent, and turned shuddering away.

" Do not ask me !—do not ask me ! " he murmured, passionately.

Chandos staggered slightly ; he was very weak.

" Is she dead ? "

"Would to Heaven she were!" said Lulli, with a force that thrilled for the moment with the fierce vengeance of the south. The gentle dreamer, who would have pardoned the cruelest wrongs done to himself, could hate and could avenge where those he loved were wronged.

"Hush! I *have* loved her," said Chandos, faintly. "What of her? I can bear all *now*."

"She is Lord Clydesmore's wife."

The answer was ground out between Lulli's teeth; he loathed, as he had loathed the unknown lover of Valeria, the woman who had abandoned and the man who had supplanted Chandos.

Chandos swayed forward as though about to fall.

"O God! his wife!"

The words broke from him like a wrung-out cry; in that moment he remembered nothing, save the passion wherewith he had loved her, save the beauty which was given to another. He made his way with a blind swaying movement towards the door; he had no sense now except that he must be alone—alone to bear this crowning bitterness which had befallen him.

"Wait — wait!" cried Lulli, imploringly. "O Heaven! why would you have me tell you? Wait! You will come back to me?"

Chandos put him aside gently, though he had no consciousness of what he did.

"Yes, I will come back," he answered, mechanically, without the sense of what he promised, as he made his way out once more into the bitter winter air.

He had forgotten all, except that the one who should now have lain in his arms—his wife—had gone, so soon, to the love and the embrace of his rival!

CHAPTER III.

IN THE NET OF THE RETIARIUS.

LULLI looked for him in vain. He never returned. It was not that he broke, wittingly, his promise; he never knew that he had made it.

He dragged his limbs, how he could not have remembered, to the only home he owned now—a home he had not coins enough on him to keep even another night—a pent, dark, dreary chamber in one of the million houses of the crowded streets, with only one better thing in it, that it was so high, so near the clouds, that a clear space of the winter skies looked down on it, and the cold serene radiance of a few stars could be seen from it above the jagged peaked roofs. There the illness on him flung him down; he lay prostrate many days, many nights, with no watcher beside him save the dog, except once in several hours, when the woman of the house came and filled afresh the flagon of water that he drank from eagerly, and looked at him with a pitying wonder, rather for his beauty than for his danger, and went away and left him; for she only knew him as a beggared gamester, and would have turned him, half lifeless, wholly senseless, into the streets, had it not been that, woman like, she was moved to compassion by the physical graces that no ruin could kill in him, and that touched her to pity as he lay unconscious there.

"As handsome as a fallen angel!" she would mutter to herself, while, though but an old, bent, savage, avaricious crone, she would just touch softly with her yellow horny hand the gold locks that women had used to crown with roses. "An aristocrat! an aristocrat! Mort de Dieu! how many of them I have seen die off like murrained cattle from their gaming-hells!"

So, just for sake of his fair hair and his beautiful mouth, like the mouth of a Greek god, she tended him enough to keep life in him like a flickering flame; for the rest, he lay alone in the midst of the peopled city where he had once reigned supreme, dying in his solitude for aught that any knew or cared. The winter stars shone clear through frosty nights, and looked in on him prostrate there, with his head fallen back, and his eyes without light or sense, and his chest rising heavily and wearily with anguish in every breath the inflamed lungs drew; while the dog watched beside him, moaning now and again its piteous wail, or covering with its caresses the clenched hands and the contracted brow. Winter dawns broke chill and grey; winter days rolled darkly on; winter nights passed with riotous storm or frost so crystal clear, through which the cold moon shone like a shield of steel; he lay there in his loneliness as though in his grave, forgotten, and without a friend in the midst of thousands who had feasted at his tables, in the heart of palaces where his word had been as law.   Yet the life in him would not die.

It survived through all; it recovered without aid, without succour, without other comfort than was given him by the warmth of the animal's nestling body and the cooling draught of the icy water.   Whilst he lay there, one only, beside the old brown withered crone who tended his wants in the few intervals of her daily toil, came and watched him.   One only of all those who had known him and been succoured by him discovered the wretchedness of that last retreat, and stood beside the bed where he was stretched.   Hate is swifter of foot and surer of chase than love, and will remember and search, untiring, when love has grown weary and laggard.

One only came and mounted the narrow, dark, rickety stairs, and entered the room where there was no single thing of solace or of mercy except when the clear pale light of the stars shone down from above the endless roofs ; one only stood beside the pallet where the man, whom all Europe had caressed and honoured, had no watcher but a starving dog. Trevenna stood there looking on his work, and was content with it. Philippe d'Orvâle had baffled him of his vengeance on the senseless stones of Clarencieux, but none could take from him his vengeance on the living man, whom his patient hate had slain more mercilessly than by a swift and single death-stab.

All the long years of subtle dissimulation, of carking envy, of longing thirst to destroy the peace and the brilliance of the life he pursued, of gifts accepted with greed because they were the means of conquest, but loathed and cursed, and adding by each one a stone to the load of his hatred,—all these were over and over recompensed now, here, in this darkened, poverty-bared garret in the city of Paris, where his prey, in torture and in famine, lay insensible beneath his gaze.

Of all the women who had listened to Chandos' love-words and toyed with the brightness of his hair, there was not one who now held a stoup of water to his lips. Of all the hands that he had filled with gold, there was not one now to touch with pitying caress the brow all bent and dark with pain. Of all the mouths to which he had given food, there was not one now to murmur a gentle word over his misery. Of all the throngs whom he had bidden beneath his roof, of all the lives he had made prosperous and joyous, of all the friends who had laughed with him through the long luxuriant summer day of his existence, there was not one now who asked whether he were living or dead. There was but his enemy, who looked on him and rejoiced.

Every unconscious sigh that broke from him, every movement of his fevered aching limbs, every breath drawn through his agonised lungs, every contraction that knit his burning forehead in his suffering, every look of dull sightless suffering from the blind and sleepless eyes, his foe watched, and was content.

> Quand j'émiettais mon pain à l'oiseau du rivage,
> L'onde semblait me dire, " Espère ! aux mauvais jours,
> Dieu te rendra ton pain."   Dieu me le doit toujours !

wrote the poet Moreau, dying in his youth of lack of the food dogs rejected. Chandos had thrown his bread on many waters, giving to all who asked, to all who were heavy laden, to all who lived in darkness and in want. It was unrecompensed and owing to him still. He needed it now, but none repaid it. There only remained with him his foe, who brought him the hyssop and the aloe when he died for a drop of the clear living rivers of the land he had left.

" Water — water!" he murmured unceasingly, where he was stretched in his delirious stupor. Trevenna poured some absinthe, and touched his lips with it. He shuddered, all unconscious as he was, and turned with a heavy gasping sigh from the loathsome drink, so bitter, so abhorrent to the fever-burnt dry lips that longed to steep themselves for ever in the cool flow of sweet fresh waters. Trevenna smiled.

"Beau seigneur!" he said, softly to himself, "*I* have drunk bitterness long; it is your turn now."

He lay insensible, defenceless; the width of his breast was bare, and the loud, panting, inflamed beatings of his heart could be seen where it throbbed like the passionate aching heart of a mured eagle. Trevenna laid his hand on it, and his eye glanced to a knife that lay on the deal board on which his pitcher of drink was set.

"How easy!" he thought. "But I have done better. I have killed him; but I have never broken a law. A stab there would be mercy to him; he shall never get it from me."

Chandos' arm moved where it hung over the bed, seeking instinctively, all dead to what passed or what looked on him though he was, the place whence he was used to take the cup of water which the woman of the house set by him. For sake of his beauty, she had been pitiful in the last hour, and had sliced in it a few cuts of orange to cool the thirst that devoured him. His hand wandered in a pathetic uncertainty, seeking, as a blind man's seeks, the only thing he had life left in him to long for. Trevenna moved the table from his reach, and emptied out upon the floor the orange-water. Had he written the "Purgatorio" and the "Inferno," he would have in-

vented more devilish tortures than Dante framed in
the Caina, Ptolomea, and Antenora.

The thirst, parched and delirious as the thirst of men
in the desert, consumed his victim with an intolerable
torment; his mouth was white and dry as dust: his
forehead red with the heated blood; his eyes wide
open with a terrible, senseless stare: thrown back there,
with his bare chest grand as the chest of a Hercules,
and the luxuriance of his hair tangled and tossed
and lustreless, yet retaining the beauty with which
nature had created him deathless to the last, he lay
like a young gladiator flung down in the sand of the
arena by the clinging serpentine coils of the Retiarius.
Indistinct, disconnected words broke now and then
from his lips, in the wanderings of thoughts that
in the misery of that thirst stretched far away into
dim memories of his past; to the forest freshness of
English brooks, to the deep still blue of Austrian
lakes, to the sweet music of waters falling through
innumerable leaves down the steep height of many-
coloured stone, of the grand breadth of Euphrates
rolling beneath its palms, of the silver-sheeted Danube
lying in the deep shadows of its woods, of the stilly
murmur of winding waters in the Italian spring-
tide leaf, flowing lazily and softly beneath the green
wild arums, and the tawny beds of osiers, and the
wreathing boughs of Banksia roses, and the gentle
fragrance of the young vine's flower-buds. They
were on his lips ever, in longing, fugitive, broken

memories—these scenes and hours of his past, those thoughts of the earth's fair freshness that was dead and lost to him.

Trevenna stood still and listened to the unconscious, unbidden suffering that longed for all that it was exiled from, that spoke in those broken words of all the glories of remembered hours, all the freedom of the forests and the seas, while life was wrung and death embittered by that one poor piteous want—one draught of the water that beggars might drink from every brook that bubbled. He listened; he could have listened for ever.

He thought of the night when he had ground the Paris sweetmeats into the mud of the gutter, and registered his childish vow; he had kept it to the letter. Happier than Shylock, he had cut the piece of his vengeance from the living heart of his victim, with none to stay his hand. .

The grey chilly twilight of a winter's day filled the attic; the light of the first faint moon-ray glistened on the bare walls and the naked floor; the noise, the stench, the noxious reeking air of the alley below could reach but little here—only an oath, or a laugh more ghastly than the oath, pierced the stillness of this chamber in the roof, while through its broken casement the tide of the icy night-wind poured bitterly in on the uncovered chest, on the fevered limbs, on the darkened aching brow.

There was no pang of conscience in the watcher

there—no memory of the friendship that had trusted, of the loyalty that had saved him ; no thought of his own fraud, of his own baseness. He only remembered what this man had been in the splendour of his promise, in the gladness of his youth, in the brilliance of his renown ; and looked at him lying thus, and was content. When the net had wound its coils, and the strangled limbs were powerless, and the strength reeled and fell under its twisting, writhing meshes down into the sand, the Retiarius had no pity, but he looked upward to where the shouts of " Euge ! " and the turned-down hands decreed with him no mercy to the vanquished, and he plunged in again and again the fangs of his trident, seeking the last life-blood ;— so it was now with Trevenna. His net had been deftly flung, and had brought his adversary down, blinded and paralysed ; but he would never have wearied of stabbing again and again, while there was life to feel.

He turned reluctantly away : he could have lingered there whilst there was a pang to watch, a sigh to count. He heard the footfall of the old Auvergnat woman heavily treading over the bare boards. She touched his arm—a hideous, brown, wrinkled, shrivelled being of nigh eighty years, with avarice in her black glance, and a horrible old age upon her.

" You know him ? " she asked.

" I know a little of him," he answered, indifferently.

"You had better not keep him here longer than you can help; he may get you into trouble."

He roused her fears and her selfishness, that even this miserable hand might be withheld from easing the suffering they looked on. The Auvergnat looked at him in terror.

"With the police?"

Trevenna nodded and shrugged his shoulders. The old creature, steeped in Paris vice and devoured with Paris avarice, set her teeth hard.

"By the Mother of God! I would have turned him in the streets days ago if he were not as beautiful as a marble Christ."

Trevenna laughed, a loud, coarse, jeering laugh.

"His beauty! You old crone, what can that be to you? If you were twenty, now——"

She turned on him her darkling and evil glance.

"Women are fools to their tombs. I cannot hurt him; I should see his face for ever."

Trevenna shrugged his shoulders.

"If you wish to serve him, get him let into some pauper madhouse. It is the only thing you can do for him."

She shuddered a dissent.

"They would shear all *that* in a madhouse!" she said, drawing through her hard withered hands the silken fairness of his hair. "When I was young, I would have given my life to kiss that gold—when I was young!"

The words lingered half sullenly, half longingly, on her lips; the memory made her touch gently, almost tenderly, the locks that lay in her horny palm. She felt for him; almost, in a way, she loved him— this battered, evil, savage old creature of Paris; but she would strip the linen from his limbs to thieve and sell, for all that.

"Send him there all the same," said Trevenna. "It is the only place that will shelter him now; except one, to be sure—the Morgue!"

And with these last words to rankle and fester, and ripen if they should, in the soul of the old beldam who had all to lose, nothing to gain, by the life of one whom she had robbed of everything, Trevenna went lightly down the high crazy staircase that passed through so many stories to the basement; there was a more intensely victorious glance in his eyes, a smile of tenfold success on his mouth.

"My brilliant Chandos! my brilliant Chandos!" he said, half a loud, "how is it with you now?"

And he went out into the night, leaving the man who had rescued him from his prison to perish of thirst, or of famine, or of fever—to die in the streets or to live like a chained beast in a madhouse, whichever should chance to be the fruit and the end of his history.

Trevenna never laughed more merrily at the vaudeville of the Bouffes, never ate his salad with keener relish at the café Riche, never looked on at Mabille with more good-tempered indulgence for the follies which had no attraction for himself, than he did that night. Once he laughed aloud, so gaily, so long, that a friend near asked what the jest was. He laughed again.

" I am thinking of Belisarius begging an obole ; and of Henry IV., hunted and naked, and dead of starvation, at Spires ! "

His friend stared, and thought the wine was in his head. But it was not ; he was only drunk with success.

The doom of his prey, however, then at least, was not the madhouse or the grave. He rose from his bed at length, the superb frame with which nature had dowered him resisting all the stress and peril that had sought to undermine it. He wondered wearily why he *could* not die.

The woman who had brought him drink and tended him now and then, for sake of those lips like the Sun-God's, of those limbs like the Antique, had robbed him of the little he had left while he lay insensible— of the diamond links in his sleeves, of the gold buttons in his shirts, of the fine cambric of his linen, of the few traces left to him of the old luxuries of his usage. She said, when he could hear, that she had been at great cost for his illness ; he believed her ; he could not tell that her pitcher of water had been the sole thing set by his side.

Having lost what he had lost, moreover, what could the few things stolen now be to him?

Thus when he rose at last and staggered out from the wretched dwelling where he had not a coin left to keep even its roof above his head, he was literally beggared—beggared almost as utterly as any unknown corpse that lay waiting burial in the dead-house by the Seine.

Since the far-gone German days, when an Emperor vainly begged bread at the monastery he had endowed, and dragged himself to a vault to die unsepulchred, there had hardly been a fall more vast, more sudden, from the height of power to the depths of poverty.

He went feebly out into the early night, that by a chance was clear, starlit, and mild. Beau Sire looked up at him and moaned; a piteous hunger gazed out from the dog's eyes: he was famished; he had well-nigh starved through all the days and nights that he had kept guard by his master. He had not a sou left him to buy the animal food.

He shuddered as he met the wistful, uncomplaining, hungry eyes—he who had never beheld pain save to relieve or to release it! He stood alone in the busy, rapid, lighted, heedless tide of life in a Paris night, and had not wherewith to buy a crust to keep the brute that loved him from starvation. He thought with a longing agony of his promise to the dead man who had bade him live to meet his fate ; the oath was a bitter one to keep.

He almost reeled through the first street that his steps turned into ; illness had mortally weakened him, and his head swam with the booming noise of the traffic, and with the stench of the crowds. The retriever followed him feebly : famine was telling on its strength ; and, like its master, used to all luxury and to all delicacies for so long, it was untrained to want : its eyes were growing dim and ravenous.

Chandos felt his limbs fail him ; the exhaustion of severe illness was on him, with nothing of shelter, of stimulant, of repose, to support him under it. He sank down almost unconsciously on some stone steps of the narrow thoroughfare he had wandered into, and drew the dog to him with its fond head nestled in his breast ; he could not bear the mute appeal of those longing, piteous eyes. The crowds swept past him— rich and poor, chiefly the latter, for it was in a densely peopled and ancient quarter, but all bent fast on their own errands. Two or three turned their heads back over their shoulders to look at him, with his arm resting on the shoulders of the animal that pressed so closely to him ; none did more. They were the hurried pleasure-seekers and the toiling labourers of a great city ; they could have no heed of *one* misery amidst so vast a canker of universal want and greed.

The throngs passed him like a throng of phantoms;
he thought, as he sat there, of the thousand nights
when he had driven through Paris with all the rank,
with all the brilliance, of the Court of St. Cloud
around him; with no name more famous, with no
presence more courted, at Tuileries or Faubourg, than
his own.

Now he must let his dog hunger for a broken
loaf!

Where he sat, the lamp-light flashed on the collar
the retriever wore—a handsome toy of silver, with his
arms embossed upon it—a relic of his long-lost life.
The collar was of value; and the woman who had
robbed him of every other trifle would have robbed
him even of that, had not Beau Sire kept her off it
through his passionate menace of her with his mighty
fangs. His hand wandered to the padlock fastening
it; how many hours it recalled to him, that burnished glittering ornament where it gleamed under
the dog's black curls!—hours of fresh autumn morn-
ings among the woods of Clarencieux, with the whirr
of a pheasant's wing through the reddening gold
of the leaves; of breezy Scottish days, with the
splash of the cool brown water, and the flush of a
snow-white swan, and the balmy honey-smell of the
heather, while the grouse gave her note of warning
to the thoughtless grazing deer; of glowing deep-hued
eastern sunsets, where the reeds of the Nile trembled
in the after-glow, or the curling flight of the desert-

hawk soared upward above the ruins of the temples of Jupiter Ammon ;—hours when the days and the nights were all too brief for the glad luxuriance of the "life he was gifted and filled with."

The great tears gathered in his eyes and fell down, wrung slowly, one by one, upon the shining metal ; then he unfastened the collar, and rose and crossed the street to a small dark house where he saw that things were pawned—a minor, obscure Mont de Piété. He entered and laid the toy down.

"Take it," he said, faintly, yet with a new, strange fierceness in the words—the fierceness that comes with the gnawing of want—"take it, and give me food for the dog."

The owner of the wretched place stared at him, and balanced the collar thoughtfully in his hands, amazed at the richness and the workmanship of the thing offered him ; he gave one glance, suspicious, curious, leering ; but the look soon passed : he saw his first thought of theft was wrong ; he saw, as the old crone had seen, "an aristocrat" in the man who craved food from him for that costly ornament.

"It is of value—of great value," he muttered, in the surprise of the moment, balancing still with critical wonder the silver links and plates, and peering through his test-glass at the graven crest and shield.

"Give me food for him, and take it."

The words were very low, but there was something of menace in them. The man, old and, though avaricious, not dishonest, for his trade, glanced half frightened at their speaker; and, keeping the collar in his hand, stooped under his dirty counter, and drew out a plate of his own supper—good food enough, though coarse, and heaped up in abundance. The retriever devoured it as only starvation can devour.

The pawnbroker watched him with a half-stupid wonder, then took three napoleons from his desk and pushed them towards Chandos.

"Your silver thing is worth more than your dog's meat. Take those."

The collar was worth thirty, as he knew well; he voluntarily gave three. He thought himself stupendously honest; so he was, as the world goes.

A deep flush came for the moment into Chandos' face; he drew back with an involuntary gesture of repulsion. Want had not killed in him yet the patrician impulses of his blood; then, as the colour faded, leaving him deadly pale, he stretched out his hand and took it. It would keep life in him for another week.

"I thank you," he said, simply, as he bowed with his old courtly grace to the man who with wide-open eyes watched him with a fascinated amaze.

"Mon Dieu!" murmured the pawnbroker, as he turned to leave the place—"mon Dieu! how strange a man! He wants food for a dog, and he bows like a king. Well, I gave him three, I gave him three; I almost wish I had given him more." Still, even as it was, he felt by that voluntary gift of three he had been virtuous enough to deserve the Prix de Montholon. There are many in higher trades than his who consider that to abstain for a little part from all the cheating they have it in their power to do, is to attain a high degree of social and commercial honesty.

Chandos, with the retriever leaping and fawning on him in gratitude and pleasure, turned to pass from the place. In the entrance stood Trevenna.

Well clothed in dark warm seal-skins that hung lightly on him, with a russia-leather case in his hand, from which he had just paused to take a cigar, with his ruddy colour brighter, his white teeth whiter, and his keen, frank eyes bluer in the winter air and glancing gas-light, he stood in an easy comfort, in a traveller's carelessness; and on his mouth was a lurking smile—a smile of irrepressible amusement, of ironic triumph. He had watched Chandos many a time in the gambling-hell, in the midnight streets, in the opium-drunkenness, before he had stood and looked at him where he lay insensible on what seemed his death-bed. He had seldom lost sight of him; he had been the only one who remembered him; for hate is more enduring than any love. But now only for the first time Chandos knew that his gaze was on him—now when the hazard of accident had made his bitterest enemy pause at the door of the pawn-shop and look on at the barter of the silver toy.

And not in the first instant when Chandos turned and saw him, could he wholly hide the caustic mockery, the victorious success, with which he had watched this last depth of hopeless misery into which the man he had pursued had fallen ; not in that moment of supreme domination over his fallen friend could he resist the impulse that beset the single weakness lurking in his bright, bold nature— the weakness of an insatiable and woman-like avidity of hate.

He stretched out his hand with his old ready, pleasant smile ; the palm was filled with some ten or dozen sovereigns and a few crisp bank-notes just won at the whist-tables of the Jockey Club.

"Très-cher ! when we last met, you used me rather roughly because I offended you with a bit of common sense ; the direst insult to you men of genius. But let bygones be bygones. Take what you want, Chandos ; you did the same for me once. Take 'em all—do now. You won't believe how, from my soul, I pity you. Pawned the dog's collar—oh, the deuce ! Is it so bad as that ? You look as if you wanted food yourself ; why didn't you write to me ? I'm a poor man, as you know ; but still a five-pound note——"

He knew so well how to pierce with the cruelest strokes the most sensitive nerves of the nature he had studied so long and so minutely. The words might have passed on a stranger's ear as kindly meant, though coarsely phrased; he knew how more bitter than all taunts, more unbearable than all outrage, would they be to the man who stood before him.

He was not prepared for their effect.

Chandos looked at him a moment in silence, then dashed his hand down with his own clenched fist in a sudden blow that shattered in the mud the coins and notes.

"Take care! or you shall have the same on your jibing lips."

The menace was low-breathed, but it thrilled with a fierce intensity of suppressed passion. Trevenna had not calculated or remembered the change that wretchedness and desperation work in the gentlest natures; he had never thought how the softest and most pliant temper, goaded by indignity and altered by circumstance, will turn at last ferocious like a wild boar at bay.

He stooped, amazed and for the instant speechless, and picked up the scattered money from the door-step and the street (Trevenna never wasted anything; it was one of the secrets of his success); then he looked up with the insolence of superiority, the coarseness of triumph, that he could no more have spared to the man before him, than the hound will spare the stag he has pulled down the gripe of his fangs, the wrench of his jaws.

"On my honour, monseigneur, we can't stand that style now, you know. We put up with your pride when you were the lord of Clarencieux, but I'll be hanged if men will let you come it over them now. You've lost your head, that's what it is, with gaming, and drinking, and going to the bad. I'm deuced sorry for you, on my word I am—awful break-down, I know, and a good deal of excuse, still, when a man would take pity on you——"

Chandos' hand fell with a swaying weight upon his shoulder and forced him back off the step, off the stones. Under the goad of his foe's insults, under the taunting pity of the man he had saved and enriched, all the weakness of illness, all the dizziness of exhaustion, seemed to leave him; he felt as though the force of lions flowed back into his veins.

"Come out—into some lonely place," he muttered in Trevenna's ear. "Come quietly, or I shall find strength to kill you still."

Trevenna was a courageous man, but also he was a sagacious one; he knew what the gripe of the hand that held him, what the gleam of the eyes that stared into his, foreboded. He turned of his own accord passively down a solitary, gloomy, unlighted court of a dreary uninhabited fifteenth-century hotel; not far from the Tourelle de la Reine Isabeau, in the ancient Rue du Temple, where the darling of Paris was struck down by the assassins of his foe of Burgundy.

Chandos had never released his grasp upon his shoulder; he forced him slowly on and backward into the darkness of the stone-paved court. Men turned and looked at him; he had no sense of them; he only saw John Trevenna's face. Once alone there, in that gaunt black silence, he released him and shook him off.

"Now tell me why you hate me!"

The words were distinctly uttered, and were not loud; yet for the moment of their utterance, as he had done once before, Trevenna felt very near his death. But he was a bold man; he did not quail; he laughed audaciously.

"Why do I hate you? What a question! In the first place, you can't know I do."

Chandos took a step nearer to him; his eyes were black, his lips were livid.

"No lies! Why do you triumph in my ruin? How have I ever wronged you?"

Trevenna laughed again; his temper was up for once, his savage hatred had got the better of him, his caution was forgotten in the irresistible delight of flinging off the disguise he had worn so long, and taunting and cursing his fallen antagonist openly while he was powerless; even as yonder, under the House of the Image of Our Lady, the boar of Burgundy had commanded the "*coup de massue*" to the fair lifeless body that his brute envy had slaughtered in its youth.

> " I have no title to aspire ;
> Yet if you sink, I seem the higher,"

he chanted, with a malicious humour. "That couplet is true to the core. Triumph? I don't triumph. I only offer to lend you a five-pound note; and you look deucedly as if you wanted it. Of course there's something droll in such a fall as yours. I can't help that. To think of all you used to be and all you are! The see-saw of Fortune was never half so strikingly illustrated since the days of Crœsus."

There was very little light where they stood, none save such as the winter moon shed; but there was enough for him to see the face above him, and the words stopped abruptly even on his fearless lips.

He knew that for far less provocation than this blood has been shed a million times since the days of Cain.

"Answer me," said Chandos—and there was a menace in the patient words more deadly than lies in passion—"answer me. *Why* do you hate me as devils hate?"

"Can't say how devils hate! Don't believe in 'em,' said Trevenna, flippantly. His audacious and insolent temper was dared and roused; though he had died for it, he would not have abandoned his victory. "No more do you. They all say now 'Lucrèce' is a deistical work; a season later, it'll be atheistical. Trust public opinion to run all down-hill when once it takes the turn. What if I do hate you? I'm not singular. No end of men hate you, *mon beau* Chandos!"

Something of the fierce concentred passion faded

from the face on which the white moon shone; a great weariness of pain came there.

"Hate me?" he re-echoed, dreamily. "I never wronged any man, to my own knowledge. Why should men hate me? Why should you?"

Trevenna shrugged his shoulders, and shook his seal-skins with a careless laugh.

"Why? Why, hate's sown broadcast, like so much thistle-down. Why? Perhaps you robbed me of my mistress, or I envied yours. Perhaps you beat me once at écarté. Perhaps you only provoked me with your d—d languor of aristocratic hauteur; that did a deal of mischief for you with a good many. Perhaps you incensed me with the very cursed grace of your generosities, with the very royal nonchalance of your liberalities; *that* annoyed more than you wot of, too. Hate? Why, what is there to wonder at in that? If I loved you now, you *might* think it out of the common!"

And yet, were love won by friendship, loyalty, and gifts, how had he bought this man's! The memory rose in him where he stood, with the goading banter of Trevenna's ironies on his ear; yet there was too grand a fibre in his nature, too proud a chivalry in his blood, for him to smite his torturer with the past of forgotten benefits—for him to appeal against ingratitude with the rebuke, "*I served you!*"

Yet to the thoughts of both one memory unbidden rose—the memory of the summer night among the green pine-woods of Baden, when a helpless debtor, pining in the Duchy prisons, had been released by the free, loving hand of the young heir of Clarencieux.

The memory came over Chandos with a sudden pang that stilled the passion in him, and filled him only with a yearning, wondering anguish of regret.

"You hate me!" he said, slowly. "*You!*"

It was the only utterance of reproach that passed his lips; in it a world was spoken. Though every other living thing had forsaken him, he would have sworn that this man would have been faithful as the dog beside him. The rebuke, slight as it was, struck such lingering conscience as Trevenna retained, and, with that sense of momentary shame, stung afresh all his greedy triumph, his jeering exultation, his untiring mockery, into their pitiless exercise.

"Well, if I do? What if I do? You'll call me a hound that bites the hand that fed him. Basta! monseigneur; there are some gifts and caresses we can't forgive so soon as we could forgive a kick and a curse. Human nature! You loved human nature; don't you love it now? You were an aristocrat, and I hated aristocrats. *À la lanterne* with every one of 'em. Not but what I'm sorry for you—deuced sorry for you. I'll try to get you a place, if you'll tell me what you'll fill. There are lots of things they'll give you; the world heartily pities you, you know, though you *were* so imprudent. Besides, if anybody ever hated you, my poor·Chandos, they can afford to forget it now.   You can't sink lower—a cleaned-out gamester, a sotted opium-drinker, a beggar in the streets!"

The last words had scarce left his tongue in their insolence of assumed compassion, in their vindictiveness of victorious jibe, when Chandos dashed his hand back on his lips, smiting them to silence, the sole answer that he gave his traitor. His face had changed terribly as he stood and heard; the instinct of vengeance, the instinct to *kill*, had wakened in him; for the moment a very hell of crime was in him.

Trevenna's laughing, sanguine, sun-tanned features turned livid, and set fixed as in a vice; the blow stirred black blood in him. Lightly as a leopard, and as savagely, he sprang forward on the man he hated. For one instant, in the grey gloom of the old lonely court, there was a close-locked struggle; wrong and hate found their last issue in the sheer animal bloodthirst, the wild-brute, untamed instincts that live latent in all men; the next, the unequal contest ended.   Just risen from his sick bed, weak with long fasting and past illness, fever-worn, and already blind and dizzy with the single exertion of the crashing blow that he had dealt, Chandos reeled over under the fresh strength and supple science of his adversary, and swayed back heavily on the grass-grown stones of the desolate court.   The dog, which had wandered away for a moment, sprang back with a lion's bound and a lion's bay as his master fell, rushed at Trevenna, buried deep fangs in his clothes and flesh, tore him with mad **fury off Chandos, and** stood guard over the senseless and prostrate form;—none could have **put** a hand on it now, and lived.

He lay there as he had **lain in the** frozen night when Guido Lulli had found him, utterly still, utterly senseless. His face was turned upward, and the moon shone on it with a white, cold, clear light.

His foe looked **at** him, standing much as in the dim centuries **of the** Moyen Age, **a little** farther under the shadow of the tower of fair Queen Isabeau, John of Burgundy **had once** looked on in the evil night at the stone-dead **body of** the man his jealous, covetous lust of ambitious **envy had** pursued and hunted down **to the death.**

He had his victory, **so sweet to him that he** never felt the blood pour from **his shoulder, where the** retriever had seized him and dragged him off.

" How **easy to kill him now !"** he thought. " Bah ! only **fools break laws.** He will be dead soon enough ; he is worse than dead now ; he can *suffer.* I wish priests' tales were true, and souls could live. I wish his father's **could have** power to see him as he lies— see the wreck of him and the ruin."

There was **a** hard, ravenous, gloating longing in **the** thought that stretched out beyond the grave, not content with its work on **earth :** he looked lingeringly, enjoyingly, reluctant to pass away ; but it was **rare** that caution **with him** could be conquered by

passion or desire, and he knew that if he waited a
moment more the dog would be at his throat. He
looked once more with a smile—a smile of full success—then went out from the still quadrangle, leaving
the chill moonlight to settle in a broad unbroken
space where Chandos lay.

That black shade of the old Rue du Temple had
seen many murders since the night when Louis
d'Orléans was felled down there as he rode from his
tryst with Isabeau; but it had never seen fouler
murder than that which John Trevenna had done,
though he had held back his hand from the shedding
of blood, from the breaking of law.

CHAPTER IV.

"SIN SHALL NOT HAVE DOMINION OVER YOU."

THE square court, surrounded with its four blank granite moss-grown walls, with the round pointed towers looming darkly up towards the sky, was wholly forsaken; it was three parts in ruin; no one wandered there save once or twice in the length of the night, when the beat of the patrol's step sounded through it, waking its hollow echoes. It was as still as when, in the mediæval ages which saw its stones raised, the monks of its brotherhood had flitted ghost-like through its shadows; the pale moon only looked down on it, her spectral swathes of light falling across the leaden gloom of the damp lichen-covered pavement.

How long he lay there he never knew; hurled

back, but swaying over from faintness rather than from injury, he had fallen in a dead swoon, his head striking the stones with a dull sound that echoed through the silence. The fresh night-air—not cold, but stirred with a cool westerly wind—revived him, blowing over his forehead and his eyes. He had been struck down heavily, flung in wrestling by a merciless hand; but there was little sense of pain on him as he woke to the knowledge of where he was and of what had chanced; his bodily weakness had prevented the struggle and the resistance that might have been fatal to him. He looked up at the moon shining so far above, so clear, so bright, so tranquil; life seemed to have faded far away from him, and to have left him in the calmness of the grave.

He rose with difficulty—his limbs felt powerless and broken; and he staggered to an old stone bench hard by, where a shattered fountain-spout slowly let fall a stream of water that ebbed away, glistening and shallow, in the starlight over the squares of the pavement. He stooped and drank eagerly from it—it was cold and pure; then sank down on the bench where many weary and heavy laden had rested before him in the pressure of the centuries gone—in the violence and the darkness of the middle age. The dog gathered itself close against him; there was no sound of the world without, save the dull roar of the distant night-traffic and the striking of church-clocks upon the stillness: they seemed alone in the heart of

Paris—God-forgotten, man-forsaken, in the midst of the peopled world.

In the stillness, in the solemn night, with the serene luminous stars gazing down on the darkness of earth around him, the opium-mists, the brandy-drugged stupor, the delirium of exhaustion, so long on him, passed away; the thoughts of his mind grew clearer, for the first hour since the day of his ruin. An intense agony was on him—the deep, still, tearless agony of absolute despair. Yet he seemed to look on the ruin of his life as from a burial-place from which he would never rise; to look on and see the world that knew him no more, the love that had abandoned, the friendship that had betrayed him, as one dead, whose sense and soul returned to behold all that he had cherished revile his memory and forget his loss. He had no feeling of present existence; all he knew was that in the world of men he had no place, that in the hearts of the vast multitude of earth he had no remembrance, that he had perished for ever into oblivion when the stroke had smitten him down. There, in the stillness and solemnity of night, all things seemed manifest to him; apart from all that he had once known, he seemed to gaze on it and hear its pitiless course pass on, as a man lying paralysed watches and listens, having no more part or share with the humanity around him than though his shroud had covered him, having no hand to raise if his cheek be smitten, having no arm to lift if a fool mock his misery, having no lips to speak if a lie make foul mirth of his name; lifeless, and yet among the living; slain, and yet alive to suffer.

This is how it seemed to him that he was now. Breath was in him—that was all he claimed of life; in every other thing he was a corpse; felled into a grave, whence he heard the jibing laughter of those who jested at his fall, the restless feet of those who passed on and bade him be forgot, the stones flung down on him by the hands he had filled with gifts, the kisses that were welcomed by the cheek his kiss had warmed! He was dead; and as the dead he was abandoned and forgotten.

The beauty that had been his was given to the embrace of another; the caress that had been on his lips now burned as softly on the mouth of his spoiler; the roof that had sheltered him from his birth up covered the sleep and the revel of strangers; the treasures that had owned him master, and been gathered by him from north to south, east to west, were scattered broadcast over the earth; the world that he had led knew him no more, and never named his name; the women who had smiled in his eyes, and wound their wreathing arms about his neck, let their bright hair brush the bosoms and their pulses thrill to the whispers of newly wooed lovers; the men whom he had served followed the light of rising suns, and gave no heed to the eternal night that had fallen for him : all that he had loved, all that he had owned, all that he had lost, was gone to make the joy of other hearts ;—his fate was the fate of the dead.

He was forgot in his misery, as slaughtered kings are forgot in their sealed sepulchres; and his sceptre was not even broken, in pity and honour for his name, above his grave, but passed to the hands of those who dethroned him, bringing them his wealth, his crown, his treasuries, his lieges.

Of all that he had possessed, of all he had reigned over, he could claim nothing—not even a heart that had loved him.

He knew the width and the depth of his desolation as he had never known it. The man whom he had fed as utterly as he had fed the dog at his feet, when he had been starving and homeless and friendless, the man whom he had lifted from a foreign prison and served as few serve their own flesh and blood, the man who had been his guest, his debtor, his suppliant for the very bread and wine of his table, had turned against him, had deserted him, had cursed him with a foe's hate; no other thing could have told him how utterly he had sunk, how utterly had the world forsaken him.

This man had flung his scorn at him, and had reviled him with a traitor's pitiless mockery ; he knew it was the last depth of his fall, the last and the most infamous witness of his degradation—as the Plantagenet had known it, when the hound that had been reared by his hand went from him to fawn on the conqueror.

In the state to which his mind had sunk, in the world-wide wreck that he saw around him, the strangeness of Trevenna's hatred struck him little; he did not muse, as earlier he would have done, on what could be the secret and the spring of this coarse, merciless passion of enmity in one to whom his gifts had been as many as the sands of the sea, and whom he had served more truly than he had served himself. He accepted it with the hopeless apathy that comes with despair: all left him, all changed with his changed fate, all condemned him where all had caressed him; it seemed but of a piece with the rest, that the greatest of debtors should bring him as payment the blackest of ingratitude.

He had loved men so well, he had trusted them so blindly, he had benefited them so loyally, to believe in their baseness had been so impossible to his nature, and to conceive their infidelity so distant from his every thought, that, in an inevitable reaction, he now, beneath the scourge of their mockery and the time-serving of their desertion, looked for no faith amidst them, wondered at no betrayal. The woman who had nestled to his bosom with languid eyes of eloquent love and sweet words of eternal tenderness, had forsworn her vows and sold herself for the gold of another lover; he could feel no wonder that the man who had been bound to him but by the ties of self-interest and human gratitude had turned traitor **too.** In one sense **only** did the full bitterness and shame of Trevenna's **taunts** strike home to him; they showed him how low he must have sunk that this man could dare revile him. It **was** less loathing of his foe that rose in him than it **was** loathing of himself; it was less hatred of his betrayer's infamy than **it was** hatred of his own abasement. He shuddered as he thought what adversity already had made him; he dared not think what a **brief** while more might make him.

The bodily **illness** which had held **him** prostrate so long had, **in a degree,** done **him good;** it had weakened his frame, but it had **saved** his reason; it had rescued him from madness **as a heavy** fall that **makes the blood flow** from the surcharged brain may rescue the man it injures. A few nights more of **the life he had led, of** the heavy drugs, the burning drinks, the endless gambling, the hell **of vice,** the delirium in which he sought forgetfulness, and he would have been dead at the Morgue **or** raving in a madhouse. The lengthened sleep that **had** preceded the congestion of the lungs which cold and lack of food produced, and the danger in which he had lingered through **so many** days, **had** cooled and had saved him, had stilled the fever in his blood, and freed his reason from **the** half-drunk phantoms **in which it had** lost itself, and been broken and blinded for so long. He rose from his wretched bed but the shadow of what he had once been; but the look was gone from his eyes which had made the *fille de joie* in the gaming-den thrust the opium to him and bid him not live to be what he must be.

Her words came back to him now where he sat, the serene, cool night, through which the stars alone looked, stilling the riot of his mind with the sense of their own eternal calm. "What he must be!" He knew well enough what that was.

A little while more of such a life as he had led since the day of his ruin, of those hideous orgies, of that drunken stupor, of that horrible and ghastly union of poverty and intoxication, of despair and vice, and the lowest creature that crawled through the mid-night snows to devour the stray relics of offal that the curs had left, would be as high as he; a little more, and every better thing would be crushed out in him, and the vilest den would spurn him from it to die in the river-slime like a choked dog.

"What he must be!"

His head sank down on his hands as the words drifted slowly through his mind: what could he choose but be?

Had he embraced dishonour and accepted the rescue that a lie would have lent him, this misery in its greatest share had never been upon him. He would have come hither with riches about him, and the loveliness he had worshipped would have been

his own beyond the touch of any rival's hand.
Choosing to cleave to the old creeds of his race,
and passing, without a backward glance, into the
paths of honour and of justice, it was thus with
him now. Verily, virtue must be her own reward,
as in the Socratic creed; for she will bring no other
dower than peace of conscience in her gift to who-
soever weds her. "I have loved justice, and fled
from iniquity; wherefore here I die in exile," said
Hildebrand upon his death-bed. They will be the
closing words of most lives that have followed truth.

What could he be? What could the future, if
he lived for one, hold for him? Misery, privation,
abandonment, solitude, the ceaseless thirst of vain
desires, the unending void of eternal losses, the
haunting knowledge of all he might have been.
These were what faced him; these were what alone
awaited him. If he lived on, he could but look
for these, and for worse yet—he to whose beauty-
steeped senses every passing pain had been unknown,
every sight of deformity been veiled! He thought
of the old sacred legend of Herodotus; how, when
the Argive mother prayed at the Temple of Juno
in Argos for the highest blessing that mortals can
attain to be bestowed on Cleobis and Bito, her prayer
was granted—her sons fell asleep to wake no more.
He knew now its terrible truth, its eternal meaning
—he who had thought ten thousand times the span
of his rich and shadowless life would be too brief a

space to spend on earth! Death;—it would not come to him; and he longed for it as a man in a desert land, shipwrecked amidst the burning wealth of colour and the cruel wantonness of beauty round him, longs for water as he perishes of thirst.

Still yet, even yet, a pulse of life stirred that he could not with his own hand slay; it was the power of the genius in him. Dulled, drugged, stifled, paralysed, beneath the weight of infinite wretchedness, the frozen apathy of despair, the fever of vice, the pangs of famine, it was not dead, and the taunts of his foe had stung the pride sleeping with it into fresh ex_istence; with the outrage of John Trevenna some faint throb of the thoughts and the instincts of old returned. The insult of his debtor and his traitor had been the crowning agony of his passion; but it brought back life in him, as the plunge of the surgeon's steel will bring it back and cut the cords of death by the very force and suddenness of its stab.

A gentler hand could not have saved him or arrested him; the unpitying and brutal thrusts of his adversary roused him ere it was yet too late.

There, in the silence, in the solitude, with the dark walls brooding above him, and the cold winter's moon looking down, something of the grandeur of resistance, something of the calm of endurance, came on him. Should this man see him die in a bagnio? point to him as one so womanish weak that the first stroke of calamity had slain him? mock him as a

madman, who, having squandered his birthright,
flung his manhood and his mind and his soul away
with it ?

Before his memory rose that day in his childhood
when he had told his father what his future should
be made; he had thought of it ere now—never *as*
now. He saw the purple mists of the distance, **the**
golden brown of the autumn-woods in the warmth of
the sunset, the far-stretching sea growing dim in the
dying light, while away to the westward the red flush
of the after-glow lingered; the very scent that up-
rose from **the** dew-laden earth, the very breath of
the wind stirring the coils of the leaves, came back
to him; he **saw** his father's eyes look down on **him**
with a proud tenderness, a gentle **smile,** seeing **in**
him the sole successor of the finest ambitions of a
stainless and world-famous **life, the reaper** of his
ripe triumphs, the **heir of his honour** and **his he-**
ritage. "I will live **so that** the nation shall only
need **to write 'Chandos' on my** grave, and the name
will tell its own tale!" The words **in** all their
childlike visionary impulse, all their pure impossible
ambition, **all their high and** chivalrous desire, came
back upon his mind with a deadly anguish. These
had been the dreams of his youth, and he had kept
true **to** them thus !

He had been gifted with such a genius as was in
Alcibiades when he listened in love to the golden
words of his Master, or heard the shouts of the

people give him to triumph as his chariot-wheels crushed the wild thyme they threw. Should he perish like Alcibiades, in the arms of a courtezan, lost to all that earlier and holier time? A greater inheritance than that which he had squandered had been given him in his intellect; a greater suicide than that of the body would be the suicide that now was destroying the mind with which nature had dowered him.

Freedom was left him and intellect—the two first treasures of life; whilst the powers of his brain were still his, and his liberty, the poet would have said:

Then first of the mighty, thank God that thou art.

There are liberties sweeter than love; there are goals higher than happiness.

Some memory of them stirred in him there, with the noiseless flow of the lingering water at his feet, and above the quiet of the stars; the thoughts of his youth came back to him, and his heart ached with their longing.

Out of the salt depths of their calamity men had gathered the heroisms of their future; out of the desert of their exile they had learned the power to return as conquerors. The greater things within him awakened from their lethargy; the innate strength so long untried, so long lulled to dreamy indolence and rest, uncoiled from its prostration; the force that would resist and, it might be, survive, slowly came upon him, with the taunts of his foe. It was possible that there was that still in him which might be grander and truer to the ambitions of his imaginative childhood under adversity than in the voluptuous sweetness of his rich and careless life. It was possible, if—if he could once meet the fate he shuddered from, once look at the bitterness of the life that waited for him, and enter on its desolate and arid waste without going back to the closed gates of his forfeited paradise, to stretch his limbs within their shadow once more ere he died.

There is more courage needed oftentimes to accept the onward flow of existence, bitter as the waters of Marah, black and narrow as the channel of Jordan, than there is ever needed to bow down the neck to the sweep of the death-angel's sword.

He rose slowly and looked upward; the hours had fled, the city was sleeping, the busy feet of the crowds were silent, and the hush of an intense rest was on the world around him. Beneath it vice might yet riot, and misery still moan; but it was towards dawn, and the noiseless peace was unbroken; the trembling rays of moonlight shivered on the water's surface, and far above, shining from the deep blue-black fathomless vault, the lustre of the stars burned through the brilliancy of winter air—a myriad worlds uncounted and unknown. Men had abandoned and hope forsaken him; on the earth he had no place, and in human love no memory; but there, under their solemn light, their own tranquillity encompassed him; solitude lost its desolation in the eternity and the immensity of that limitless space, of that unknown deity. A lifetime suffered here—what was it? the span of a single day in those bright worlds beyond the sun. In face of that changeless and endless calm, the burden of so brief a labour might well be borne; sufficient if through travail the faintest shadow of likeness unto truth were gained. To many in their suffering that unalterable and eternal serenity of nature is pitiless, is unendurable; they find no mercy in it, no shelter, and no aid; to him it was divine as consolation, divine with the majesty of God. Above the fret and vice and wretchedness of earth it brooded so still, so cold, it stretched so boundless and so death-less out into the infinite realms of space!—from it there seemed to breathe the promise of a future when men should live " sceptreless, free, uncircumscribed ;" from it there seemed to steal the bidding, " let the world abandon you, but to yourself be true."

His foe too early had triumphed.

Though he had lost all, there were with him still the dreams of his youth ; the world forsook him, and the width of the earth stretched before him—a desert laid waste, barren and pitiless as stone, through which he must pass, wearily and in solitude, to live and to die alone; yet he arose with his dead strength re-

vived, with the calm of a passionless endurance fallen
on him.

He accepted the desolation of his life, for sake of
all beyond life, greater than life, which looked down
on him from the silence of the night.

BOOK THE FIFTH.

Seggundo in piuma,
In fama non si vien.   DANTE.

Comme il était rêveur au matin de son âge,
Comme il était penseur au terme du voyage !

Lucky men are favourites of Heaven.
All own the chief, when Fortune owns the cause.
DRYDEN.

CHAPTER I.

IN EXILE.

It was sunset in Venice—that supreme moment when the magical flush of light transfigures all the southern world, and wanderers whose eyes have long ached with the greyness and the glare of northward cities gaze and think themselves in heaven. The still waters of the lagunes, the marbles and the porphyry and the jasper of the mighty palaces, the soft grey of the ruins all covered with clinging green and the glowing blossoms of creepers; the hidden antique nooks where some woman's head leaned out of an arched casement, like a dream of the Dandolo time, when the Adriatic swarmed with the returning galleys laden with Byzantine spoil; the dim, mystic, majestic walls that towered above the gliding surface of the eternal water, once alive with flowers, and music, and

the gleam of golden tresses, and the laughter of careless revellers in the Venice of Goldoni, in the Venice
of the Past; everywhere the sunset glowed, with
the marvel of its colour, with the wonder of its
warmth.

Then a moment, and it was gone. Night fell with
the hushed, shadowy stillness that belongs to Venice
alone; and, in place of the riot and luxuriance of
hue, there was the tremulous darkness of the young
night, with the beat of an oar on the water, the scent
of unclosing carnation-buds, the white gleam of moonlight, and the odour of lilies of the valley blossoming
in the dark archway of some mosaic-lined window.

One massive and ancient house towered up amidst
many another palace—a majestic melancholy place,
with shafts of black marble and columns of porphyry,
and deep sea-piles that the canal bathed into a hundred umber tints. Long ago some of the greatest
of the oligarchy had held there their highest state;
now it was scarcely habited, left to decay, and lost
in gloom—a sepulchre of dead glories, while the insolence of foreign mirth and the shame of foreign
arms outraged the captive and widowed beauty of
the Adriatic spouse. It was lonely and unspeak-
ably desolate; with the gliding sheet of the still
water beneath its walls, and the long sombre lines of
forsaken palaces stretching beyond it on either side,
and facing it in the splendour of the early moon.
Yet it was infinitely impressive, infinitely grand, stand-

ing there with its mediæval sculptures touched with rays of starlight, and its costly marbles washed by the ebbing of the tide.

At one of its lofty narrow casements a man leaned out into the fragrant spring-tide air; he had risen from close studies in the chamber within—vast in space as a king's throne-room, barren in garniture as a contadina's hut—to watch the fading of the sun, the sudden loss of all the wealth of colour in the grey hues of evening; and he lingered still, now that the night had wholly fallen. In that stillness, in that soft lapping of the water, in that glisten in the distance of the silvery lagune, in that scarcely stirring wind filled with the breath of opening blossoms, there was a lulling charm—there was the echo of a long-lost youth.

His face was of a great beauty; though many years had passed over it, time could touch and could dim it but little; but in the eyes there was the exile's weariness and the deep thought of the scholar; on the mouth there was that certain look which comes of bitter pain borne, of strong victories wrung from calumny and poverty and hard defiance—such a look as Dante might have worn, yet less harsh, though not less mournful, than the Florentine's. He looked down on the deep and sleeping shadows, on the gliding darkness of the canal below; the sweetness of the young night, the Adriatic fragrance of the sea-wafted air, brought him a thousand memories across the desert of long years.

Through his mind floated such thoughts as wearied
Cleon :

> Indeed, to know is something, and to prove
> How all this beauty might be enjoy'd is more ;
> But, knowing naught, to enjoy is something too.
> Yon rower with **the** moulded muscles there,
> Lowering the sail, is nearer it than I.

There had been a time when every breath of life
had been for him enjoyment, rich as the god's life of
Dionysus. In moments such as these he longed for
that dead time, as the poet Ovid, in the ice and
winter storms and snow-bound forests of his Danubian
exile, longed for the golden sunlight, for the purple
pomp, for the glad idolatry of the vine-crowned land
that knew his place no more.

"Am I any nearer the ambitions of my youth
than I was twenty years ago?—am I as near?" he
thought. In the voluptuous hush and fragrance of
the Venetian night his years seemed cold and fruitless and heavy laden.

Where he stood, in the dark arch of the window,
the measured music of oars beat the water ; beneath
the walls several gondolas glided ; on the silence rose,
chanted by the mellow voices of young Venetians,
a hymn of liberty. They might pay to their tyrants
well-nigh with life for its singing ; yet that knowledge gave no tremor to the cadence that rang so bold
and so clear in the stillness. Passionate yet unspeak-
ably sad, rich as the world of colour that had just

passed from the world, but melancholy as the breathless stillness of the calm lagunes, the ode of freedom
was sung by the lips of those who knew themselves
slaves—young fresh voices, the voices of youth and
of vivid ambition, yet touched to a deeper meaning,
and vibrating with a hopeless desire; for they were
the voices also of forbidden hope, and of thoughts
held in bond and enchained. It was the "Io tri-
umphe" of liberty:

> Thou huntress swifter than the Moon! thou terror
> Of the world's wolves! thou bearer of the quiver,
> Whose sun-like shafts pierce tempest-tossèd error
> As light may pierce the clouds;

but also it was the lament of Leopardi; the lament
most weary, most utterly desolate of all upon earth;
the lament of men whose hearts ache for lofty aims
and noble fields, and whose lives are denied all purpose and all effort—of men whose country is in
thraldom.

The chant ceased; all the many and melodious
tones which had risen on the night and swelled louder
and sweeter down the canal, till the boatmen far off
heard the echo and gave it back, were suddenly
silenced, as a choir of song-birds will cease at noontide. In the prow of the foremost vessel a young
Venetian rose, the gleam of his auburn hair and the
kindling light on his face like some old painter's
Gabriel or Michael yonder in the gloom of the ancient
churches. He lifted his eyes to the arch of the case-

ment where he stood up in the white tremulous lustre of the moon.

"You have striven for the freedom of thought and for the liberty of judgment," he said, simply. "Venice, who has lost them both, loves you for that which you have loved, and gives you thus the only homage she now dares."

Without pause, without a word more, the rowers bent above their oars, the gondolas floated down the dark surface, the young impassioned faces of the singers turned backward with a fond and reverent farewell as their vessels swept into the shadows so deep, so rayless, underneath the walls of the abandoned palaces : it was all they had to give, that song of freedom in a fettered land.

He to whom they gave it thought it more than the gift of crowns laid at his feet. It touched him strangely with its suddenness, with its meaning—this gratitude rendered to him by the young, pure, patriot-voices of those who might pay the cost of that night's utterance with the pain of captive's bondage or of exile's banishment. It was more worth to him than any diadem with which the world could have anointed him—this recognition of what he sought, this knowledge of why he laboured.

It came to him as answer and rebuke to the thoughts which had been with him as that unbidden music rose upon the night. To enjoy was much ; but to seek truth and labour for freedom might be more.

"One fetter of tradition loosened, one web of superstition broken, one ray of light let in on darkness, one principle of liberty secured, are worth the living for," he mused. "Fame!—it is the flower of a day, that dies when the next sun rises. But to do something, however little, to free men from their chains, to aid something, however faintly, the rights of reason and of truth, to be unvanquished through all and against all, these may bring one nearer the pure ambitions of youth. Happiness dies as age comes to us; it sets for ever, with the suns of early years: yet, perhaps, we may keep a higher thing beside which it holds but a brief royalty, if to ourselves we can rest true, if for the liberty of the world we can do anything."

For he was one of those who, to the cause of freedom and of truth, bring the wealth of their intellect and the years of their life, and receive but little requital save a sullen reverence wrung from an unwilling world, and the railing bitterness of the crowds who abhor light and hug error and tradition close. His words stirred with shame the hearts of nations steeped in lust and lethargy and the greed of gold; and they awoke to hoot and hiss the one who dared rouse them from their torpor, or arrest them in their money-changing. His thoughts sank down into the unworn hearts of youth, and they shook themselves free from ashes of superstition and the chains of creeds; and the priest of superstition cursed him. His utterance probed the surface of the world, and, piercing its panoply of wordy falsehood, brought to it the clear keen light of scepticism and truth; and the world was weary of him, it slept so much more soundly beneath the veil and in the darkness. He loved men with a pity and a tolerance no trial could exhaust; he would have led them, if he could, to the search and the knowledge of other things than their gold-thirst and their paradise of lies; and they turned back to their treasuries of money, to their granaries of hypocrisies, and would have none of him. Their ears were wilfully deaf, their eyes were wilfully blind, their feet loved the trodden paths, their hands were busy grasping their neighbours' goods; they wondered at and they reviled him; they would not follow to the mountain-air he bade them breathe; they stayed in the mud, seeking a coin. He was alone. The world gave him fame grudgingly, reluctantly, because it could not withhold it longer; but it left him alone and condemned because he saw no holiness in the shrine of gold, and no right divine in the tyranny of tradition.

He was alone; eagles that love the high light-penetrated air, that has no mist and clog of earth-born dust, must ever dwell in solitude. Yet now and then there came to him, as there had come from the voices of fettered men to-night, an echo of his own thoughts, a recognition of his own labours, and these sufficed to him.

Where he leaned now, in the fragrant Venetian night, with the southern song of liberty still seeming to linger above the waters, and the moonlight full upon the decaying grandeur of the forsaken sea-palaces, he thought of the words of Dante, written in exile, as he lived in exile now.

They who labour justly for the sheer sake of truth find no present reward; will they hereafter find it? A weary question—one to which men never yet have gained an answer.

CHAPTER II.

IN TRIUMPH.

THE stars, as they shone on Venice, shone likewise farther northward on one of the mighty labyrinthine ink-black cities of labour. The heavy pall of smoke loomed over the forests of roofs, of chimneys, of factories, of churches; the bells of the latter were chiming with incessant joyous pealing clangour, bells that rung a chime called of God every seventh day in the midst of the worship of Mammon, bells put up in many a steeple, iron offerings to Deity by iron hands that wrung the last bitter drop out of poverty, and clammed the last starveling of labour, and bought redemption cheaply by a sop to a parish priest.

The bells were rhyming wildly, with no pretence,

happily, that it was in the honour of Godhead now—tossing upward through the weight of murky air wave on wave of changing sound, of riotous triumph, of passionate, **mirthful**, random, uncouth music like the harmony **of Thor's** great hammers. Under the sea of iron-echoing noise vast crowds pressed tumultuous, **in a grim triumph like that** of the metal melodies. **Their** hard, keen, indomitable faces were **sharp-set as the knives they made, were** massive as the iron they worked; **and on** them **was the flush and the pride of victory. It was on the night of a** great **election, an** election that had followed in Lenten time on a sudden and unlooked-for dissolution—an appeal to the country as agitating as **it had been** unforeseen; and they had brought **to the** fore their champion, **their idol, the most** famous of all his party. In this vast **city of Darshampton** there was but one **name and but one** sovereignty—his. The people **had crowned him; and who should** dare to discrown ?

In one of the chambers of **a** magnificent hotel, he stood in **the dusky red** glow of the sunset that burned through the smoke-laden atmosphere, and fell **about** his feet as though it, too, were eager to seek him out and smile **on** him—this man, omnipotent in **all he** undertook. A crowd of friends were about him, breathless in congratulation on **what was but a** repeated triumph, waiting in delighted warmth of welcome **on one in whom they** saw a deity more

potent than all the gods of Semitic or Archæan creeds
—the deity of a supreme Success. Throngs had been
about him from earliest days—throngs of friends, of
flatterers, of men who believed in him honestly, and
would have fought for him to the death had need been
—of men who believed in nothing except the divinity
of success, and followed that idolatrously in him because they saw his acumen never fail, his fortune never
change. The city would give him its banquet to-
night; his party brought him devoted gratitude and
ecstatic pride, the country bestowed on him scarce less
admiration; young men looked to him as their leader,
elder looked to him to reap the harvest of the seed they
had sown in the future; the aristocracy dreaded, the
plutocracy bribed, the multitude adored him. He was
a great man already; later on he would be a greater
—popular beyond all conception, triumphant in whatever he essayed.

The shouts and the cheers of the populace swelled
louder and louder; the clamour was hoarse, Titanic,
almost terrible in its imperative power, as the voice of
the People always is when once it thunders through
the land—imperative for murder as imperative for
bread, mighty and resistless alike in both. Here it
rose with one accord, with one word—his own name.
They had brought him in—those men with their
horny, supple hands, and their blackened, resolute
brows, and their limbs like the limbs of the old
Berksækers, those men of the Black Country, who

grasped so doggedly at truths sharp as steel, yet grasped but at half-truths, and, so blinded, reached but hatred of an Order when they thought they grasped at liberty for Mankind. The shouts swelled louder and louder, more and more full of peremptory d · mand; they had brought him through, or thought they had, and clamoured for their idol.

He humoured them ever as a lion-tamer humours his cubs, that he may cut the claws, and grind smooth the teeth, and make the brave beast lie down passive as a spaniel at his beck, and turn to profit the world's terror when he shows how docilely he guides the wild tawny desert-king, that at his bidding would leap forth and tear and slay.

He went out on the balcony, and the din of the acclamations rolled up to the red evening skies like thunder. In the large square before the building, and in the transverse streets that crossed and met, the dense multitudes were gathered, wave on wave of human life, surging in in swift succession, and stretch-ing far and wide away beyond the sight, like a stormy and restless sea. Their dark faces, swarthy and be-grimed, shrewd and stern, were turned upward to the balcony with an eager pride and pleasure, while from the brawny chests of the iron-workers that tremendous welcome rang. The sun shone more burnished red in the crimson, heavy west, and, slanting in broad, glow-ing, dusky streams of light athwart the misty gloom, fell on that ocean of upraised faces, and across the eyes of the man they honoured—eyes so keen, so mirthful, so unerring, so full of sagacious life, of triumphant victory.

"He is the man for the Future," said one stalwart worker, with the **breath of the** furnace-blasts and the blackness **of** the iron-foundry upon him, yet who read Bentham, and Fourier, and Mill.

One, less book-wise and more world-wise, pierced **nearer to the secret of** success, to the root of popularity, **as he answered:**

"He's more: he's the man **for the Present.**"

"And the man for the **People!**" shouted a third, behind them. The words were caught up and echoed on **all sides, till they ran** through the **packed thousands** like **electric fluid; till from** the whole of the swaying **gigantic** mass the words broke unanimously, rising high above the pealing of the bells and the strife of the streets, hurling his name out in that grim, passionate, furious love of a multitude which has ever in it something, and well-nigh as much, of menace as of caress.

He nodded to them with a pleasant familiar smile —such a smile as a **boy** gives to his favourite and unruly dogs; then **he stood** more forward against **the** iron scroll-work of the balcony, looking **down** on that movement beneath him, and **spoke.**

Not for the **first** time here, in Darshampton, by many, the ringing, metallic clarion-roll of the voice they knew **so well** stilled them **like magic,** thrilled

them as hounds thrill at the notes of a horn, and held
them in check as the horn holds the pack. He spoke
as only those can speak who have been long trained
to the public arena, who have studied every techni-
cality of their science and every weakness of their
audience, who have brought to it not only the talent
of native skill, but the polish of long usage, the power
of assured practice. He spoke well—keen, trenchant,
vigorous, humorous oratory, English to the backbone,
coarse in its pungency withal here as it could be
scholarly elsewhere, striking to the heart of its subject
as surely and as straightly as the arrow of Tell to the
core of the apple. There was a breathless silence
while he spoke, the trumpet-like tones of his ringing
voice penetrating without effort to the farthermost of
the listening throngs, the Swift-like humour and wit
shaking sardonic laughter from the brawny chests of
his hearers, the biting and incisive reasoning drawn
in by them as eagerly as town-dusted lungs draw in
the salt fresh breezes of the sea. He was their
master, though they thought themselves his electors
and creators; and he played at will on them, as a
strong skilled hand plays on a stringed instrument,
moving it to what cadence he chooses. They listened
in devoted silence, only broken by tumultuous cheer-
ing, or by the hoarse gaunt laughter, that was ominous
as any curses, raised against what they hated. He
spoke long, though so succinctly, so pungently, that
the minutes of his speech seemed moments; then

ceased, while the red sun-glow still strayed to his feet, and the chimes of the bells swung wild delight, and the shouts of the populace teeming below deafened the air with his name.

He laughed to himself as he bowed many times his thanks and his farewell; then sauntered from the balcony into the lighted and crowded room, glancing back at that shifting sea of upraised, earnest, hard-lined faces in the dusky heat of the fading sun.

"D—d rascals, every one of you, my friends," he thought, "or out-and-out fools; God knows which. Rave about oppression and the wrongs of Capital to Labour, while you send your children to sweat, at five years old, in furnaces, and threaten to kill your brother if he don't join your trade union, and strike when he's told; clamour for the rights of man, and worry your brains after political econo-mies, while you think all the 'rights' centre in scribbling your name in a poll-book, and talking mild sedition in a tap-room! Oh, you precious fools! how we use you, and how we laugh at you!"

For he was not even wholly true to those who were so true to him; and he had no belief even in their thorough, heartfelt earnestness, erring from im-perfect vision, and distorted from imperfect educa-tion, but sincere and true in its widest errors.

They thought they had made him what he was; he knew that they were his tools, his wax, his weapons.

He glanced back once on to the vast oscillating crowd in the reddening angry sunset mist, and the laugh of a consummated victory, the insolence of a secure triumph, was in the backward flash of his eyes, mingled, too, with a certain proud power, a certain exultation of self-achieved distinction. His name was still echoing to the skies from the lungs of the close-packed throngs.

"Who dare sneer at that name now?" he thought; and there was in that thought the glow which Themistocles felt when they who had exiled him as a nameless thing of the people, to wrestle with the base-born in the Ring of Cynosarges, welcomed him in the city of the Violet Crown as the victor of Salamis, the slayer of Persia.

Then he went within from the stormy clangour and the scarlet flush of evening, and was feasted through that night by the men of the mighty town, nobles who hated him bearing their part in his honour, rivers of wine flowing to his toast, the crowds of the streets knowing no theme but his present and his future, the nation on the morrow saying, as the city said to-night, "He is a great man; he will be a still greater."

BOOK THE SIXTH.

———◆———

From the world as it is Man's, into the world as it is God's.

COWLEY.

Sie ist volkommen und sie fehlet
Darin allein dass sie mich liebt.

GOETHE.

CHAPTER I.

" PRIMAVERA ! GIOVENTŬ DELL' ANNO !"

Down at the foot of the mountain-slopes reaching
to Vallombrosa, hidden away in the deep belt of the
chesnut-forests, was a little Tuscan village. Sheltered
high above by the pines of the hills, and veiled from
every glance by the thick masses of the chesnut-leaves,
no strange foot ever scarcely wandered to it. It was
out of the route of travellers; it had slumbered here
for ages: it had been here when Milton looked on the
Val d'Arno; it had been here when Totila thundered
at the gates of Rome; it had been here when Plautus
caught in the colour of his words the laughter, the
mirth, the tavern-wit, the girls *à libre allure*, the wine-
brawls, and the Bacchan feasts of the Latin life; it
had been here through all changes, but it had never
changed. Belike, it had been sacked by Cæsar, razed

by Theodoric, visited by Stilicho, plundered by the
Franks of Carl; but it was still the same, surviving
all ruin, and covered in the spring-time with so dense
a leafy shade that the grey tint of its stone, the red
brown of its few roofs, showed no more than the
oriole's nest through the boughs. The purple plums
of the olives ripened and were gathered, the red osiers
changed to tender green, the grapes were garnered
with the vintage-tide, the cattle came down the hill-
sides when the sun sank low, the chesnuts turned to
ruddy brown, and broke their husks and fell upon the
moss; a few lives were born, a few lives were buried.
These were all the changes known there, the changes
of the night and day, of the seasons of the year, and
of the coming of life and of death. The light of the
after-glow shone on it, the scorch of the later summer
parched its fields and woods, the snows of winter lay
upon its hill-top and gleamed between the darkness
of its pines, the breath of the spring breathed the
flower-glory over its land, and uncurled the white
spiral blossom of its arums in the water-bed; but
through wars and rumours of wars, through the
Campaign of Italy as through the wars of the Great
Captain, through the ravages of the Cinque Cento,
as through the raids of the Goths and the Gauls,
the little woodland nook of Fontane Amorose remained unaltered, as though the foot of Dionysus, when it had pressed its sward, had bidden its
blossoms keep an eternal bloom," and the Dryads

and the Satyrs, driven from every other ancient haunt, still lived beneath the green **fronds of its** trailing plants, **and** laughed amidst the **bronzed gold of its** autumn vines.

It was in the " mezza notte d'Aprile," beloved of painters, hymned of poets, which **makes of all the** southern **land** one fresh and laughing garden. Upward yonder, higher still on the hills, there was some little chillness lingering still, and the air blew keener through the aisles of pines; but here, **midway** in the sloping of rich mossy green sward, deeply sheltered by its beeches and chesnuts and by the slopes of its firwoods, the delicious spring of Italy was in its fairest, with the purple orchid glowing **in the noon, and** the delicate **wind-flower fanned by the breeze,** and the young buds **of the** vine opening in the clear and perfect light. **A few miles from the clustering** dwellings of Fontane was a grove of beech-trees, always, **save at the height of** noon, dark **as** twilight; for the branches were dense, **and the** trees towered massive and many. **Yet in the heart of them was a** nook **fit for the couch of a Naïad—fit to have had laid down** in it the fair lifeless limbs of Adonis. **In the** shade **of** the leaves the moss and grass were ever fresh; the sun-tan of mid summer never brought drought there; anemones and violets, and all wild flowers that bloom in Tuscan woods, filled it with odour and colour, and through it welled the bright clear water of a broken fountain, **so** old that under

neath its moss might still be traced the half-effaced
Latin inscription. By it perhaps Virgil once had
leaned, or Claudian rhymed his epic; at its spring
the beautiful evil lips of Antonina might have drunk,
or, lying beside them, Lucretius might have thought
of the Etrurian shades, looking far down into those
deep rayless aisles of beech, sublime and sad as his
own genius. Where the water rippled, losing itself
amongst the mosses and the orchids, a glory of sunlight came, touching to silver the wing of a wood-
pigeon poised to drink, lending a warmer blush to
the white wild rose as the rifling bee hummed far
down in its violated chalice, and shedding its ripe gold
on the hair of a young girl leaning motionless
there.

The birds, fearless of her presence, paused in their
flight to glance at her; the nightingales, thinking
it night in the beech-shadows yonder, sung her their
softest songs; the butterflies alighted on the flowers
her hands held;—they knew her well, they loved her;
they were her only playmates in the long Italian day.
Arum lilies, and the pale-green blossoms of ivy, and
anemones glowing crimson, and the emerald coils of
moss, were in a loose sheaf on her lap; she sat in a
day-dream, watching the mystical flow of the water as
though its patient music could sing her the hymn of
her future.

She was very young, but on her beauty was the
Tuscan glow; and she had already the tall, slender,

yielding, voluptuous form of the south. In the hair, like a chesnut that has the fleck of the sunlight upon it, in the deep eyes with their blue-black lustre and their dreamy passionate lids, in the lips so soft, so proud, so mournful, in the brow, broad and thoughtful like an antique, in the brilliance and the light upon the face, were all the southern types; it was only in the fairness of the skin that something more northern might have been fancied; in all else it was the rich and sunlit loveliness of Italy.

Her hand rested on the stone that bore the Latin words, all covered now with the wild growth of ivy; her gaze rested on the water sparkling so bright in sunshine here, flowing so dark beneath the grasses there; the sheath of woodland wealth rested listlessly on her lap. She leant there, in her childhood's carelessness, in the classic solitude, against the black shades of the beech-woods that closed her in as in a temple, and only let the flood of sun pour down across the ruined Roman fountain and the countless flowers at her feet.

She was fair as Sappho while yet love was unknown, and a child's laughter amidst the roses of Ionia was only hushed now and then by vague and prescient dreams; she was fair as Héloïse while yet only the grand serenity of the Greek scroll laid open before her eyes, and no voice beside her had taught a lore more fatal and a mystery more mournful than the wise words of Hellas.

She was very lovely, **motionless** here where no sound came except the lulling **of** the water and the gliding noise of a bird's wing, where the tender green of blossoming vines hung coiled above **her** head, and where the deep bronze of the beech-belt drew round her the gloom of the night.

Where she leaned thus, one passing through the denseness **of that** gloom saw her, unseen himself, and **paused; he** thought of Proserpine amongst the **flowers, ere the** cruelty of fate fell on her. The young **life and** the grass-grown **ruin, the aisle of colour** and sunlight, **and the** mass **of** enclosing shade **were a** picture and a poem in one—**the** gladness **of a** Greek **idyl,** with the **mystic** darkness **of a** northern Saga.

Once he would have lingered there, **drawn the ivy-wreaths from** the hands, wooed the **eyes from their musing gaze, paused** beside her in the **leafy peace— once, in** the days of his youth. Now he looked an instant, thought how fair she was, and passed onward **down his lonely path far into the** beechen shadows.

CHAPTER II.

CASTALIA.

Suddenly, without a warning, the radiance of the late day clouded, the stormy cirro-stratus whirled in angry turbulent masses, the grey nimbus-clouds swept up with instantaneous movement, like the ranks of an army hurrying to battle; one of the tempests of the south broke over the spring-tide peace of hill and valley. Rainless, furious, driving down the hill-sides, flashing in flame through the depths of the woods, rending off the shoots of the vine and the buds of the olive, blinding the trembling cattle, breaking the fast-rooted pines like reeds, rolling its thunder down the mountain and over the plain till the earth shook and the end of the world seemed come to the peasants crouching beneath their roofs, well used though they were to the sweep of the hurricane, to the blaze of the skies. Before the mules could patter along the stony roads, before the contadine could reach homeward as they came from antique Pelago, before the workers could leave the olive-fields and vineyards, before the mild-eyed oxen of the Apennine could be driven through the rank hill-grass, without warning the mighty clouds gathered, the night fell, the fires ran down the heavens, the storm broke!

Through it, as best he might, he who had an hour or two before passed through the moss-grown path of the beech-woods, made his backward way. He had seen it gather as he crossed the broad stretch where the cross stands, and the view of the Val d'Arno lies unfolded in all its beauty; but before he could retrace many steps of his road, the full force of the tempest was down. It was now peril to life and limb to be out in its fury: the melon-plants were torn up by their roots, the twisted olives writhed into tenfold contortion, the peaceful bubbling waters turned into angry torrents, the young trees were up-rooted and hurled down the steep descents; the darkness was impenetrable, except when the lightning lit the whole land in its glare, and the rushing of stones, and of boughs, and of saplings, as the wind tore them up and whirled them on its blast, roared with a thunder only drowned in the peals that shook from hill to hill, and echoed through the solitudes of the forests.

He could not even tell his road; he had lost its
certainty in the blackness around; the woodland
paths were all so similar, the tracks ran all so much
alike under the pines, and stretching towards Vallombrosa, that he told with difficulty how near or how
far he was from the refuge of Fontane Amorose, or
from the shelter of his own house-roof. All that he
could do was to retain his footing against the fury
of the hurricane, and to make head as best he might
against the force that drove him back at every step,
and the deafening din that rioted around. Unknown
to himself, he had wandered back once more into the
beech-glades, and was lost in their impenetrable shades,
instead of holding on his upward road along the hill-
side through the pines. As he went, feeling his way
slowly through the dense hot gloom that was like the
gloom over earth and sky when the lava-torrent of
Vesuvius bursts, he trod on some fallen thing that
his foot crushed ere he felt it. He stopped and
stooped to it; he thought it might be some frightened
hare or some large bird struck in the storm, and en-
tangled in the yielding, clinging moss. The darkness
was dark as that of a moonless midnight; he had no
sense to guide him but the sense of touch. The
grasses and the flowers, all bruised and beaten, met
his hand; then, as it moved farther, it wandered to
the loose trail of some floating hair, and passed over
the warmth of human lips and the outline of a wo-

man's cheek and bosom. He thought of the Tuscan child whom he had seen in the sunset light.

The heavy tresses lay in his hand; he could not tell whether she were living or dead, she was so still in the darkness. He passed his hand gently over her brow, she did not move; he spoke, she did not hear; he drew her loosened dress over her uncovered chest, she did not feel his touch. There was warmth from the lips on his palm, there was a faint pulsation in the heart as he sought for its throb; that was all. Else she lay, as one dead, at his feet in the blackness of the driving storm, in the din of the echoing thunder.

The fire flashed from the cleft skies; the blaze of an intolerable light poured down. In it he saw her features, and the broken stone of the Latin ruins, with the water gliding into its deep, still pool. She was stretched senseless on the very grasses amidst which she had leaned in her summer dream; her eyes were closed, and her breathing was so low, so lingering, that it seemed each breath might be the last she drew. He paused a moment, leaning over her with the thick wealth of the hair lying in his hand; he could not leave her, and succour there was none. With little thought, save such an impulse of pity as that in which a man might raise a fawn his shot had struck, or a song-bird his foot had trodden on, he stooped and raised her in his arms. Her head fell back, her limbs were powerless, she lay passive and unconscious in his hold; forsaken here, she must perish; death was abroad in every blast, in every flash. He hesitated no more, but leaned her brow against his breast, and thus weighted went on his toilsome and perilous way through the beech-glades. He knew his road now; that was much; and he was not very far from his own home. He forced his passage slowly and with diffi-culty through the denseness of the woods. It was a tedious and dangerous toil; her long hair blew in his eyes, her burden chained his arms, the great blasts blew against him with the blow of a sea-wave; the forest now was sunk in the ink-black gloom of night, now alive with lurid points of flame; his sight was blinded, and his strength sorely spent. But still as he went he sheltered her, and he pierced his road at length through the aisles of the beech-wilderness till he came into the broken arches of what had once been stately Roman courts. So far near his refuge, he paused a second to take rest; the vivid lightnings filled the arcade with their glow, the peal of the storm rolled above; he leaned against a marble shaft and looked down on his burden. Her head rested on his breast as peacefully as though she slept upon her mother's heart; the long dark lashes swept her cheek; her lips were slightly parted with a warmer breath. There was a touching sanctity in the un-conscious rest, a plaintive appeal in the extreme youth, and in its death-like calm.

"Poor child!" he thought, "she may live to wish

she had been abandoned there to die in the peace of her childhood."

In other years his lips would have called back the sleeping life with a caress; now he looked on her with a passionless pity, gentle because profoundly sad, sad because she had so much youth, and that youth was a woman's.

Then he went onward through the shattered arches that were canopied and covered with impenetrable ivy and feathery grasses tinted to every hue in the flashings of the light, and entered by a low side-door the first court of a Latin villa half in ruins, crossed the court, and passed into the first chamber. It was long and lofty, and had in it the decay of a patrician greatness; fragments of a perfect sculpture were upon the walls, a fresco, in hues fair as though painted but yesterday, covered the ceiling, the pavement was of mosaic marbles; these were all of its old classic glories that time had left untouched: for the rest, it was an artist's studio, a student's library, strewn with papers and with books, with here and there a cast or bronze; at the far end a lectern with a vellum manuscript open upon its wings, and in the midst an Etruscan lamp swinging from on high, and shedding a subdued silvery light and a soft perfume on the gloom. Here he brought her, and laid her gently down upon the cushions of a couch. She knew nothing of what was done with her. He went to a flask of Montepulciano standing near, poured some of the wine out, and touched her lips with it. She drank a little, by mere instinct; the warmth revived her; her lids trembled, then unclosed, and her eyes looked out with a dreamy, bewildered sightlessness.

"What is it? Where am I?"

He bent to her soothingly, speaking her own Tuscan.

"Have no fear, my child; you are safe now. I found you in the storm, and brought you here."

Her glance met his ; consciousness came to her, the colour flushed back into her face ; a shyness, half awe, half shame, was on her.

"You saved my life, eccellenza! How can I thank you ?"

"By telling me you are unhurt."

She looked at him with that awed wistfulness, that earnest wondering gratitude, of a child.

He touched the bright masses of her hair, moving them back from her brow—she was so young; he caressed her with his hand as he would a wounded bird.

"I fear you are in pain? There is a bruise on your temple; and you were senseless when I found you. Do you suffer now?"

She sighed—a sigh rather of rest and of wonder than of pain.

"Oh no! not much. You brought me from the forest? How good! how merciful!"

She stooped her head with the supple grace of the south, and kissed his hand with the reverent supplica-

tion and thanksgiving of a young slave to her owner;
he drew it from her quickly.

"My child! do not pay me such homage for a mere
common charity. What creature with the heart of a
man could have left you to perish alone? The blow
must have struck you down senseless. Was it from
a bough, do you think?"

She shuddered with the memory.

" I cannot recollect. The storm came up from the
back of the woods before I saw or thought of it; it
burst suddenly, and as I went something struck me
down ; whether it was the flash or a fallen branch, I
can remember nothing since, till I awoke—here."

She lifted herself a little, and glanced round the
chamber with the startled wonder still in her eyes, as
of one who wakes from a deep sleep in a strange
scene; her glance came back to him, and dwelt on
him with a venerating marvel and admiration : she
knew his face well, though until that day he had never
seen hers. Her sweeping lashes were weighted and
glistening with tears as she looked—sweet, sudden
tears of an infinite gratitude for her rescue, and to him
by whom she had been saved. She was very fair in
that moment.

Her hair, all loosened by the wind, fell backward
and over her shoulders, like a shower of molten gold ;
the warmth of the chamber, and the surprise of her
waking thoughts, gave a glow like a wild rose to her
cheeks. Some of the ivy-coils that she had dropped

in her haste to rise and flee from the storm had caught
in the gay colour and the white broideries of her
simple picturesque dress;—an artist would have given
a year of his life to have painted her as she was then,
in the shadowy chiar'oscuro of the lamp-light, in the
marble waste of the far-stretching, half-ruined chamber.

A dim fugitive memory wandered before him with
the glance of her eyes—a likeness that he could not
trace, yet that pursued him, rose before him with the
earnest, haunting beauty of her face. Far down in
his past it lay; he could not disinter it—he could not
give it name or substance—but its shadow flickered
before him. She was like something remembered,
like something recovered—this strange young Tuscan
girl whom chance had thrown across him.

"You are tired and exhausted; lie still," he said,
gently, as she strove to rise. "They shall bring you
food—I need some myself; and in an hour the storm
may lull, perhaps. May I ask who it is that my roof
has the honour to shelter?"

She looked at him still with that wistful wondering
homage; she was shy with him, and the language
of courtesy was unfamiliar to her—it was very new to
her to be addressed so.

He smiled.

"What is your name, *poverina?*" he asked her.

Her eyelids drooped, the hot colour deepened in her
face; she hesitated a moment.

“ They call me Castalia.”

“ Castalia!—a fair and classic name!   And what else ? ”

“ Nothing else, eccellenza ! ”

Her voice was very low; her head sank, the tears glittered thickly on the length of her lashes. In the answer she had told him all the history she had.

He was silent a moment, regretful that he had pained her; his voice was very tender as he spoke again.

“ And your mother—is she living ? ”

She shook her head.

He looked at her with a deep pity, this child with the brilliance of southern suns about her, and a fate so lonely and so blighted at the outset.

He asked her no more ; but, as a Tuscan woman answered his summons and brought into the chamber a tray of fruits, and maccaroni, and truffles, with some flasks of Italian and Rhine wines, he served her with his own hands as assiduously, as reverently, as any would serve a queen.   And as the rest and the food revived her more and more, and more and more restored the animation to her lips, the lustre to her eyes, she seemed, in the antique classic Doric charm of the silent chamber, like some gem of the old Venetian Masters set in the white coldness of the marble walls ; like some lustrous, gold-leaved, Italian flower sprung in its bud from the grey solemnity, the sublime decay, of Roman ruins.

He wondered whence she came and what she was —this Tuscan child with the grace of a daughter of the Antonines, who was without a name; and once more the memory which had haunted him rose again, not to be grasped, but lost in the mazy shades of a far-distant past.

The storm was at its height, there seemed little chance of its abatement; the mighty din of its thunder rolled like the roar of a hundred battles, and the moaning and trembling of all the beech and chesnut woods were heard on the stillness; she shuddered as she listened.

"Ah! I should have been lying dead in all that terror now, but for your pity!"

"Do not think of it," he answered, soothingly. "Let the storm rage as it will, you are safe here with me. Tell me, where is it you live?"

She looked at him with an intense sadness, very strange upon the glow and glory of her youth; and though the flush grew hotter in her face, it was proud and still in its pain.

"Illustrissimo," she said, softly, for there was a breathless awe of him upon her, mingled touchingly with a spaniel-like trust, "you ought to know whom your house shelters; it is only just. I have no name —I have no history. My mother died when I was a few months old; she came a stranger, and the village knew nothing of her, only this—she was not wedded. The Padre Giulio and his mother adopted me; they have been very good. The name they found on me was Castalia. I have nothing more to tell."

The simplicity of the words lent them but the deeper sadness; the restrained pain, the half-haughty, half-appealing shame with which she spoke them, gave them but the stronger pathos. They touched her listener greatly.

"Thank you for your confidence, my fair child," he answered her, with a pitying tenderness in his voice—she was so young to be already touched with life's suffering and the world's reproach! "You do not know your history; there is room, then, to hope it a bright one."

She shook her head.

"Illustrissimo, how? It began in shame; it will end in a convent."

"A convent? Better the tomb!"

He spoke on an impulse. To cage her to that living death of the veil seemed barbarous as to shut away in darkness, till it died, one of the golden-winged orioles that fluttered through the length of a spring day below the slopes of Vallombrosa.

"Yes! better a thousand times!" she answered him, with a sudden vibration of passion that told how surely passion would wake in her one day. "In the grave one sleeps unconscious! But forgive me, eccellenza; I weary you. Let me go.”

“Go! with the storm at that height? You would go to your destruction. No living thing could pass from here to Fontane in such a night. Wait awhile; it may lull presently. And give me no titles of deference; I can claim none.”

She looked at him wistfully, with a shy surprise, like that with which a forest-bird glances at a stranger.

“You must be a great lord?” she said, softly and hesitatingly.

He smiled, something wearily.

“My greatness—if I ever truly had any—departed from me long ago. I am no noble. I am little richer than your peasants of Fontane.”

She glanced round the chamber: to her, after the bare simplicity of the Fontane hamlet, the frescoes, the sculpture, the mosaics, though they were but the relics of Latin ruins, made it seem a palace; then her glistening meditative eyes—eyes divine of the south —dwelt on him.

“You are lord of yourself, at least?” she said, lingeringly, with the naïf expression of a child.

“I have but a rebellious subject, then,” he answered, with a tinge of sadness that did not escape her. “But, *poverina*, you look feverish and tired. I have been thoughtless for you. You must have been terribly hurt by that blow, I fear. Are you in pain?”

She smiled at him—a smile of infinite patience and sweetness, that brought back in his thoughts once more a memory he could not follow.

" Not much ; it is nothing."

She would not confess that, in truth, an intolerable pain ached through her bruised temples, and that an utter exhaustion was stealing fast upon her.

" Lie still, then," he said, bending over her ; " the tempest is at its worst now. Take no heed of me, but sleep, if you can. Your eyes are too heavy and too hot, and I have let you talk when you should have been at rest."

She thanked him softly, and obeyed him ; the colour grew richer in her cheek at his touch, but she offered him no opposition ; she watched him with a reverent, wondering homage ; she revered him already like a king, like a deity.

He had saved her life, and he had brought her here to this mellow light, to this delicate temple-like chamber, to this dream, as it seemed to her still, of classic beauty, of hushed repose, that had followed on the tumult of the tempest like an enchantment. She had passed all her young years in the chesnut-shadows beneath Vallombrosa, and she had far too much innocence, far too much faith, to think of harm that could be done her in this solitude, to feel anything but a sublime, devoted trust in the stranger who had saved her life. Moreover, the weariness that was growing on her, the sleep that weighed down her eyelids, the reaction from the shock and peril of the night, left her little sense save of a lulling peace that surrounded her, of a voice that soothed her like music, of a wish to be silent and still, and keep unbroken this soft charm.

He left her, and went to the lectern at the farther end of the room, where the vellum scroll lay, a disputed manuscript of Boethius; he leaned his arms on the desk, he bent his eyes on the Latin words of the last of the Romans, of the man martyred for too much truth. On the wide stone hearth some pine-logs were burning, for the evenings were chilly, though the days were so warm; the aromatic odour of the lamp filled the room with a sweet, faint incense; the shadows were deep in all the farther parts of the hall, only about the hearth was the ruddy, flickering glow of the pines; all else was in gloom. The roar of the storm was almost ceaseless, and the drenching rains broke above the low Latin roof like a waterspout. He heeded them little; his thoughts were gone back into the studies that filled his days and nights. She heeded them no more; an irresistible exhaustion had weighted her eyes, till they closed unconsciously; she lost all knowledge of where she was, and slept.

The hours passed; he almost forgot that he was not wholly alone. The volumes about him were many, and rare, and old; the classic treasures of dead empires and buried freedom were before him; their eternal charm so old yet so vernal, their thoughts so familiar, so long known, yet never sounded, as it seemed, in all their depths, enchained him in their compensative beauty. He was such a scholar as the world lost of late years at Damascus, when Henry Buckle died of fever, with those last words of love for his labour on his lips: "My book! my book!"

The hours passed uncounted; the thunder had somewhat lulled, but the winds were a hurricane, and the drenching downpour of rain scoured the land and howled through the pine and the beech woods. It was a night which broke the mountain firs like saplings, and wrenched up the grey writhing olives by the roots, and laid the young birds stone dead by the score. No human thing could venture out in it and be sure of life. The twelfth hour struck from the campanile as the lull of a moment succeeded to the roar of the storm; he lifted his head from where he bent over the lectern and looked at the young companion chance had so strangely brought there. In the glow of the embers she lay, in her delicate, richly-hued beauty, a child in her innocence and her tranquil rest, far more than a child in her grace and her charm—a thing of light, and life, and colour, and youth, in the cold, classic solitude of the lonely and half-ruined hall, whose cracked mosaic had been worn by the passing of so many banished feet that had trodden through their brief day, and had glided onward down into their tombs. He watched her with an indefinable pity, with a fugitive, intangible remembrance pursuing him; her brief story was so mournful, and the memory that pursued him was so strong, though he could find it no clue, and would give it no substance. As a chord of music, as a flower blooming in a desert-place, as a sound of harvest-chant or spring-bird's singing, will bear us back to long-gone hours, so the sight of her bore his thoughts backward to years that were sealed for ever—thoughts that thronged on him, many, and embittered by their own dead sweetness, as the thought of all that he will never again see come on the exile with the mere scent of faded leaves brought to him from the summer woodlands that hear his step no more.

In them he was lost, as he leaned against the broad bronze wings of the lectern-eagle, with his eyes on the ring of ruddy colour that circled her like a halo. The storm shook above the low flat roof of the Latin villa, breaking on it as with the force of a waterspout. He roused himself and went near her.

"She cannot go out in such a night as this," he thought.

She slept still, softly as a child, the long black fringes of her eyelashes lying on her flushed cheeks, a proud, resigned sadness like the memory of her stained birth and lonely fate on her face. He was loth to break her rest, yet he knew that to let her sleep on here would be to let the coarse tongues of the mountain-peasants touch even her defenceless childhood. He stooped and passed his hand lightly over her brow. At the touch, slight as it was, she wakened instantly; the blue-black lustre of her eyes startled into consciousness, the flush on her cheek bright as the scarlet of japonica-blossoms. She started up, ashamed.

"Oh, eccellenza, forgive me! I have been asleep!"

He smiled kindly at her alarm and her penitence.

"Naturally, after your danger and your fatigue. It was the best restorative you could have. It is midnight now, and the storm is scarce lessened——"

"Midnight?" she murmured, terror-stricken. "The Padre Giulio will be so wretched; what will he think? Let me go—pray let me go."

"Impossible; you would go to your certain death. I could not venture myself in such a night; you hear the hurricane. You must remain with me."

"With you?" she repeated, under her breath.

"Surely, I would not let a dog leave my roof in such weather as this is. Besides, you are miles higher on the slope here than Fontane; the return to the village would be impossible for those far hardier than you."

She looked at him with a wondering awe; he seemed to her such an emperor as Marcus Antoninus, who had laid down his pomp and come to dwell awhile like other men. The deep-blue, weary, brilliant eyes that gazed on her made her think of the serene, imperial eyes of Augustus.

" I am a total stranger to you, it is true," he said, gently, misinterpreting her silence; "but you are not afraid to remain in my house? I am only here for a villegiatura, and the place is desolate enough, but it will at least give you shelter."

She lifted her head with the proud grace that would have paled and shamed the grace of many royal women.

"Afraid? Afraid of *you*? What could I fear? You saved my life—it is yours to command. All is —I cannot thank you enough."

The words were very touching in their liquid Tuscan, in their complete innocence, and in their perfect trust.

"You have nothing to thank me for; a mule-driver or a charcoal-burner must have done for you what I did," he answered her, his voice unconsciously softening. "And now go to rest; you want it. I will send the women to you, and they shall remain in your chamber; for you are not well enough to be left alone."

"Ah, eccellenza, how good you are," she mur-mured. A few years older, and she would have been grateful to him in silence, better knowing the motive of his words. "But indeed I am strong now; we, below Vallombrosa, have the strength of the mountain-air, and—shall I not trouble you with staying here?"

"Far from it; you bring your own welcome, like

the birds that come and sing under our windows. Good night, *poverina*, and sleep well."

He held his hand out to her; she was but a child to him, and a child who had been sheltered on his breast through the driving of the storm. She stooped with the exquisite softness of movement of southern women, and touched the hand he gave her, lightly and reverently, with her lips.

"I would thank you, eccellenza, but I cannot."

She did thank him, however, better than by all words, with that hesitating touch of her young lips, with that upward glance of her eyes, languid with sleep and fatigue, yet lustrous as the Tuscan skies by night—eyes that seemed to him to have some story of his past in their depths.

Then he summoned the women to her, peasants who dwelt in the villa, and she left him.

He, having surrendered to her, though she knew nothing of it, the only habitable chamber that the half-ruined villa afforded, stretched himself in the warmth of the pine-logs on the wolf-skins strewn before it. She had brought back to him, why or whence he could not tell, memories that he would willingly let die—memories that, through the length of weary years, burned still into his heart with un-utterable longing, with intolerable pain.

In the loneliness of the old classic hall, in the leaping light of the pine-flames, throngs of shadowy

shapes arose around him—the shapes of his past summoned by the light of a child's smile.

She meanwhile lay wakeful, yet dreamy, gazing
out at the unfamiliar chamber and the swaying figure
of the peasant-woman keeping **watch over** her, and
nodding in her sleep. Her thoughts were steeped in
all **the wonders of** legendary lore, and she fancied
some enchantment had **been wrought** in her since,
out of that awful forest-darkness, **she** had been
brought to this charmed stillness in which **only one**
remembrance was with her, the remembrance **of the**
musing, lustrous, weary eyes that had looked so
gently on her, of the voice that had soothed **her**
terror and her pain **with** an accent softer **than she**
had ever heard. She thought **of him,** and thought,
as one other had once done before, that he was
like the Poet-king of Israel, **but** having known the
bitterness of abdication, having known the ingratitude of the people. Then her **musing** became **a**
dream, and, with a smile upon her lips, she slept
under a stranger's roof till the tempest had passed
away **and the dawn** was bright. As she awoke, the
morning **had risen.** The sun broke in full glory over
a splendid **mass of** purple cloud and tumbled storm-
mist that **glowed** in magnificent colour beneath the
newly risen rays. The earth laughed again even
amidst her ruin—her ruin **of crushed** olive-buds, and
uprooted saplings, **and** trees rent asunder by, and

X 2

nests flung down, with the young birds killed, and the mothers flying with piteous cries over the wreck; but the wheat-sprouts were too low to be harmed; the vines, though they trailed and hung helplessly under the dead weight of rain-drops, were still only in blossom; the water-courses made the wilder, merrier music, filled to overflowing, and laying in swathes the rank grasses of their beds; the mules began to patter over the broken paths, picking their careful way over the dislodged boulders of rocks and the deep channels of brimming brooks. Beneath Vallombrosa the morning was fair and sun-lightened again, deadly though the tempest had been overnight, and rough work of destruction though it had wrought. With the sun she rose, her youth, like the youth of the spring and the earth, the brighter for the storm and the danger gone by. There was the flush of waking childhood and of past sleep upon her cheeks, and her eyes had the gladness of a wondering dream in them, as she found her way, marvelling if she dreamed a fairy tale, down some broken marble steps and out into the air.

CHAPTER III.

"GIUVENTÙ! PRIMAVERA DELLA VITA!"

THE full light poured into the open loggia before
the half-ruined courts and halls of the Latin villa.
Within, the one spacious chamber, with its frescoes
and the mosaics, its books and scrolls, was bare
enough. But the world of blossoming spring, of
morning mists, of lavish foliage that opened out before it, made ample amends for any poverty and
decay of the interior; and it was perfect for a villegiatura, this deserted place that Roman pomp had
once filled in Augustan days.

In this loggia, reading, her host sat—a man no
longer young, though as yet there was no silver
amidst the fair and golden length of his hair; a man
of a grave grace, of a serene, meditative dignity of
look and of movement that had in it something that
was very weary, yet something not less grand, not

less royal : he might have been a king in purples rather than what he was—an exile, and poor.

The book was open upon his knee, but his eyes were not upon it for the moment; they were resting on the gardens without—gardens wild, forsaken, un-cultured, but only the more beautiful for that, with dark waters winding under laurel-thickets, and gum-cistus, and ilex, and pomegranate, and Banksia roses growing at their will, and, all ivy-coiled and covered, broken fragments of arches and statues and fountains. What he watched in them was the passage of the young Tuscan flitting through them with the free-dom of a chamois in her step, and all the languor of a dew-laden flower in her loveliness.

Sixteen years beyond the Apennines bring woman-hood; they had brought it to her in the loveliness Nature had dowered her with, but in all else she was young as a child; she who had never wandered from the chesnut shadows of her village, who had but dimly heard of another vast world beyond the beech-woods, who had known no friends but the birds who sang to her, who had known no pleasures but to watch a blue-warbler shake his bright wings in the myrtles, or to look deep down into the heart of a pas-sion-flower, and build a thousand fancies from its mystic burning hues. She was a child with the beauty of a woman; there could be no greater peril for her.

He thought so as he saw her in this deserted

garden. Art had no handling with her; the pure hill-air of Tuscany had made her all she was; and she had the abandon and the unconsciousness of some rich-plumaged bird, now floating softly through the sunlight, now pausing on the wing, now alighting to drop drown in happy rest in a couch of feathery grasses.

He gazed at her as she wandered through them, that exquisite ease in her step which many a royal woman has not, which a contadina may have balancing on her dark imperial head a pannier of water-melons. The lizards did not hurry from her, but watched her with curious eyes; the timid hares let her stoop and stroke them; the old owls blinking in the ivy let her lift her hand and touch their crests; the wood-doves flew about her and pecked the buds from the boughs she held up to them.   She bent over the black swollen water, and saw her own reflexion laurel-crowned as the branches met above her head; she gathered the lilies of the valley, the buds of Banksia roses, and the young green ivy-blossoms, and crowned herself with them till the wreath was too heavy and shook all her glistening hair downward in a shower of gold, like a picture of Flora.   Then, lastly, she sank to rest on a grey rock of fallen sculpture, the crown of flowers still above her brow; and after the glad, thoughtless pastime of a child, the proud and profound sadness that usually in repose was on her face succeeded it with a charm not the less great because so sudden.

It was like 'the sudden fall of evening over the
brilliance and the glow of her own Tuscan landscape.

As he saw it, he left the loggia and went towards
her. She did not hear his step till he had approached
her close; then she sprang up with the swiftness of a
fawn, and with words of gratitude, made only softer
by the awe of him which lent her its delicate coy-
ness.

"I have been watching you for the last half-
hour, Castalia," he said, gently. "I am glad you
could find such companions in my flowers and my
birds; there is little else here fit for your bright
youth."

She coloured under his gaze, and put her hands up
hurriedly to remove the dew-laden wreath of bud and
blossom; she had forgotten it till his speech brought
it back to her thoughts. He put out his own hand
and stayed her.

"Not for worlds! I wish a Titian lived to paint
you; you look like a young priestess of Flora. But,
tell me, what spell have you that tames the lizards,
and stills the hares, and brings all the birds to your
hand?"

She lifted to him her musing eloquent eyes, grave
as a child's when he pauses to think.

"I do not know, eccellenza, unless—it may be because I love them so well."

His face grew a shade darker and yet softer; her words recalled the fond belief of his own youth.

"You think love begets and secures love? I thought so once."

"And was it not so?"

"No; but—that knowledge should not kill love in us; there is much that is worth it, if there be much that is not. Because a viper turns and stings you, it would be wild vengeance to wring the wood-pigeon's neck."

He spoke half to his own thoughts, half to her; she regarded him with a reverent, grateful, wondering gaze; in her little beech-forest nest of Fontane she had never seen anything like him. She who had known but one bent old priest, and brown brawny muleteers and vintagers from whom she shank as the white sea-swallow shrinks from the hard beak and cruel pursuit of the kestrel, thought almost he must be more than mortal.

"I ought to leave you, 'lustrissimo?" she said, hesitatingly. "I have troubled you so long."

"Do you wish to leave me?"

Her eyes opened more lustrous than ever in their surprised negation.

"Wish? Oh no!"

"Well, do not leave me yet, then. Come within, and let me see, though no Titian, if I can paint you with your crown of flowers. Your Padre Curato will feel no anxiety; I sent a messenger to him to say you were here."

The gravest contrition stole over her face; she looked penitent as a chidden child.

"Oh, 'lustrissimo! I had forgotten him. How ungrateful, when he is so good! How selfish one grows when one is happy."

The naïf confession amused him.

"Then are you happy with me?"

"Eccellenza," she said, under her breath, "it seems to me that I have been happier than in all the years of my life."

The reply pleased him. He had always loved to see happiness about him.

"I am glad it should be so. And do not believe that happiness makes us selfish; it is a treason to the sweetest gift of life. It is when it has deserted us that it grows hard to keep all the better things in us from dying in the blight. Men shut out happiness from their schemes for the world's virtue; they might as well seek to bring flowers to bloom without the sun."

He spoke again rather to his own thoughts than to her; but she understood him. This young Tuscan, lost amidst the chesnuts beneath Vallombrosa, had in her the heart of a Héloïse, the mind of a Hypatia, though both were in their childhood yet.

"Eccellenza," she said, hesitatingly, "that is true. If we keep light from a plant, it will grow up warped. When they condemn, do they ever ask if what they condemn had a chance to behold the light ? Perhaps — perhaps if my mother had been happy, she would not have been evil, as they call her ? "

The colour burned hotly in her face, but her eyes were raised in wistful entreaty to him; it was but very vaguely that she understood the shame that she was made to feel was on her birth, but very dimly that she comprehended some vast indistinct error with which her dead mother was charged.

The question touched him with great pity.

" *Poverina !* " he said, caressingly, " do not weary your young life with those subtilties. You do not know that error lies at all upon your mother's history; who can, since you say that history is wholly unknown —even to her very name? It may be that the thing the world—your little woodland world, at least— blames in her was some unrecognised martyrdom, some untold unselfishness. At all events, be she what she will, *you* are stainless and blameless ; all you need seek is to be so for ever."

She looked at him with a look of passionate, of intense, yet of restrained feeling, which told him how well she would love some day, and how bitterly she would suffer.

" I thank you, eccellenza," she said, her voice very low, " more for those noble words than for the life that you saved me."

The brief answer was very eloquent—eloquent of her nature and of her gratitude. He said no more, but led her within to the old hall, only fit for a summer residence for an artist, or a scholar sufficiently content with its classic charm and forest wildness to bear its scant accommodation. An easel stood before the open colonnade facing the gardens; he paused before it, and glanced at her. A lovelier theme never lured any painter's brush with the fresh crown of the lilies and rosebuds and light green blossoms of ivy shaking their dew upon the gold-flaked shower of her hair. He looked at her; then he threw aside the colours he had taken up.

"Twenty years ago I could have given your picture there," he said, half wearily. "Now I have not the heart to paint you, my fair child. I have not the great inspiration—youth."

Twenty years ago he would have found no hour more beguiling than that spring morning with the young Tuscan, bringing the bloom of her beauty and of her crown of flowers out on the canvas; now it only recalled to him all he had lost.

A shadow stole over her eyes; he saw it, and turned back to the easel.

"Are you disappointed, *poverina?*"

She looked beseechingly in his face.

"I never saw any paintings except those in our little chapel."

"No? Well, then, I will try and give you your desire."

He took the colours and brushes up again, and,

standing before the easel, sketched her as she leaned against one of the pillars of the colonnade, the rich glow and warmth of her young face but the brighter for the whiteness of the lilies and the deep green of the leaves that circled her hair. He had both the skill and the habit of Art, and the impassioned brilliance of her beauty, with the coronal of blossoms weighting her forehead with the weight of all diadems, rose gradually under his hand out of the sea of brown opaque gloom on which it was painted. The hours passed, and the picture grew; it beguiled him for the time of heavier cares, and won him out of deeper thoughts; yet ever and again, as he lifted his eyes and glanced at her, the weariness which had made him turn from the task came over him. He thought of so many golden hours, when faces as fair had bloomed to fresh life thus on his canvas, and the glory of his youth had been with him to lend its sweetness to the eyes, and teach the language of love to the lips, of those he painted. The soft labour only recalled to him so many days that were dead.

The noontide was intensely still, the heat of the sun quivered down through the open arches of the colonnade: the picture grew clearer and richer beneath his hand, and the blossoms faded where they crowned her hair. She untwined them, and touched them mournfully.

"Ah, eccellenza, they are all dying!"

He smiled, not without sadness, too, though it was for deeper things than the flowers.

"Never mind; you have had their sweetness. Be content with that. Nothing endures."

"But it is better never to have had them than to see them withered!"

"I doubt that. If we should have been spared much pain, we should also have missed much joy."

His thoughts were with other things, though he spoke still in the figure of the flowers. He had seen his own crowns wither and fall and be trodden under foot, yet he would never have worn them. She looked at him in silence, reverently, wonderingly; she mused on what his history could be; she thought him a king in exile. So, in a sense, he was.

There was an infinite shyness of him in her that gave her tenfold more charm; it was so innocent and so full of religious veneration. He seemed to her like the archangels of her church, so full of majesty, so full of pity. She thought with him of all the grand, serene, lonely lives that she had read of in the Latin legends.

He rose and turned the easel to her.

"Castalia, do what even wise men never do—see yourself as you are."

She came forward and looked, as the sun fell full on the work of a few hours, and her countenance changed as by magic; a breathless surprise was on her lips, a scarlet flush upon her cheeks, the light of an immeasurable admiration and amaze beamed in her eyes. She stood entranced at the likeness of herself, as, with its diadem of blossoms, it gazed out at her from the brown shadows of the background.

"Well?" he asked her, smiling.

She turned to him bewildered and beseeching.

"Oh! 'lustrissimo, can it be? Am I as beautiful as *that*?"

"Did the river and the fountain never tell you so before?"

Her head drooped, the colour in her cheek deepened; her innocent delight had had no thought of vanity, but at his words she remembered what she looked on was—herself.

"And yet, it *is* beautiful!" she murmured, very low, as though in apology. "And if I be really like it——"

"What then?"

A prouder, more passionate glory flashed into her face; she lifted her head with the royalty of a daughter of emperors, mingled with a great softness of regard.

"Then, I think, if I could once see the great world I might reign there, and I might win some love, and not be scorned as peasants scorn me here. Would it not be so, eccellenza?"

He paused a moment; the words touched him to compassion. How little she knew that her nameless loveliness would only bring her in the "great world" a sovereignty and a love that would be but added shame! Nor could he tell her.

"Would it not be so, eccellenza?" she asked him, eagerly again.

"Yes," he answered, slowly; "doubtless it would. But do not wish it, if you be wise. Your diadems would not be so pure as the one that lies withered there; your brows would soon ache under them, and for the love——"

"Ah!" she said, softly, whilst the glow faded, and her eyes filled with tears as she spoke with the pathos and the guilelessness of a child, "I long to be loved! All the children of Fontane have their mothers, who look brighter when they see them near; but I am all alone. I have been alone so long!"

The words had an intense and touching piteousness in them; a harder nature than her listener's was would have been moved by them. How could he find the cruelty to tell her that the chances were as a million to one that the only love she would ever meet in this world beyond the pine-woods, to which she vaguely looked as the redresser of her wrongs, would be one less merciful to her even than the bitterness and loneliness which now visited on her innocence and her youth the unproven error of her dead mother? Twenty years before he would have heard her with little thought, save to let his lips linger on the brow whence the faded ivy-buds had fallen, and murmur to her the tenderness which her unawakened heart longed for, as an imprisoned bird longs for the shelter of summer leaves and the whispers of summer rivers; now such a thought as this was distant from him as the wide unknown world was far from her.

But pity her he did, profoundly. This nameless, motherless child, with her radiant grace and her proud instincts, was as desolate as any chamois-fawn lost on the hills, and driven as an alien from every herd with which it seeks a refuge.

"You will have love, some day, *poverina*," he said, gently, "and as much as you will; you will hardly lift such eyes as those to ask for it in vain."

She sighed, and her head sank lower, while she looked still at the painted likeness of herself. She was unaware of any tribute to her beauty in his words; she thought he meant that some, one day, would pity her.

"Ah, signore," she answered, wearily, "where is the worth of love, if with it is scorn?"

The thoughtless taunts and the careless jests which among the peasantry had been cast at her from her birth up as a foundling—rather in the mothers' jealousy of her face and the children's resentment of her love of solitude, than from any cruelty or any real contempt—had sunk deeply into her nature, rousing rebellion and disdain well-nigh as much as they caused sorrow and a vague sense of shame.

He saw how great a shipwreck might be made of her opening life, even from the very purest and loftiest things in her, if this outlawry banned her long—if this passion of mingled defiance and humiliation were fostered by neglect. He spoke on that.

"Scorn! Why dwell on scorn? It is unworthy of you. It is a word that may bring a pang to those who merit it by their own ill deeds; it need have no sting for any other. Keep your life high and blameless, and you will afford to treat scorn with scorn."

She did not reply to him with words, but she flashed on him with an answering glance the night-like lustre of her eyes, in an eloquence, in a comprehension, in a promise that accepted his meaning far more deeply and more vividly than by speech. He saw that she might be led by a cord of silk; that she would not be driven by a scourge.

He stood a few moments in the shadow of the colonnade, later, when she had left him, looking at the painting that had grown out of the deep sombre backwork by the work of his own hand, the head alone luminous, from the veil of gloom around it, with its spiritual radiance, crowned by that wealth of flowers; he looked, then turned it aside towards the wall, so that the richness of colour no longer smiled out of the opaque shadows, and went within to his solitude. That face, gazing out from the darkness under the diadem of woven blossoms, seemed like the phantom of his own dead youth.

CHAPTER IV.

"seigneur! ayez pitié."

Never in the rich days of the Cinque Cento, or the
Dandolo age, when the cities of Italy were filled with
pomp and mirth and music, when the mighty palaces were wreathed with flowers that lent their
bright blush to the white stone and glowed over the
black marbles, when the dark arches framed hair
like the gold arras that draped the balconies, and
lips ripe as the scarlet heart of the rose that glowed in
their bosom, and eyes that sent men to far Byzantium,
or to the oaths of the Templar, with the riot of burning thoughts which drove their steel with fiercer thrust
into the Paynim foe—never amongst those "dear
dead women," whose lost loveliness the poet mourns,
was any beauty rarer or more lustrous than that of
the young Tuscan, who had grown up under the

forest-shadows below Vallombrosa, scarce more tended, not more heeded, than one of the passion-flowers that burst into its glorious bud unseen by any eyes, above the broken stone of some ruined altar of Pan. Though her years were so few that the fulness of her beauty might yet be scarcely reached, she had already the splendour of a Titian picture on her, the superb grace, wild as a deer, proud as the daughter of Cæsars, that here and there still lingers, as though to verify tradition, in the women of Campagna or of Apennine.

The loneliness of her childhood, the consciousness of a ban placed on her, the haughty instincts which had wakened in self-defence against the shafts of scorn, the solitary and meditative life which she had led, had lent her a certain patrician pride, a certain thoughtful shadow; a wistful pain sometimes gazed out of the depths of her blue-back eyes; a lofty rebellion sometimes broke through the dreaming gladness of her smile. She was happy, because she was young, because she was sinless, because she had the innocence which finds its joy in the caress of a bird, in the radiance of a sunset, in the mere breath and consciousness of existence; but she had the pang of wounded pride, the burden of a scarce-comprehended shame, and the vague, bitter, impassioned longing of a mind too ardent and too daring for its sphere; and these gave their character to her face, their hues to her youth; these made her far more than a mere child, however lovely, can be. She was like Héloïse ere her master had become her lover, and while her eyes, as they gazed on the Greek scroll or the vellum Evangeliarium, were brilliant with the light of aspiration, and dark with the thoughts of a poet, but had never yet drooped, heavy with the languor and burning with the knowledge of love.

From the aged priest she had learned all his scholarly lore that plunged deep into the life of the past, and drank deep of Latin and Hellenic culture; he had loved the rugged roads of wisdom, the unfathomed sea-depths of knowledge, the buried treasures of cloister folios and of crabbed *copia*—she had loved them too. With no other in the obscure hill-side, to which fate had condemned him, to give him sympathy or understanding in these things, the stern old man had taken eager pleasure in steeping with them the virgin soil of a young and thirsty mind. In the bare, grey, narrow chamber of his dwelling, with its single lancet-window through which the mellow sunlight crept through from the cloudless skies, the fair head of the child Castalia, with its weight of burnished tresses, had bent above the huge tomes and the century-worn manuscriptum for hour on hour, like Héloïse in the cell of the Canonry. She had a passionate love of those studies; and whilst they filled her mind with great and impersonal thoughts, they did much to console her for her fate, and much to enrich her intelligence far beyond her years and her sex. They and the beauties of the earth and the seasons were **her** sole pleasures. The priest's mother, under whose roof she lived, was nearly ninety years, decrepid and harsh, who, well as she loved her foundling in her heart, could be no aid or **associate** to her. With the peasantry, the people who maligned her unknown parent, she would have no converse in their flower-feasts and their vintage celebrations. She lived alone, with the learning of dead ages and the fragrance of a forest-world.

Some, such an isolation would have maddened or ruined; Castalia, with a singular vividness of imagination, and a proud patience beneath the passionate warmth of her nation, had received through **it a** higher nature than any other and happier life could have developed.

She was a poem, with her aristocracy of look that might have sprung from some great race like **the** Medici or the Medina-Sidonia, and with her slight, sad, all-eloquent story, that needed no detail to fill it up; with her touching desolation of circumstance and of destiny, and her brilliant youth that in its elasticity and its enthusiasm broke aside all barriers of doom and pain, and found its careless joy God-given from a song-bird's carol, from a cloister-scribe's **story**, from the tossing of a sea of green rushes in the wind, from the dreams **of an** outer world, unknown and glorified in fancy into paradise. She was a poem in the spring-time of her life and in the spring-time of the year.

The smile of women's eyes had no beckoning light for him, the whisper of women's allurement no sorcery for his ear; he had been a voluptuary in an earlier time, but he had passed through bitterness and poverty, and sensuous charms had ceased to hold him. Yet there was enough of the poet lingering in him to make him vaguely feel some memories of youth, and some tenderness of pity arise, as he looked on the bright head that he had painted with its diadem of flowers, on the opening life that he had found in this beechwood-nest. Had chance not thrown her on him, he would never have sought her; brought to his protection, to his compassion, she won her way to him in the spring of the divine Tuscan year as some forest-fawn whom he should have found wounded and beaten in the storm might have come to his hand in after-days, and been caressed for sake of its past peril and its present gratitude.

He had sought the seclusion of the old Latin villa for the isolation which he, a writer and a thinker of whom the world spoke, often preferred to the life of cities, under grey Alpine shadows, in still Danubian woods, by olive-crested southern seas, or amidst the Moorish ruins of a Granadine landscape. Wealth he had none—he was poor; but as

each young year awoke in its renaissance, he liked to
have around him the richness of colour and fragrance,
the beauty of the earth's dower, that needed no purchase, but could be made his own by each who loved
it well enough to understand its meaning.

In the monastic twilight and silence of the old
classic hall, the painting with the crown of flowers
glowed brightly and vividly like a living thing from
out the gloom; and with the deep studies and the solitary thoughts which had heretofore usurped him,
the memory and the presence of this fair child
mingled—not without a charm, a charm which had
in it something of recollection. The remembrance
was fugitive, and he could never bring it clearly
before his knowledge; but it was there, and strong
enough to make him seek more of her history. The
search was futile—there was no more to know; her
mother had died, mute and nameless, and whence
she came there was no record—there was not even a
suggestion—to show or to hint. One thing alone was
certain; her mother had worn no marriage-ring, and
the only word marked on the child's linen was the
single one—Castalia.

The woman had been of great beauty, the peasants
said, though worn and haggard, a southern beauty,
with eyes that burned like flame, and a terrible wandering look; but she had been utterly exhausted
when she had reached Fontane, and had lain almost
speechless, until in the middle of the hot, heavy,

tempestuous night she had looked with a glance that
all could read from the face of the priest to the
sleeping form of the child, and then had sighed
wearily and restlessly, and died.

The blank in the history made it but the more
mournful, the more suggestive. An exceeding pity
moved in him, as he heard, for the life ushered in
in such abandoned desolation, and for which there
seemed no haven open save the cloister—a fate as
barbarous for her radiant and impassioned loveliness,
which not even the melancholy of her fate could
dim, as to wring the glad throat of a song-bird in
the full rush of its forest melody. With him at
least she was happy—she who had never known what
happiness was, except such forms of it as the sweet,
irrepressible intoxication of the mere sense of existence which youth gives, and the joys that a vivid
imagination and a passionate, poetic temperament
confer. In his presence she was happy, and he could
not refuse it to her. Few days passed without his
seeing her, in the beech-grove where he had first
glanced at her by the broken fountain, in the
pine-woods sloping up towards Vallombrosa, in the
deserted gardens or in the ruined hall of his own
Latin villa. He had no thought in it save that
of compassion, even whilst her lustrous eyes vaguely
recalled him his past ; and in the untutored thoughts
that had fed in these hill-solitudes on the legacies of the Hellenic schools and the literature of

the Renaissance, he found the wakening intellect of
a Corinna. Love had long been killed in him; it was
a thing of his youth, never, he believed, like that
youth, to revive, and no touch of passion mingled
with the pity she aroused in him; but that pity was
infinitely gentle, and to her the most precious mercy
that her life had known.

In her home, silence and austerity reigned with the
stern simplicity of the primitive church. From the
peasants she met with, at best a good-natured insolence that was to her instinctively imperial nature
worse than all neglect; from him alone she met with
what ennobled her in her own sight, and filled her
towards him with a passionate gratitude and veneration that was only not love because no knowledge of
love had dawned on her, and because an absolute sub-
mission and awe were mingled with it. To her he was
the incarnation of all sublime lives that she had
dreamed of over the stories of Plutarch, and Tacitus,
and Livy, of Augustin, and Acacius, and Basil;
to her he was as an emperor to his lieges, as an
archangel to his devotees; all grand and gracious
things to her seemed blent in him, and all lofty and
royal lives of poet, saint, or king with which her
memory was stored, seemed to her met in his. It was
not love that she bore him; it was something infinitely
more unconscious and more idealised—it was an
absolute adoration.

She did not know why the hours were a dead

worthless space unless they brought her to his presence, why the mere distant sound **of his voice** filled her heart with a joy intense as pain, why any suffering he had bidden her would have been sweeter than any gladness, why the forest-world about her wore a light it had never had before:—she did not know; she only **knew that all the** earth seemed changed and transfigured. He was not blind to it; it touched him, it beguiled him, it pleased him; it was very **long since anything had** loved him and been the happier for his smile; **it was very** long since these softer, slighter things had come into his life, and **they had** a certain charm for him.

There had been a time when all women's eyes had gained a brighter light at his approach, though that time lay far away in a deserted land; yet in some faint measure it revived for him, as he saw the silent welcome, more eloquent than all words, of this young **Tuscan's** glance; and **to him** she was but a beautiful child to be caressed, without deeper thought.

"Eccellenza!" she said, hesitatingly, one day that **he had** paused by her beside her favourite haunt by the Roman fountain in the black belt of the beechwoods, "you **tell me that I** have talent—you **say** that my voice, when I sing the Latin chants that you love best, is music the world would love too. Would they do nothing for me *in* the world?"

That "world" was **so vague, so far** off, so dim, so glorious to her! She could not have told what she thought lay beyond those chesnut-belts that she had never passed; but her ideal of the unknown land was divine as Dante's of the City of God.

He answered her slowly;—he knew the fate to which her defenceless and nameless beauty would there be doomed; but he could not find the heart to break her fair illusion.

"They might—they would; but you are better and safer here in your mountain shelter."

A quick sigh escaped her.

"Oh no!"

"No? How can you tell that? You do not know what would await you. Be happy while you may, Castalia; the world would crush you!"

She looked at him wistfully, while a grander power and aspiration than the mere longing of a child for "fresh fields and pastures new" gleamed in eyes that with a little while would burn with passion as they now glanced with light.

"It is only the weak who are crushed. They could not scorn me for my birth and loneliness if I forced them to say, 'See! fate was harsh to her; but God gave her genius and endurance, and she conquered!'"

The words and the tone moved him deeply: the fearless youth, with its faith, its fervour, its courage, its sublime blindness of belief, recalled to him his own.

"Ah, Castalia!" he answered, gently, "but the

world loves best to dwarf God and to deny genius.
And genius in a woman! Cyril's envy stones Hypatia, and casts her beauty to the howling crowds."

Her head drooped, but the look of resolve, though
shadowed, did not pass off her face.

"Perhaps! Yet better Hypatia's glory won with
her death than a long, obscure, ignoble, useless life!
You say, be happy here, 'lustrissimo : happy! when all
my future is the convent?"

It was a great terror to her that monastic doom to
which the priest inexorably condemned her future;—
other provision he could make none for her. She
was so full of vivid, luxuriant, abundant, glowing life.
Life was to her an unread poem of such magical enchantment, an ungathered flower of such sorceress-
charm;—and nothing opened to her except that living
tomb!

He gave an involuntary gesture of pain.

"God forbid! Some fairer fate will come to you
than that. To condemn *you* to a convent-cell! it
would be as brutal as the captivity of Héloïse."

A brooding weariness passed over the beauty of her
face.

"But Héloïse was happier than I should be. She
had been loved once!"

There was no thought in her as she spoke, save the
longing for tenderness ever denied her, and an in-
stinctive comprehension of the passion and the sacrifice of Paraclète.

Where he leaned against a beech-stem above her
his hand touched her hair lingeringly and tenderly,
as it had done when he had brought her through the
storm—like a touch to a fluttering bird.

" You would love like Héloïse, Castalia ? "

She drew a deep soft breath ; she was always
awed with the despair and the beauty, half mystic,
wholly sublimated to her, of that eternal tale.

" Ah ! who would not? That alone is love !
' Quand l'empereur eût voulu m'honorer du nom de
son épouse, j'aurais mieux aimer être appelée ta
maîtresse !' "

The words of Héloïse on her innocent lips, which
uttered them with no thought save of their devotion
and their fidelity—their choice of slavery to her
lover rather than of imperial pomp with any other—
had an eloquence and a temptation greater than she
knew.

He sighed almost unconsciously; it was the love of
which he had dreamt in his youth—dreamt, and never
found.

" Castalia! you make me wish we had met
earlier !"

The words escaped him involuntarily. She lifted
her eyes in wonder: his meaning she could not
guess.

" Earlier, eccellenza !—why ? "

He smiled; he was glad that she failed to understand him.

"No matter!   What is it you are reading there?"

She lifted him the book; an Italian translation of an English romance—"Lucrèce."

A shadow, weary and heavy, came on his face as he glanced through the pages.

"You know it?" she asked him.

"Yes, I know it."

"I love it so well!" she said, passionately. "It was left here by chance years ago, by some travellers going through to Vallombrosa. It is beautiful —it is like the life of Héloïse! It moves me as the winds do when they make their music through the woods, and seem as though they called on men to cease from evil and remember God."

The words, fantastic, yet very eloquent in the Tuscan tongue, while her eyes grew humid, and the colour on her cheek grew warm as the scarlet heart of a pomegranate, were perhaps the truest homage the work had ever known.

He closed the book and gave it back.

"Since you feel it so, you give the author his best reward."

"But you must think it great, too?"

"No; it is very imperfect. No one knew that better than he who wrote it."

"It is perfect to *me*. And who was he—its writer?"

"You see his name there."

"Yes, his name; but his fate——?"

" Was, they say, a very common one. It was the fate of Icarus, who thought himself a winged god and fell broken to earth."

" He never fell ignobly," she said, below her breath. " He strove to rise too high, perhaps ; and those who were earth-bound envied him, and shot him down as hunters shoot an eagle ; but whoever wrote that book would only gather strength from any fall."

He answered her nothing. A little later, and he spoke of other things.

The spring deepened into early summer ; he had been seven weeks in the Latin villa since the day he had found her in the storm, and he saw her often. He was beguiled with her, and the thoughts of her cultured fancy, all untinged by the world's taint as they were, had a certain charm for the scholar, not less than her personal loveliness had a charm for one who had been, as the world held, a libertine. But either passion was dead in him, or her defencelessness lent her sanctity in his sight ; for no warmer word or glance than that of a pitying and pure tenderness ever came from him to teach her either his power or hers.

She knew nothing of his history, not even his name ; to the peasantry he was simply " the stranger." He was sojourning here for the villegiatura, and into his solitude none had ventured until she had been taken there by the hazards of the mountain weather.

Muse on what could be his history she often did, but to question him on it she no more would have thought of than, in the old legends of her church, those whom angels visited thought of pressing curiously upon their reverenced guest. She followed other words of Héloïse: "En toi je ne cherchai que toi, rien de toi que toi-même." It was he who was the idol of her thoughts; what he was, whence he came, she never sought to know. The kingship of the earth would not have seemed to her an empire too superb for him to have forsaken. She would have believed whatever he should have told her of himself—save evil. As it was, he told her nothing; and he spoke her language and the dead Latin, which was equally familiar to her, so that he might have been a Tuscan by birth, or, as her fancy — imaginative to extravagance— sometimes could have almost conceived, have lived in those ages of Augustan Rome or Gracchan Revo- lution, of which he loved best to converse.

Utterly at his mercy she was; of peril to her from him she had no conception—what he had commanded she would have obeyed implicitly; of her own danger she was profoundly ignorant; and that he could have erred she would have no more believed than the simple fanatics of her native beech-woods would have believed in the error of the saints and seraphs to whom they prayed. The very difference in their years, wide as it was, lent an additional charm to their intercourse, and even an additional danger, since it lent it also an apparent and fallacious security.

Later on that same day, returning through the forest above Fontane to the ruined villa, where he lived in the ascetic simplicity of a man whose only riches lie in his own intellect and in the books that he can gather round him, he saw her again, as the sudden break in the wall of leaves and the sudden descent of the rocky pathway brought him to a grey antique broken bridge that spanned what was now little save a dried water-course, orchid-filled, with a narrow glimmering brown brook under the flowers. She was leaning over the parapet, resting her arm on a basket of fruit. There was the indolent, reposeful grace of her southern blood in the attitude, but there was also something of depression ; and while a joyous light flashed into her eyes, he saw that they had been dim with tears. He paused beside her.

"Castalia ! what has vexed you ?" .

"An idle thing, eccellenza."

"Nothing is idle if it have power to wound you. Tell me."

A proud pain, that was half of it scorn for itself and half the impatience to repay scorn, was on her face as she raised it.

"It is my folly to *be* wounded ! But as two contadine passed me awhile ago, they thrust out their lips with a smile that was wicked, and looked at me. 'Altro ! like mother, like daughter !' And I knew that they meant disdain at me and at her; and my heart ached because I could not *revenge*. Revenge is guilt, the **Padre Giulio says**; it may be, but **when they** mock at her it would be very sweet to me."

The strength of southern vengeance gleamed for a moment over the softness of her youth; he saw how easily **the noble nature** here might be driven to desperation and **to** guilt. If the **lash of** scorn fell **on her,** it would never chasten, but it would goad **and** madden into rebellion, perhaps into recklessness.

"*Poverina!*" he said, caressingly, "evil be to **those** who cause you one moment's pain. Does so much coarseness and cruelty exist even in **your primitive** valley? But do not heed them, Castalia; these women are beneath your regret; and, remember, calumny can only lower us when it has power to **make us** what it calls us."

Her glance gave **him** eloquent and grateful comprehension.

"Oh, signore! it is not *their* scorn **that I heed;** it is only—I am afraid that it may bring **me yours.** And death would be more merciful to me!"

The **words touched him deeply,** more deeply than he showed; **for he sought to turn her** thoughts from herself, as he took her hands **in his own and looked** down into the splendour of her eyes.

"Castalia, never fear that. I honour you for what you are, my child. Your mother's error—if error it were—can never rest upon you; and the world **is** often sorely at fault in its judgments. It condone its thieves, and condemns its martyrs. But you are rash to attach so much value to my opinion. You do not know who I am—whence I come—what my history may be."

"But I know *you*. Had I sought to know more, would you not have thought me unworthy of so much? The fable of Psyche is so true; where doubt has once come, faith is dishonoured."

He smiled at the fable she chose, and her insight into human nature.

"Right. I think Eros was justified in taking wing and in never returning; but still there is such a thing as prudence. How can you tell that some guilt does not rest on me ?—that I come here because I am a marked and disgraced man; that I may be utterly unlike all you believe me ?"

She looked at him proudly and yet sadly.

"Eccellenza, those who bear guilt do not look as you look; and, whatever you be, you are *great*."

"No! I told you I am a fallen Cæsar, and dropped my purples long ago."

"But his purples are the least part of Cæsar's greatness."

"Not in the world's estimate. Come, let me see you homeward."

He raised the load of yellow gourds and luscious summer fruits, glowing amidst leaves and wild flowers, as he spoke; she tried to take it from him.

" Oh, illustrissimo ! do not do that ! *You* must not carry a burden."

" I have carried many," he said, half with a smile· She looked at him still, with that reverent, wistful look ; she wondered what he had been.

" You have ?   But they must have been the weight of royalties, then.   Give me the fruit !   Pray do not take it for me !"

" Castalia, an emperor is bound to serve a woman. We have that lingering chivalry amongst us at least.'

The rocky road wound down under beech-boughs, and over green turf, and into the twilight of dense woods, till the aërial campanila of Fontane rose in its delicate height like a frozen fountain out of the nest of leaves.   The Tuscan sunset, in all its glow, was just on earth and sky as they entered the valley where the white spire and the masses of chesnut-wood stood out against the intense blue of the early summer heavens.

" Coleridge cried, ' O God, how glorious it is to live !' " he said, rather to himself than to her, as they came into the roseate radiance.   " Renan asks, ' O God, when will it be worth while to live ?' In nature we echo the poet ; in the world we echo the thinker.'

The light was gone, the twilight fallen, as he left her at the little châlet where the charity of the church sheltered her.   He drew her to him with an involuntary action of tenderness.

" Castalia, good night !"

Her eyes looked up to his in the shadows heavily flung around them by the bending boughs. The infinite beauty of her face had never been more fair; almost unconsciously, something of the softness of dead years revived in him; he stooped his head, and his lips touched the flushed warmth of her cheek in farewell. The kiss startled her childhood from its rest for ever; with it the knowledge of love came to her.

A sudden consciousness, a sudden alarm, quivered through her; her heart beat like a caught bird, in a sweetness and joy, that made her afraid at their terrible strength, and made her tremble before him as though criminal with some great guilt; she stood like an antelope that in its wild shy grace only tempts the hunter the more: what she felt had a strange awe for her, and as strange a rapture. Though given only in a compassionate tenderness, the caress had taught the meaning of passion; her colour burned, her eyes sank under his.

At that instant the tread of a heavy step was heard on the silence; she fled instinctively, fleet as a fawn, into the deepening shadow of the arched and open door; he turned away and went back up the woodland road to his own dwelling. Fronting him, in a faint ray of dying light that slanted through the wall of chesnut and of cypress, the old priest stood, his grave, austere features rugged as the riven rock.

"Give me a word with you," he said, simply.

He whom he checked in his path looked up and paused; he had scarcely seen, and as scarcely thought, of the self-appointed guardian **of Castalia.**

"A word with me?   Assuredly."

The priest looked at him with searching **eyes,** in which there was still a great sadness and a great appeal.

"Whoever you **be,**" he said, briefly, "whether great, as I deem by your bearing, or no, I speak to you not as to one owning authority, nor as one holding myself God's command, but simply as man speaks to man."

"Say on."

"Then I say, have **you** thought what it is you do now?"

"**Do?**   I fail to understand you."

He spoke patiently still; but there **was** a touch of intolerance in the tone.

"I will make my meaning plainer, then," said the **Italian,** who had in him the temper with which Savonarola upbraided the Triple Tiara, and preached the ruthless doctrine of renunciation. "**Do you mean** to ruin **that young** life?"

"God forbid!"

He meant it in utmost sincerity, and surprise was the strongest feeling in him **for the moment.**   The disavowal softened the Tuscan.

"Then do you know that they speak evil of her on **your score?** Do you know that, through you, they say **the** shame of her mother is **hers?**"

His face grew dark.

"They lie, then; utterly! Teach your flock more charity to youth and innocence, holy father. And let me pass; I cannot wait for this catechism."

The Tuscan bent his head with a certain dignity.

"I thank you for that denial. *I* did not need it; her eyes are too clear beneath mine. Yet allow me a few words more. You give her no love, probably; but you are already far more her religion than the creed I have taught her from infancy. How will you use your power over her?"

He was silent; his thoughts were little with the speaker; he was thinking of the lips that had trembled beneath his own.

"You may lead her where you will; I confess it you! You, a stranger, who saw her first but a few weeks ago, have a force to mould and to sway her that I never won—I who have reared her and succoured her well-nigh from her birth," said the Italian, with a bitterness in which was a yearning pain. "It may be that I have seemed harsh to her; it may be that I have missed my way; that, while I strove overmuch to shield her from her mother's error, I forgot to woo her trust and her heart—I forgot that a child, and a woman-child above all, needs love and needs indulgence. It may be that I erred. Be it so or not, you can command her; and I can no more stay her from your sorcery than I can check the winds. Yet you say you would not blight her life; you speak as though you had pity on her. You say you leave her innocence sacred; but will you, then, rob her of peace? You say you will not lead her to dishonour; will you not spare her also the bitterness of a knowledge that must destroy the virginity of the heart? You say the slanderers lie; will you not, then, be wholly merciful, and leave her, as she learns to love you too well? You can make her the plaything of an hour—but it will only be at the price of her whole future."

He stood silent still while the old priest spoke. The appeal surprised him, and awakened many thoughts that had never before dawned in the compassion and tenderness he had felt to Castalia—to this young girl who looked at him with such spaniel-eyes of love, and brought him back so many memories of his youth. He had not thought of cost to her.

"Your lips touched hers to night," pursued the Tuscan. "The woman who has once felt shame under a caress has already lost half her purity. You gave her in that a memory which will burn into her heart with humiliation every time that she thinks of you. You may mean her no injury now; but you are one who has lived long, doubtless, in the pleasures of the world; how will it end if you remain near her?"

He raised his eyes, where they stood in the early evening light falling so faintly through the parting in the barrier of cypress, and looked full at the Italian.

"You plead with *me* for her; to what fate do you condemn her yourself? The cloister? Have you ever thought what it is to bury her in that tomb which cannot claim even the repose of the graves of the dead?—to bar her out from light, and laughter, and melody, and joy?—to chain her loveliness where no kiss shall ever meet her own, no heart beat on hers, no eyes see her smile, no lover seek her embrace? Have you ever thought what you will do when you seal down such luxuriant life as hers to beat, and struggle, and desire, and pine, and wither, and perish alone? Yours is the cruelty—not mine!"

The Tuscan's furrowed cheek grew paler; he was too deep a scholar to be a fanatical churchman, and in his close, stern, rugged soul he cherished Castalia tenderly.

"I mean no cruelty—Christ knows. But I have no other shelter for her, and there, at least, she would have innocence."

"Innocence forced and untempted! what is it better than sin? Let her take her chance in the width of the world, let her even know trial and poverty and temptation, let her be a wanderer and a beggar, if she must; but leave her the free air, and the forest liberty, and the human love that is her right, and the possibility at least of joy!"

The Italian sighed wearily.

"I strive for the best; and my cruelty is not as yours. I would save her at least from actual pain

you—if you do her no worse thing—will bind on her
a passion and a regret that will consume her to her
grave. I know her nature; and though she has the
innocence, she has not the inconstancy of a child :
she will not *forget*. There is but one way to spare
her : leave her."

He was silent a while longer, as the priest's words
ceased, and there was no sound save the falling of a
water-course rushing downward through the gloom
and through the leaves.

"I will leave her," he said, at last, "if you in
turn give me your word never to force her life into a
convent ? "

The Tuscan bent his head.

" I promise."

"So be it. I will make her no farewell; let
her think me heartless, if she will; so she will best
forget."

Then he went upward alone through the evening
shadows, along the slope of the hills to the loneliness
of the Latin villa. In the gloom of the deserted hall
the picture of the diadem of flowers alone gleamed
radiant as a ray of the moonlight fell across it. He
paused before the painting, and a sudden pity stole on
him.

The promise that he had given had a certain pain
for him. It was not love that he felt for her. There
had been too great a darkness on his life for the softness of that passion easily to revive ; but he had found

a pleasure in once more, after lengthened solitude,
being the subject of that sweet, reverent adoration;
and she had inspired him with an unspeakable compassion for her fate, which could not let him muse
without anxiety upon that fate's inevitable future.
There had been a time when the lavishness of his
gifts and the influence of his word could have lifted
her into happiness as easily as a flower is transplanted
into sunlight from the shade; but that time was far
away.   He felt the hardest pang of poverty to those
of generous nature : he had *nothing to give.*

He had offered the promise, and he would redeem
it, because she was motherless and defenceless, and
therefore sacred to him ; but he stood and looked at
the flower-crowned painting with a pang of regret.

"It is a harsh mercy that he asks of me," he
thought ; "and yet what else should be the end?
Love is no toy for me now ; and she is worthier of a
happier fate than to be the passing fancy, the consolation of an hour, to a worn and wearied life."

On the morrow, ere the sun was high, he was far
from Vallombrosa.

END OF VOL. II.

LONDON:
PRINTED BY C. WHITING, BEAUFORT HOUSE, STRAND.